HIGH PRAISE FOR MELANIE JACKSON!

"Melanie Jackson is an author to watch!"
—Compuserve Romance Reviews

THE SELKIE
"Part fantasy, part dream and wholly bewitching, *The Selkie* [blends] whimsy and folklore into a sensual tale of love and magic."

—*Romantic Times*

"A page-turning paranormal romance."

—*Booklist*

DOMINION
"An unusual romance for those with a yen for something different."

—*Romantic Times*

NIGHT VISITOR
"I recommend this as a very strong romance, with time travel, history and magic."

—*All About Romance*

AMARANTHA
"Intriguing . . . Ms. Jackson's descriptions of the Cornish countryside were downright seductive."

—*The Romance Reader*

MANON
"Melanie Jackson paints a well-defined picture of 18th-century England. . . . *Manon* is an intriguing and pleasant tale."

—*Romantic Times*

SURRENDER TO THE MAGIC

Cyra forced herself to loosen the grip she had in Thomas's hair. She would trust. She might as well. Her small hands were no match for the strength in him if he turned the beast loose upon her.

Thomas shuddered, as though hearing her decision to place her trust in him, and finding it both exquisitely pleasurable and yet also horrifying.

"You've seen the monster, you know he's there, but still you come to me. It seems miraculous." His voice was so low that she almost couldn't hear it. "But is this salvation, or damnation? Or just trickery, the magic seducing us both for its own ends?"

"I don't know," Cyra whispered. "I don't care. Heaven or hell or enchantment, all I know is that I want you. Please," she said for a third time.

Other books by Melanie Jackson:

OUTSIDERS

MELANIE JACKSON

LOVE SPELL   NEW YORK CITY

For all my friends and family who see the goblins too.

LOVE SPELL®

November 2003

Published by

Dorchester Publishing Co., Inc.
200 Madison Avenue
New York, NY 10016

ISBN 0-505-52567-4

Author Note

My apologies to the residents of Sin City for destroying their town. But, if there was ever a city where goblins would choose to dwell, it is there. Such a glittering jewel would cause unhealthy excitement in their greedy little hearts. They would covet the town above all others for its wealth and eye-catching brilliance. Thus is the nature of the green beast. Fortunately, this is only a book, so your real-estate values have not actually been driven down by goblin occupation.

I need to say another thank-you—to my husband for suggesting the unlikely world of goblins as a setting for a romance. It's weird, but it works.

Lastly, it will be obvious to anyone who is familiar with anything having to do with explosives that I know absolutely nothing about bombs. I am unenlightened and therefore my story is likely riddled with technical errors. Please let us both remain so. When Hollywood snaps up the book and makes it into an action film, they'll fix those pesky details.

Hope you have fun in goblin town. If you would like to know more, please visit www.lutinempire.com. Viva Sin City!

Prologue

The man, recently called Malcolm Fayre, was dressed in the remains of a black tuxedo and dress shoes. His hair was black. His mood was also dark and somber as the night he ran through.

He had been afraid, at first, that he wouldn't escape Sin City with his news. But he had managed to find a gap in the magical fence well away from the guarded gates and now he was free, running through the desert under the moon, temporarily and blessedly alone with the snakes and scorpions.

It wouldn't last. The coyote was coming. And then the bear. He'd seen their shadows from the corner of his eye, stalking him even as the poison burned in his veins.

But if he were lucky, and the goddess inter-

1

vened, he might be able to reach Ianna Fe's legendary *tomhnafurach* before anaphylactic shock set in. He wasn't certain where the abandoned faerie hole was, but he had to somehow find it. If he didn't get help soon, amnesia and then paralysis would take him.

His enemies would find him and eat him then, gobble him up body and soul. And no one would know what the goblins were doing in Sin City. No one would know about Fornix.

Not until it was too late to stop them.

Already the man's thoughts were beginning to blur and run together. That was bad. He kept repeating his name, which was an anchor but also an incantation that kept him in control. He was Thomas Marrowbone, the quiet man. He had to remember this. It was very important. *Thomas Marrowbone, the quiet man.* All his other names and identities didn't matter. They were meaningless shadows, without the ability to command. But Thomas Marrowbone was a name vested with power, power given to him by his heritage and feared by his enemies.

His lips pulled back in a rictus grin as he ran; his lungs dragged in gasping breaths of the surrounding dry, dead air. It did little to feed his muscles. Under his shirt, the small medallion of the goddess thumped repeatedly over his breastbone as though attempting to jump start his failing heart. The small pain kept him resolute and running.

The trick to endurance in this sort of situation was not to embrace the notion that death was inevitable. Such negative thinking brought with it a sort of blind panic to the spirit that was irrecoverable, unreasoning, final. That way lay madness, and it would kill Thomas quicker than any goblin poison. He had gone that road once and would not even think of it again.

Fortunately, the body's strongest instinct was for survival, and this would carry him forward even if his mind succumbed to the goblins' toxin. It—the beast inside his flesh—would make his legs run until they could run no more. He had to keep heading west. If he kept his back to the sun when it rose, he would be all right. He had time yet.

Time.

It was the human age of instancy—ruled by microwaves, cable TV, and the Internet. Humans assumed that these machines regulated the universe. But magic wasn't regulated. Nor did it function on human time or live by human rules. Thomas was fortunate in that respect, because a human body would have given in to the pain and died long since. But, being fey, he knew from history that he could go on suffering for a long, long time . . . until the bear and coy-

3

ote ate him. Or until the sun burned him up. That cruel light loved by humankind had killed more of his kind than any war or disease.

Humans. Even in their world of vast databases there were many things they did not know. Goblins had a code of silence and secrecy the CIA could only envy . . . until the goblins took them over too. And goblins were willing to spend money on their goals. They poured wealth into their projects like they owned their own mint. Which, of course, they did. They had recently taken over Sin City and set up their own goblin Costa Nostra. What a racket. Tourists happily vacationed there and paid for their own doom.

Fragile fools! They were too ignorant even to fear. Because they didn't know the enemy like he did. He'd paid for his intimacy with the *lutins* in blood—not all of it his own.

Thomas looked up as he ran. At night, the sky was full of stars. By day, it would be empty and lonesome. Already the night was beginning to fade and the tiny lights were winking out one by one.

It was hot, but nowhere near what it would be after the sun rose. Temperatures would climb above 120 degrees before noon. This landscape would be a dry stone furnace, a crematorium without flames.

The thought frightened him, but Thomas would have to endure until the goddess sent aid.

It was fortunate that his shoes' soles were made of leather. Rubber would melt and leave a clear trail for his trackers. Of course, running shoes wouldn't have blistered his feet and made them bleed. When his feet got bad and his socks couldn't hold the blood, he'd have to stop and bind them. But not yet.

Thomas ran on.

As dawn stole over the horizon, Thomas jumped down into a steep dry wash, hiding as best he could from the light that would slowly steal his strength and will and maybe even his mind. He fell more than twenty feet, but his ankles held up to the impact and he never slowed his pace.

Faster! Faster!

Beneath his shoes, dead branches and thin chips of shale snapped like ancient bones, and vipers hissed at him with dry voices. He flew by.

Fee, fi, fo, fum, Thomas Marrowbone has to run.

He had to. Coyote would soon smell the blood of the quiet man, and coyote was swift. And anything the coyote tracked, the bear would kill.

Chapter One

Einsteinian scholars had it all wrong. *Tempus* didn't always *fugit*. No, in some instances time could slow to a crawl and then stop altogether. A large, life-shaping error could be frozen into an eternal moment, where it remained to inflict itself on you—forever—in practical fact and in ever-enlarging memory. It was one of the lesser-known torments of the damned that could happen to a person even before she died.

"And let me testify, O Lord—*where the hell am I?*" Cyra looked first out the front windshield and then out the Honda's dusty side window, forgetting that her side-view mirror was gone. It had been knocked off by a boulder last night before she had finally given in to the faint voice of reason and stopped driving through the moonless dark.

"Damn." The Honda was in rough shape. Cyra and the red Civic had gone steady since high school, and it had been a reliable vehicle, outlasting boyfriends and even her parents' deaths. But though it was a trooper in the city and as fuel efficient as any car could be, it never had been made to withstand the rigors of cross-country travel. Especially not now that Cyra was in Nevada and going off-road.

Cyra chewed her lip, her hands tightening on the wheel. But what other choice did she have except to indulge in auto abuse? Her finances wouldn't stand for a jeep rental—not that she was sorry for what she'd done to Larry. That goblin-sympathizing, two-timing, fiancée-hiding, credit-stealing bastard deserved what she'd done to him!

It wasn't *that* part of her frozen memory that she regretted. She experienced scalding glee when she pictured the tines of that Neptune ice sculpture stabbing Larry in the butt as he crashed into that prenuptial table loaded with lobster and champagne.

But the parts that came after and just before . . . those were bad. They still gave her nightmares every time she drifted off to sleep. Finding out that her research—two years of it— had been stolen by her lover had done something to her brain. The betrayal had blasted new

7

pathways to dark parts of her soul. That rat-bastard Larry had actually published her paper under his name—and then expected her to be grateful for a mention in the acknowledgments!

And then, to discover that the institute they worked for was being run by goblins—and that she had been in their pay! It was all too much.

But the truth will set you free.

"Ha! Free." Cyra swallowed hard. Taking goblin money was bad enough, but thinking about how she had slept with this two-faced creature named Larry made her physically ill. What had happened? He had seemed so normal, and then one day he had come to her apartment a changed man—cold, secretive.

Maybe it was when the unmentioned fiancée—Little Miss Magnolia Blossom, aka Lydia Clarice Beaumont-Armstrong—came on the scene. That would explain the change. Partially. But while Cyra had at first hated the idea of her—and was admittedly insanely jealous of her golden skin and golden dress and golden life—she had to admit the expression on the poor girl's face when Cyra had crashed her engagement party and shoved her fiancé into the buffet would always haunt her. She had wanted to hurt Larry, not Lydia.

What was worse, it had all been for nothing. The truth had *not* set Cyra free. No one believed her about the goblins—not her employers, not her friends, not weepy Miss Magnolia Blossom, who had been thinking of nothing but Larry's punctured ass and all the ruined lobster she couldn't even feed to her dog because he had a delicate stomach and seafood always made him ill—and *what was she going to do?*

Well, that part about no one believing her wasn't quite true. No one believed her except that strange, skinny man in the black sweater with the white, spongy skin that looked like uncooked dough. He had slipped a business card into her hands as he shoved her into a taxi and told her to get out of town while she still could. *He* didn't think Dr. Cyra Delphin had flipped her lid. He didn't look at her like she was some pathogenic organism that should be quarantined and studied.

Of course, she hadn't followed his advice. She was in the right. She would not flee. People had to be warned. Larry had to be stopped. The thought of what he might be doing with her research was terrifying.

Larry! Even now the thought of him conjured anger—anger so vast and deep that she could drown in it. She vomited it up like Lydia's dog did lobster. It was anger made of every ugly feeling she had never allowed herself to have, and many that she knew intimately from childhood

9

but had never wanted to feel again. There was shame and guilt and hate . . . and there was something new: contempt, for herself and what she had become. Since her parents had died, she was like some worker bee in a hive with no individual identity, never questioning what she did or why she did it. She had no goals except those set by her employer. Her work, bequeathed to her by her parents, had started as something wonderful to nurture, had grown into a demanding and jealous lover, then became her master, and finally the tyrant that ruled and owned her life more surely than the moon ruled the tide or the sun owned the day. Little by little, her mind had been set to discriminate against emotion, against humanity really. It was as though her memories—her very sense of self—had been assassinated one brain cell at a time and replaced with worker drones that labored only for Bracebridge. She almost deserved to be betrayed by that jerk for being so inhumanly soulless!

But you aren't really human, are you? Do you even have a soul?

"Shut up." But it was an excellent question. Had she embraced her research at Bracebridge because deep inside she felt that she had no connection to—not even the *right* to—anything human?

10

Larry had certainly encouraged her in this dehumanizing effort, guiding her every step of the way. Under his tutelage she'd gotten really good at lying to herself, at believing the illusions of camaraderie their work provided and that it was enough. It was only now that she could recognize the hunger that had been growing inside of her. She was starving for some meaningful contact—some intercourse with humanity—and all there was to feed it at Bracebridge was more illusion.

Of course, the blinders were off now. There would be no more sitting down to dine off Larry's mirages. The blast shield was open and there was nothing to protect her from the glare of her stupidity and Larry's betrayal. *Bastard!*

"Rat bastard," she snarled, when thinking the words wasn't enough. She stepped on the accelerator and pointed the car at Larry's phantom image, letting the bumper tear him to red shreds that flew in all directions. "Take that, you unreal prick!"

Another deep rut assaulted her tires, recalling Cyra to reality with a sharp blow to the head as she bounced off the roof of the car. She instantly slowed, taking a few calming breaths. She had to watch that. This was no time for a breakdown or a blowout. She had to think—calmly, logically—about what had happened and what she was doing. She couldn't exactly recall *why*, but it was important to stay calm, to think about what had happened, to understand . . .

Her thoughts skipped backward.

Well, her actions after the disastrous engagement party were certainly understandable and logical. Unable to endure the sight of her former lover, she'd transferred to another department and tried to brazen it out. There had been a lot of support for her among the rank and file. In fact, only hours after her rampage among the lobsters, the first of the floral tributes had arrived at her office. Then they had started coming to her home too—several every day. Soon, there wasn't room for all the floral thank-yous from people who hated and feared Larry, and she had to start giving them away because they reminded her of a funeral. She also had given up tipping the flower deliverymen. She'd been going broke.

The human higher-ups, those who might have been sensitive to her case because of what they perceived as a nervous breakdown after Larry's personal betrayal, had been angered however. They saw Cyra as a magnet for unrest among the wage slaves. At The Bracebridge Institute, they informed her, they studied mass hysteria and psychological chaos. They did not participate in it. They would have fired her then and there, but orders had arrived from on high—from goblin headquarters, no doubt—and she'd been transferred again to an outlying office fifty miles away and encouraged to get in-house counseling. It had only been when her exile wasn't enough to end the female secretarial uprising, and when Cyra had refused to let any of her colleagues poke around in her brain, that she'd been let go.

She'd gotten another job immediately. But it had only lasted until Larry called and hinted to her new employers that she was mentally unstable and a security risk.

There'd been another job after that one, but the pattern repeated itself. Her contemporaries had started calling her Carthage because she had been sacked so many times. She'd become an amusing by-word in the research community, and worse, notorious enough to finally make the news as a colorful, local crackpot. She knew she was being hounded, driven toward some awful end. But she couldn't see the pattern, the path her invisible enemies were herding her down.

Well, whatever their plan, and however impermeable their invisibility, she was certain that this was all Larry and the goblins' doing, all their fault—even if no one would listen. She now understood the frustration of conspiracy theorists who couldn't make anyone believe them.

After a while she'd found that she was walking through city streets, staring at people with suspicious eyes and wanting to slap anyone who looked even mildly inquisitive. She'd started fantasizing about doing Larry physical harm. Mentally, she'd rehearsed killing him. Her favorite method was feeding him feet first into a wood chipper.

At the urging of concerned acquaintances, she'd tried traditional feminine relief for a lover's betrayal: shoe-shopping, new lipsticks, a change of hairstyle, excessive chocolate consumption, even a shock-therapy trip to a leather bar for an S&M fashion show. None of it distracted her from her growing thirst for revenge. Hatred had become omnipresent. Larry had evicted her from her life, from her work. Her loathing of him coated her tongue. It was a cataract over her eyes that blinded her to any joy. It consumed her thoughts and started eating her soul.

People had begun suggesting she needed more than career counseling, that she should try lithium or maybe Prozac. They avoided her because she couldn't have a normal conversation anymore. Her every sentence was like a hurled rock. She'd become a devout conspiracy theorist and hated the world because she knew—or imagined that she knew—it was secretly being run by goblins.

Cyra understood elements of what was happening to her. It was part of her work to understand the brain and recognize the signs of its disintegration. Rage was the result of a cocktail of chemicals—triggers—flooding the brain and causing its synapses to fire. In disturbed people they fired erratically. In her . . . Well, her brain synapses weren't firing really. It was more like they were exploding. She had thousands—*millions*—of cherry bombs going off in her head, shorting out her pre-frontal cortex, strafing her reason and keeping it pinned down in an obscure corner of her brain where it could not aid in her fight for sanity. She knew the situation was aberrant, unhealthy—but knowledge didn't help. She couldn't stop herself from thinking the things she did.

Finally, one day, in an act of lonely desperation, she'd dug out that business card the pale man in the black sweater had slipped into her hand the day he hustled her out of the country club. All it said was: HUMANS UNDER GROUND. That and an e-mail address.

Feeling that she was out of options, and probably losing her mind, she had written to the e-mail address. They had sent her to a website.

And now she was running away to join the malcontents' circus. Or maybe the French Foreign Legion. She wasn't at all clear on what she would be doing for H.U.G., and had already started to have some regrets at following the anonymous, digitized voice's instructions about decamping her home in the middle of the night without telling anyone where she was going. Every mile she traveled inland made her feel more lonely.

Still, what else was there to do? She was alone. No parents, no lover, no friends, no research, not a shred of decent reputation to wrap herself in.

Cyra sniffed, but she refused to actually weep. If she ever started, she wouldn't stop until every tissue she had was saturated. Only she didn't have any tissues with her, just her short sleeves, so crying was out of the question. Anyway, it was far too late for tears.

She hit a stone in the rutted trail and the wheel was nearly jerked from her hands. There was a loud clattering and Cyra looked back to see some pitted metal pipe disappearing behind her. It was probably the muffler, but she wasn't going back for it. It was too damned hot to stop. And the thing had needed replacing for months. Really the noise was no worse than before. There was no one to be annoyed by it anyway.

Cyra wiped a hand over her eyes and then down her T-shirt, leaving a damp smear over the rubber decal. At one time, the sentiment had amused her: *Do not meddle in the affairs of dragons, for you are crunchy and taste good with ketchup.* Nothing amused her now.

She was tired, so very tired and perhaps a little dehydrated, though she didn't feel thirsty. And she was beginning to see things now that the sun was wheeling to the west. Maybe it was lack of sleep or some weird desert optics, but she was seeing little darting shadows at the corner of her eyes, movements in places where no living thing should be. Once she thought she saw a coyote, but it had moved too fast and had been too large to be a real animal. Later she had seen a bear. Only, there were no bears in the desert. And, of course, when she had turned her head to take a good look, nothing had been there. Nothing at all. Just stone and sand and relentless sun.

"I should stop and nap." But there was no shade anywhere. The car would be a sauna in five minutes if she turned off the air-conditioning. And she just wanted to get this trip over with.

When the man appeared directly in front of her, she almost didn't step on the brakes. He was, after all, probably just another illusion, a hallucination brought on by sleep deprivation. But then she noticed his tattered tuxedo and his cracked lips, which pulled back from his teeth as he called to her to stop. The battered lips decided her. That was too much detail for a mirage.

She slammed on her brakes, but her car continued to skate over the sand. It stopped only inches from the stranger, dust boiling into the air. The poor man keeled over right on the hood of the vehicle, his thin body folding in on itself like a house of cards hit by a gust of wind. His head hit with an audible thump and his sweat-dampened cheek began to sizzle on the hood.

"Oh Jeez!"

Cyra jumped out into the breath-stealing heat and quickly hauled him off of the sheet of burning metal. She staggered under his unexpected weight as she wedged her body underneath his arm and towed him toward the passenger door. At that point, it was hard to say whose legs were shakier.

He looked thin—long and lanky—but he might as well have been packed with sand. Certainly keeping hold of him was like trying to grab grains of the stuff. As his muscles failed

18

and his arms swung loosely, it became almost impossible to get him into the car without banging something on the blistering frame and damaging him more.

"Hurry," he whispered. "It burns."

"I'm trying. Help me out a little here!" she gasped, cramming him into the passenger seat. "What the hell happened to you? What are you doing out here?"

The man groaned but tried to arrange his limbs in the thin shade of the dashboard. Cyra helped stuff them inside and then slammed the door, hard. The door wouldn't latch any other way.

She rushed back around to her side of the car and climbed in. Knowing it would strain the Honda beyond what it could endure, she nevertheless turned up the air-conditioning before reaching under the passenger seat for her bottle of water. Armed with liquid and cool air, she turned to take a good look at the dark stranger she almost had run down.

Her first glance at his face was a shock. His eyes were light—a true gold that shone like a wedding ring. His skin was reddened by the sun but obviously usually very fair. His hair was black, black as any midnight that had ever been, and grew past his shoulders. All his features—eyes, ears, lips—had an exotic upward

19

tilt. Cyra had never seen anyone like him.

"Help me," he whispered again. His voice was weak, but somehow he did not seem pathetic.

"I am," she said quickly, and held the bottle to his lips. She tried not to spill any of the fluid. She only had one more bottle and was still almost a hundred miles from where she needed to be.

"So, let me guess. You're out here working on your summer tan and lost your way back to the cabana. Or were you out looking for long lost silver mines, planning to make your fortune off lost treasure?" Cyra flinched as she heard her own words. She hadn't meant for her voice to be so acidic. Blaming the victim for being hurt— she knew better. She made an effort to soften her tone, but it didn't work. And her words came from a deep, unexplored part of her mind. "Or maybe you are trying to cross the species barrier by becoming the world's first human lobster."

That was a bad choice of words. Mentioning lobsters made her think of the rotten son-of-a—

Ruminating! She was ruminating again. Larry wasn't important now. She had to focus.

"Thank you," the soft voice whispered when the man was done swallowing. Then: "Who are you, pale stranger in the wasteland?"

"I'm Cyra Delphin," she answered, surprising herself. She had been instructed by the voice on the phone to use the name Susan Hanson for her trip and had, up until this point; managed not to forget her instructions.

"Delphin? Then you are of the *See Fe*." He nodded slowly. "But you are far from home."

"Huh? From where?" She shook her head. "I'm not from Santa Fe. I'm from Monterey. In California. Look, I think you've been out in the sun too long. I've got to get you to a doctor. Somehow."

The golden eyes looked at her, staring through to the back of her skull where they rummaged around in her chaotic thoughts. Something touched the base of her brain and Cyra went into shock. The man didn't look dangerous. He appeared, in fact, rather waiflike. But something about him made her want to shiver in spite of the heat. She wanted to shiver, but couldn't.

"You don't know, do you?"

"Know what?" she asked, beginning to frown. A small headache was starting to pinch between Cyra's brows. She felt dizzy. She quickly swigged some water.

"It doesn't matter now. I am sorry, daughter of the sea, but as they say, 'needs must when the devil drives.' I am Thomas Marrowbone, the

21

quiet man." He drew a slow breath and then ordered: "Say my name. Now."

Her ears began to buzz and her heart to beat erratically.

"What?" she whispered. It was as though adhesive had glued her mind shut and her eyes open, so that she was forced to see but could not comprehend.

"Say my name."

"Thomas Marrowbone," Cyra heard herself repeat obediently, rubbing at her temples where her brain seemed to be trying to escape the confines of her skull. It was pressure, like a storm front, making the tympanic membrane throb.

"Thomas Marrowbone, the quiet man," he said again. Thomas raised a shaking hand and began to rub his own temples.

"Thomas Marrowbone, the quiet man," Cyra said a final time, the hissing in her ears getting louder. But some of the pain eased. She would have been grateful, but she knew that somehow she had just surrendered much of her will to this stranger.

"Good. Now, do you see those rocks to the left? The red needle sticking into the air?"

Cyra turned her head and peered through the bug-spattered windshield. "Yes."

"Drive there."

"But . . ."

"Do it."

Cyra knew she shouldn't. It was the wrong way. There wasn't even a road leading to the rock. But . . .

"Do it, Cyra Delphin," the voice whispered, as he took the water bottle from her. "My strength is running out. And the goblins will be coming. The coyote, the bear . . ."

Cyra did begin to shiver then. Her hands were shaking badly as she turned down the air conditioner and put the car back in gear. She was aware that her will had just been completely hijacked by her passenger. It was like he had given her a psychic spinal block and she was now partially closed off to mental and physical control of her own body. She'd probably be really angry about that later. After all, she was always angry these days and this was a gross violation—a rape almost.

She wanted to demand of this man that he tell her who—*what*—he was that he could do this to her. But the words wouldn't come. Fear, or something, closed her throat and stilled her tongue.

Goblins. The coyote. The bear. Those words suddenly scared her badly. Maybe she wouldn't be angry with Thomas Marrowbone, whatever he was. Maybe there finally *was* an emotion stronger than her rage.

As she drove, Cyra's eyes sought the patches of shadow, making sure that none of them actually moved. Of course, the terrible part was that she was certain that sometimes some of them did shift the moment she looked away.

Chapter Two

"Stop here," Thomas said. His voice was weaker but still commanding. Hope had given him a last burst of strength. Thanks to this lovely, lost sea fey they would make it to sanctuary after all.

Cyra stopped the car, obviously grateful to be in the shade of the stone needle. Sweat had been running off her for the last several miles, and she had been unable to let go of the steering wheel to wipe it away. Thomas was sorry about her physical distress.

"Help me out," he whispered, and Cyra obediently opened her door and came around to his side of the car. He did his best to struggle upright, but he still needed her support. The desert heat was like a hammer blow, a breath of hell. It was the fire hour, sunset, the time when the sun died, painting the desert with blinding light.

"We are going into a cave now. There is no need to be frightened," he said gently, trying to prepare her for the *tomhnafurach*. It would probably not reject her since she was fey, but the place would still feel alien to her, and her ignorance of her own supernatural nature made her vulnerable to magical illusions.

This woman was a mystery, really. How was it possible in this day and age that she did not know her true nature? Thomas hadn't thought it feasible for any fey in this era to actually go through life thinking himself human. Unless Cyra had been orphaned at an early age? That was what had happened to—

"I don't see a cave," she said, glancing back over her shoulder and interrupting his unhappy thoughts. She had been doing that a lot. Apparently she sensed that they were being followed. Perhaps she was looking for coyote and bear. They were what the goblins would send to kill Thomas since they themselves were hydrophilic and couldn't survive long away from water.

"It is just ahead," he answered, already feeling stronger. Simply getting near the *tomhnafurach* was supplying him with new strength. The abandoned faerie hill had obviously been

26

lonely, and it was eager to guide them inside. It was letting him borrow its stored power.

He would have to be cautious. These *tomhnafurachs*—or *shians* as they were sometimes called—had a way of gobbling up time. Normally he wouldn't mind a nice long stay, but it was imperative that he get a message to the others and let them know about the goblins' plot as soon as he was healthy enough to travel. Already Lilith, the Goblin Queen, had extended her labyrinth deep into the desert. She would be to Yucca Mountain in only a few weeks, and then General Fornix's plan would be implemented.

"My skin is so dry and salty," Cyra complained suddenly, sounding fretful. "I must look fifty."

"No, you don't." She wouldn't look fifty when she was fifty. Cyra Delphin didn't realize it, but she would still be beautiful at ninety and a hundred—and two hundred. Like Ninon de L'Enclos she would be intriguing men well beyond the normal human lifespan. If she lived through the next few days.

Of course, she might not be pleased with the news of her heritage. Ignorance of one's nature was often an anesthetic. Thomas wasn't sure if he should take it away. He would decide later when he was rested.

27

The *tomhnafurach* opened its stone door as
they approached, showing them an easy path
inside. With every step, Thomas got stronger
and he was able to take some of his weight back
from Cyra. He knew he was heavy, even for
someone with this woman's strength.

"It isn't dark," Cyra whispered. Thomas
couldn't tell if she was awed or alarmed, and he
didn't want to intrude any further into her
mind since it caused her such pain to have him
there. He'd violated her enough already.

"No, it wouldn't be. We are expected. The hill
lit the fires for us."

The *tomhnafurach* had indeed lit its ancient
hearth fires in a glorious welcome. The grand
chamber was filled with orange light, which
danced merrily on the ceiling and walls.

"O come magic that in the colors of the rainbow lives, for as I pass I worship." Thomas
spoke the ritual words easily, the incantations
coming out automatically, though it had been
nearly a century since he had been inside this
kind of faerie hole. As soon as he decently
could, and remain polite, he asked the hill to
seal the door behind them and lead him to the
healing waters he required.

Though impatient and curious, Cyra stood
still while Thomas chanted and sketched runes
in the air. His control of her mind wasn't total,

but it was still effective enough to keep her from panicking at his strange behavior. Another wall shifted open, showing Thomas where he needed to go; yet he found himself pausing, again distracted by Cyra's presence.

She was slender, with chocolate hair and brown eyes as was common among the selkie women—though usually they did not bob their hair. She wasn't boyish looking, however. She definitely had enough curves to challenge her jeans' restraints. And, as for her t-shirt . . . Thomas read it and smiled slightly. The slogan was very wise, but it didn't stand a chance of being read while her body was in it. Male eyes would always see breasts before wisdom.

Thomas shook his head. This was stupid. He was wasting valuable time staring at a woman. He had to get to the holy waters and start to heal. Being inside this hill where its time distortion ruled had slowed the progress of the poison in his body, but it hadn't stopped it. He was dying.

"Come with me," he ordered. The words were a command, though his tone was as soft a lullaby. "There is nothing to be afraid of."

"I'm in a cave in the desert with a total stranger, and it looks like we're having a barbecue with the devil," Cyra mumbled. "This is just jim-dandy. Nope, nothing here to be afraid of."

"No devils, I promise."

"Uh huh. Then, exactly what sort of mosh pit is this place?" She turned to look at him, her mind fighting hard against his control and to gain some understanding.

"'Mosh pit'?"

"Where are we?" she asked again.

"We are in a faerie mound," Thomas answered, taking pity on her bewilderment and answering truthfully, even though it wouldn't mean anything to her. "One that was abandoned long ago. If you think you can refrain from acting stupidly, I will give you your will back. Would you like that?"

"My will?" Her brow wrinkled. "Don't be a moron. Of course I want my will back."

Thomas laughed silently and then eased off some of his control. He turned back to the hidden door.

"Come on, then. We must go down to the water."

Cyra perked up at the mention of water.

"Can I have a bath?" she asked.

"Yes, if you like." Thomas turned and started down a corridor lit with glowing torches. The floor was smooth and glassy as though made of polished obsidian. He slowly let go of more of the magical compulsion he had placed Cyra under, but was ready to resume control if she began to panic.

"You said that *the hill* lit these fires? Aren't you maybe anthropomorphizing a little? Don't you mean the seven dwarves, or trolls, or whoever lives here did it?"

As the echoes of her voice died away, Thomas could hear the slow drip of water. *Salvation!* In the desert, there was no greater blessing that could be bestowed.

"No one lives here," Thomas told her again. "Not anymore. All of Ianna Fe's people died during the Great Drought that followed the Solar Event. And you better hope there aren't any troll squatters."

Cyra ducked her head. She didn't like to think of the time of the solar flares. What had simply caused skin cancer in many humans had killed off most of the pure-blooded fey.

"Ianna Fe?" She asked, feeling that she should remember this name from childhood but unable to recall it. So many of her childhood recollections were deeply buried.

"Yes. She was not as famous as Tatiana or Mab, but she was still a queen."

"Oh." Then: "Thomas, you'd tell me if you were a nutcase, wouldn't you?"

Thomas again smiled, though it hurt his lips.

31

"I would tell you if I knew I was insane."

"But would you know?" she asked.

"That is, of course, the pertinent question. What does your intuition tell you?" He stared at her intently.

"My intuition is flat-lined. Just like my brain. I can't believe what I'm seeing. It must be another hallucination."

Thomas began to ask her what she meant by her use of the word hallucination, but just then the tunnel opened into a large underground chamber that held the healing pool. There were no torches since the water itself was luminescent.

"Ah!" Thomas breathed in the cool air, which extinguished some of the fire that burned in his lungs.

He began to undress.

Cyra watched Thomas strip, half horrified and wholly fascinated by her abductor's lean, long-limbed body. Pale scars decorated his back in a pattern of scales.

He wasn't human! Well, *duh.* She already knew that, didn't she? No human could do what he'd done to her mind. At least, she didn't think that it was possible. Even at Bracebridge they hadn't progressed that far with mind-control. The good news was, he wasn't a goblin either. She wasn't certain how she knew this, but the certainty was there.

More fascinated than fearful, Cyra slowly approached Thomas and the glowing blue water.

Her life had taken an abrupt left turn, and she wasn't sure how she felt about it. Part of her was maybe a little relieved that she hadn't made it to H.U.G.'s western headquarters. She had a sneaking suspicion that Humans Under Ground was a lot like the mafia, or maybe the priesthood: When you were in, you were in for life. And who wanted to spend that life in something called Humans Under Ground, anyway? That would make her a . . . what? A Hugger? A Huggite? A Huggee? Jeez! And what if they meant that underground part literally? It wasn't a thought that filled Cyra with any happiness whatsoever. She had always lived near the sea, on the open shore.

She was a little angry, too, she realized suddenly. But only a little. Thomas had done something to her—laid a spell on her or something. But, in a way, she was thankful that had happened too. His mental manipulation had finally cut through her rage and severed the knots of fury that had bound her to a stupid form of revenge. Even with Thomas still partially in her brain, she was thinking more clearly than she

33

had in weeks. Whatever Thomas Marrowbone was, he seemed fairly benevolent.

Of course, he was sick and needed her help. He'd probably say or do anything to ensure her cooperation until he was better.

"If you want to bathe, remove your clothes," he said, stepping with bloodied feet into the softly churning water. He sighed heavily and waded out into the pool. He kept his back to her.

Cyra thought for a moment. Normally, she wouldn't consider undressing in front of a stranger. But whatever Thomas was doing to her head made it okay for her to take her clothes off and join him in the lake. And she really, really wanted to bathe in those eerie blue waters. They looked so calm and peaceful and cool.

Shrugging, she undressed.

"Thomas, I thought I saw a coyote and a bear earlier in the day," she said, stepping into the deliciously cool water. It felt like nothing she had ever known. She waded out quickly until her body was decently covered. No bath had ever felt half so wonderful.

"I'm not surprised. They would not have been able to conceal themselves from you."

"They wouldn't? Why? What are they?"

Thomas turned to face her. His eyes appeared to be glowing, but a decade of pain and worry had dropped from his features.

"Because you are fey. Selkie, but still fey."

Cyra didn't voice her usual automatic denial of this statement. She had avoided thinking about her mixed blood since her parents had sat her down as a child and explained how dangerous it could be to reveal herself to others in their human community. They also had been researchers—scientists—and their jobs had required they carry high security clearances, something that would not be easily granted to those of mixed blood.

She also had a sudden memory of them taking away her security blanket—only it hadn't been a blanket really. It had been been some kind of skin. She had cried for days when that happened. . . .

Of course, she could have embraced her magical side when she reached adulthood. Her parents were dead by then, and there had been no way to hurt them with a defection from their beliefs. And the Humans With Disabilities Act had been expanded to include protections for those of mixed magical blood. But, by then, Cyra had been used to living as a human. And once she had worked at Bracebridge for a few months, she realized at some level that revealing her true nature would probably get her moved to the other side of the microscope. The people at Bracebridge would have pressured her to volunteer for their mind-control experiments—just as they had after her breakdown. In the beginning, she might not have minded so much because the mind-control trainees were doing excellent work diagnosing physical ailments in sick patients, and she could have been of great help. But that part of the program had been shut down in favor of attempting to actually manipulate patients' thoughts and actions. Deep in her heart, Cyra had always doubted the wisdom—and morality—of this goal, even if it would eventually allow patients to give up terrible behaviors like smoking, drug use, or pedophilia.

And things had changed for the worse since. Cyra's whole world had been turned upside-down and dumped on the floor where she now had to confront the whole ugly chaos. Maybe it was time to start being truthful, at least with herself. If she couldn't put her brain in order, what chance did she have of rescuing her life? Could it really hurt that much to admit just who and what she was?

"I know I'm . . . different," she said at last, making as much of an admission as she could in a stranger's presence. She quickly turned the subject away from herself and back to a more immediate worry. "So, we are running away from these animals? Are they some sort of—I don't know—supernatural menace?"

"They are the goblins' hunters, yes," Thomas answered.

His eyes were unblinking and his face awash in unearthly blue light. He was eerily beautiful even if his words were not. Yeah, this one was pure trouble. Cyra could see it in his eyes—those golden, compassionate eyes! A woman could easily lose control to him. Enthusiastically even. Give him a little time to work his magic, and she'd shout *whoopee* while rushing toward her doom.

" 'Goblins' hunters.' Swell. So, how do we thwart these evil goblin minions? I didn't bring my rifle or silver bullets." She made her tone flippant. While she was going to try being more honest with herself, she wasn't ready to face up to her genuine fear just yet.

Or lust.

Lust?

"We don't thwart them right now," Thomas answered. "We avoid them while we travel to Death Valley."

"Death Valley? You know all the real garden spots, don't you?"

Thomas smiled and sank beneath the rippling water. Cyra could see his golden eyes for a moment, even when the water had closed over his head. He was truly spooky, in a handsome sort of way.

"What if I don't want to go to Death Valley?" Cyra raised her voice, certain Thomas would hear her through the water if she did.

Valley . . . valley . . . valley . . . the cave echoed back at her. Thomas didn't answer, even though he rose suddenly directly in front of her. How had he gotten that close? He must be part eel to move so quickly.

"*Why* are we going to Death Valley? What's waiting there?" Cyra asked softly, her face only inches from Thomas's chest and the odd silver and gold medallion that rested there. The skin on his breast also bore the faint pattern of lacy scales. She had an urge to touch him to see if the flesh was ridged.

"We're going to Death Valley to find help," he answered, looking down at her. His expression was unreadable, but she had the feeling he was trying to puzzle her out. Good luck to him. She didn't understand herself anymore, either.

"Help with what? The coyote and bear?"

Thomas shook his head.

"The coyote and bear are small problems really."

"They are?" Cyra swallowed and asked reluctantly: "Then, what's the big problem?"

Thomas leaned his head to one side, studying

her. He finally said: "The goblins in Sin City are tunneling toward the Yucca Mountain nuclear waste storage facility. They are going to build a bomb. Possibly several bombs."

Cyra took the news like a blow to her head, but her incipient panic died as soon as it was born. Thomas had clamped down on her brain again.

"They are tired of living in the desert and want some beachfront property?" she guessed, again half annoyed that he had dared enter her mind, but also relieved that he had aborted her hysteria before it swallowed her completely.

"Exactly." His tone was reasonable even as he implied impossible things. "They want humans out of California so they can control the seaports. They figure that a couple of dirty bombs should do the trick—what's a little above ground radiation to goblins? It might make them a little uglier, but Lilith, for one, doesn't mind that."

Lilith. The queen of Sin City. Larry's real employer. She was camera-shy and the mainstream media didn't talk about her much, but the information about her empire was there, if one started digging.

"But we'd retaliate," Cyra pointed out, trying to deny Thomas's words even when she somehow knew refutation was impossible. This man did not lie. "If they launched a nuclear attack, we'd exterminate them."

"The humans would. *If* they ever realized it was anything other than a tragic accident at a nuclear power plant. Unfortunately, it would be a long time before anyone could get close enough to investigate what had happened."

"But someone would know that the waste had been stolen. They'd put it together."

"Why would they? With the goblins stealing stuff out of the supposedly sealed chambers, and the military under the command of General Fornix swearing nothing was missing and no one had entered the facility—who would necessarily suspect bombs and not several unluckily coincidental nuclear accidents? And if the goblins generously offered to step in and help with cleanup in the moment of crisis . . ."

Cyra stared at him for a long moment.

"I think my deodorant is beginning to fail."

"You're fey. You don't need it." Thomas waited to see what else she would say. She tried to think of something intelligent.

"Can they really *do* this?" was all she could come up with.

"They think so."

"And we can't go to the authorities?"

Thomas spread his arms wide. "Which authorities? The goblins own all the police in Nevada. The governor is a goblin. Lilith has contributed heavily to the campaigns of every politician she could find. She owns at least half of the House and Senate."

"But surely the military—"

"The man in charge of Yucca Mountain, General Fornix, is a modified goblin. The goblins have gotten so good with their plastic surgery, they can now pass for humans. No one has ever questioned Fornix's bona fides—and I doubt anyone ever will. We'll do what we can to warn the appropriate parties, of course, but we will likely be seen as cranks. I don't wish to alarm you," Thomas said, only to stop at her snort of horrified laughter. He laid two fingers just below her jaw as though checking for her pulse. "All right, I don't wish to alarm you *more*, but this isn't the first time the goblins have tried to wipe out humankind. The authorities didn't believe us the last time, even when presented with proof. It is standard policy among humans. If the threat is too large to manage, deny it and pray it goes away. I have no faith that this occasion will prove any different."

"Well, holy mother of God—"

"Goddess," Thomas corrected, touching his medallion. "We worship the goddess. May as well pray where it will do some good, Cyra."

"Goddess . . . Well, why not? I'll take help

from anyone. And speaking of help, you need to go to Death Valley to get some?"

"*We* do, yes. And we need to be fast and lucky, or we won't get there."

"Both fast and lucky at the same time? You don't want much, do you? I mean, you've seen my car. Prayers and rust are all that's holding it together."

"I want . . ." He looked into her eyes, then said in a tone of mild surprise: "I want things that are probably impossible . . . unless they're meant to be. But obviously I am not thinking clearly and need to sleep." He fell silent.

"Thomas, do you believe in Fate?" Cyra asked, looking away. The man's gaze, even when not directing her will, was too much, too powerful.

"Oh yeah. But I try hard to avoid her." Thomas stepped around Cyra and started for shore. He seemed much healthier than before; and his tone was again matter-of-fact. "Come on. It's time to eat."

Cyra shrugged, muttering, "I suppose the hill is going to provide us with food too?"

"After a fashion."

Cyra shook her head. "You can let go of my brain now. I won't hyperventilate or anything," she promised. "The Yucca Mountain thing just caught me by surprise."

"I thought I would wait until you had dressed," Thomas said. After a moment, blue water streaming from his body and hair, he walked out onto the glassy shore. His feet were completely healed. "It'll spare you some embarrassment. I can tell that you are not used to being naked around people."

Knowing he was right, Cyra hurried after him. She was glad he tamped down on her discomfort. Unable to resist, she stole a peep at him as he leaned over to retrieve his clothes.

He wasn't circumcised. He wasn't flaccid either.

"Feys never are," he said quietly, and started dressing.

Never are what? But she didn't ask it out loud.

Blushing, in spite of Thomas's partial control, Cyra hurried to her clothing.

"I don't know if you're a nightmare or a miracle," she said to herself, then was horrified to hear the mound's acoustics amplify her voice.

"I'm only miraculous in bed," Thomas responded without looking at her. "And then only sometimes. It takes someone a little bold to truly enjoy me." He was calm as he fastened the studs of his shirt. He added: "I rarely stick around long enough for anyone to acquire the taste."

"A love-'em-and-leave-'em miracle in bed, and a nightmare everywhere else? Interesting."

"So I've been told."

Cyra wished she knew whether he was joking.

Chapter Three

As Thomas slowly pulled back from her mind, Cyra found herself again able to think clearly and logically. Neither Thomas nor anger was interfering with her thought processes. Cyra was almost wholly herself again. Almost. It was reasonable to assume that after the events of the last few weeks, she probably wouldn't ever completely return to the life she had known before. It was impossible.

"What happened, Cyra?" Thomas asked quietly, conversationally. "What drove you into the desert and away from the sea? You must have needed to leave badly, to come without your skin."

She answered easily: "I . . . I'm not sure now. It's all kind of hazy—like how you feel after an accident. I was so angry . . ." Her voice trailed off as she began a long-delayed inventory of her accumulated thoughts. There was a lot to sort through because the rubbish had been amassing. Her brain had locked up events, unable to discard any of its bad thoughts. She sighed. "This is important, isn't it? The hand of Fate or something."

"Probably. I cannot believe that your presence here—a fey—is accidental. And anything planned by Fate or goblins needs careful consideration."

Knowing Thomas was right, Cyra turned her mind inward, searching for answers, for patterns, for something that would suggest a place to begin her tale. Thomas didn't move or urge her to haste as she sorted through her thoughts.

"Was it just anger?" he finally asked, when she was unable to find a place to begin.

"No," she answered immediately. She realized it was true. "Something happened to me."

"Recently?"

"Yes. But that was another thing. This—the wrong thing started a long time ago."

Cyra sat down to tie her shoes but remained sitting after she was done, her knees almost touching Thomas. Oddly enough, in this moment she felt closer to this stranger who had hijacked her than anyone else on the planet.

"When they took your skin," he guessed. "Was that when you forgot you were fey?" He gave her a gentle look.

"I don't know. I never really acknowledged that I was. Mom and Dad—they didn't want me to." Cyra felt as though she were confessing to a priest and that perhaps absolution would come. It made discussing the painful details easier, more purposeful. Maybe she would be able to talk about *before.* "They never admitted that they weren't human. I think—now—that they were afraid to. Especially, they were afraid for me."

"But blood will out," Thomas said. "Deny it and you go mad. Especially if you are alone."

Was that what had happened? Had she been temporarily insane—finally driven there by years of self-denial?

She thought back. The memories came easily and without pain, and she realized that Thomas was helping her to remember by filtering out the more tender emotions before they reached her gut and caused physical reaction.

She had been a cheerful child, a natural optimist. Next to her, Mister Rogers was a nihilist, Mickey Mouse a depressive. She had been sunshine. Her father called her Joy because she brought pleasure to everyone she met. Until she was five and started kindergarten, she

47

didn't know that her real name was Cyra.

But then she had gotten a little older and started to change. The difficult task of submerging her identity had begun in middle school. It had gotten worse as she entered her teens. Once she hit puberty, it became even harder for her to conceal who and what she was. Simply avoiding the subject of her differences from other people wasn't enough; she began lying to herself.

But though she didn't talk about it, she noticed on an almost daily basis the ways in which she was not like other kids. She never got sick like her friends did. Any wounds she received healed quickly and did not scar. She could exercise longer than they could, and without tiring. She was, in fact, stronger than most of the boys her age. A lot stronger.

She also had difficulty being away from the sea. Visiting friends in the valley was physically painful for her. And she had felt that she had to hide all this, even from her parents, who did not want to know their precious daughter was unhappy. So she smiled and played the flute in band, went to speech and debate meetings, ran for student council, and constructed elaborate reasons why this was all a perfectly normal way to live.

Of course, she never went out for sports,

never signed on to the cheerleading squad, never competed at anything where her greater dexterity and strength might be revealed. Yet even with these precautions, the lies about her humanness grew thin and then transparent. She was lucky—inhumanly lucky. It was as though she were influencing events so things always went her way. And instead of feeling awe or pride in what she could do, she began to see her physical and mental gifts as being more than *different*. They were a cause for shame and guilt. And later, for fear. She spent her school years in a state of constant apprehension that she would betray herself and her parents, that their shameful secret would become known: She was an alien masquerading as human.

Later, after her parents were gone, there had been other reasons not to let anyone know what she was, chiefly her job at Bracebridge, and Larry.

Larry! The thought of him was still annoying, like wet sand in a bathing suit. Still, annoyance was a vast improvement over the devastating fury she had felt before. That rage hadn't been like her at all. If Cyra had stayed in Monterey, she might actually have done him some physical harm. It seemed now as if she had been possessed by a demon, or invaded by some foreign power. They probably should have made her a case study at the institute instead of firing her . . .

Cyra straightened and drew in a shaky breath. Once again, she felt like she had received a blow to the head. They *had* wanted to make a case study of her.

"Your intuition speaks at last?" Thomas asked. "Do we have a pulse?"

"Oh my God—Goddess," she corrected, looking at Thomas with wide eyes, her psychic concussion probably apparent to him.

Had they really done it? On purpose? Had they actually been using some kind of mind control on her? Was the whole thing—Larry, the firing, the persecution—some controlled experiment? Was that possible?

"Maybe," Thomas answered, and Cyra realized that she had spoken aloud. Thomas could probably also see some of the images in her mind. "The goblins have been spending money on more than politicians. Mind control is a top priority for all the hives."

Cyra laid trembling hands on the glassy black floor, instinctively trying to ground herself as her world spun away. It was bad enough to know that Thomas had been in her head, but Larry? The goblins—those six-limbed, thinking cockroaches?

Thomas reached out and covered her hand. His fingers were blessedly warm. Out in the pool a fountain rose, its waters twirling happily, as though they were rejoicing at her painful enlightenment.

"I slept with him—loved him. Could he really have done that to me?"

"Of course he could. He works for the goblins. The man has no morals—assuming he is a man and not a goblin replicant."

"Replicant? You mean Larry was replicated? Replaced? He's a modified goblin?" She swallowed. "But that would mean that the real Larry was dead, wouldn't it?"

"Probably not dead enough," he muttered. "Most replicated humans donate their DNA willingly. But cheer up. I don't think you did love him, whatever he is. And be glad for that. Feys who actually manage to love do so until they shuffle off their nearly immortal coil."

His tone was brusque, but something in Thomas's manner, a sadness but also a sudden remoteness, told Cyra that he had known such a loss firsthand.

"Did they . . ." She licked her lips. Her mouth was suddenly dry. "Did the goblins do it because they knew I was fey—as sort of a preemptive strike before I discovered who really

51

controlled the institute? Or did they do it out of sheer malice?"

Thomas's eyes were grave but kind.

"It's a real possibility that they chose you because of your nature. Goblins don't often get the chance to practice dark arts on magical beings. The temptation to use you would have been almost irresistible. That you were ignorant of your own nature, repressing it, would have been a plus to them. A trained fey would not be so easily manipulated."

He didn't say anything more, but Cyra sensed his indignation at her parents for having done nothing to prepare her so that her magical nature could not be turned against her. She considered defending them, but didn't have the energy.

Cyra thought some more, trying to look at things unemotionally. It was difficult because thinking of her parents always made her sad and frustrated. They had taken her skin away and done all they could to suppress her magic so that she would grow up as human as possible. Nothing they had done was meant to hurt her—but it had.

A verse popped into her head.

Yesterday upon the stair
I met a man who wasn't there.

He wasn't there again today—
I think he's in the CIA.

Only he wasn't in the CIA, was he?

"Was that man really from Humans Under Ground?" she asked suddenly. "Or was he a goblin too?"

"That man?" Thomas repeated. He refrained from riffling through her memories to find the man's identity, though they both knew he could have.

Cyra explained about the pasty, doughy man claiming to be from H.U.G. Again, Thomas's face was impassive, but she sensed that he was disturbed by her story.

"I don't know, Cyra. That is a very interesting question," he said slowly. "Interesting and disturbing either way."

"Swell. So, just to sum things up"—Cyra attempted a smile, but knew it was only a grimace—"I am a fish entirely out of water."

"Not a fish. A water fey. Probably part selkie," Thomas corrected.

"Fine, a water fey. Plus, I am probably the victim of a mind-control experiment, and also might have been walking into a goblin trap. And now that I've gone missing, they are probably searching for me with coyotes and bears."

Thomas nodded reluctantly. "Or something."

"Swell." Cyra started to rise. "I don't suppose it would help to join a witness protection program and move to Brazil?"

"No, humans can't help you. But wait," Thomas said; then he leaned forward and reached beneath his damp hair. A moment later he held his goddess medallion out to her. "Take this and wear it, Cyra. It will help. You know, I didn't think it was possible, but you might actually need more protection than I do."

She blinked.

"Thomas, I can't—"

"Take it. Please. We'll both feel better. Let me do what I can to protect you."

Cyra's hand shook as she accepted the medallion. She stared into the peaceful and loving face of the goddess. There was power there, tranquility and protection.

"Thank you," she said sincerely, moved nearly to tears by the gesture. It had been so long since anyone had been kind to her, and she didn't know how to react. Bursting into tears seemed excessive, but she wanted to.

"Put it on," he urged.

"Okay." It took her a moment to find the clasp because it kept tangling in the thick hair that curled at her nape. Once found, she was unable to guide the ring into the tiny lock.

"Allow me," Thomas said, leaning forward.

His fingers were quick and warm where they brushed against her flesh. "It isn't a skin, but maybe it will help."

Perhaps it was simply suggestion, a placebo effect, but Cyra felt much better having the goddess medallion close to her.

"Thank you. I've been feeling a little like Alice down the rabbit hole," she said. "I wouldn't be at all surprised to find some bottles of potion lying about saying 'eat me' or 'drink me'."

Thomas gave her an odd look.

"What?" she asked. "What did I say?"

"Nothing. That isn't a bad analogy really. And, as I recall, Alice wasn't particularly afraid in her adventures. You don't seem to be either."

"Oddly enough, I'm not. Not now. Though the freak-out factor may go up if I start seeing white rabbits and mad hatters." She stopped joking. "Thomas? When I saw the coyote and bear . . ."

"Yes?" His eyes were alert.

"Do you think they were after you? Or were they really after me?"

Thomas smoothed back her hair and adjusted his charm so that it lay between her breasts, just over her heart. The gesture was not sexual, but it still made Cyra's heart beat faster.

"Let's hope we never know the answer to that.

Let us never discover whether they wanted you or Malcolm Fayre."

"Malcolm Fayre?" Cyra repeated. Then she realized somehow that he was referring to himself. "Why that name? I thought you were . . ." She stopped before saying his full name, recalling that it had been some sort of spell.

"Malcolm Fayre is a version of my name—a middle name and a title." He paused, then added: "My full name, in English, is Thomas Malcolm Marrowbone. I am also known as the quiet man. Malcolm Fayre was not the most subtle of aliases, I grant you, but every time one of them used it, the use of part of my name put them a little more in my power. It didn't confer the sort of compulsion that saying 'Thomas Marrowbone' could to manipulate them, but it was enough to give me a small edge while I was down in their goblin city."

"Are you going to stay in my head?" Cyra asked, not angry or frightened anymore now that he was just a shadow at the edge of her mind, but she was still rather curious about his intentions and plans for her.

He hesitated a moment, then said truthfully: "Yes. For a while."

"Why? Is it because . . ." This question was harder. "Is it because there is something else in there too? Something the goblins put in my brain?" That was a terrible thought.

"I don't see anything obvious," he assured her. He also didn't pretend not to know what she meant. "No suicide spells, no program to murder someone. But you have a hole in your psyche. Your magic is beginning to wake up, and until you learn to control it, you will be vulnerable to whatever stronger will comes along and decides to attack you. A gifted magician could even steal your power."

Cyra's brows pulled together. "A breach? Because of my missing skin?" she guessed.

"Yes. But don't worry about it. As long as I'm here guarding the gate, no one else will be able to get at you. I have to set up a defense for you before anyone tries anything. I've learned that with goblins, it doesn't pay to be reactive."

Cyra nodded, but she wasn't happy.

"You don't like me in your head?" he asked. Then, more stiffly: "Do I feel unbearably alien?"

"It isn't that," she told him, laying a hand on his arm. Stupidly, she wanted to comfort him for having to do what he did to her. Maybe it was some version of the Stockholm Syndrome. "It's just that I'm not used to thinking of myself as being weak-minded and vulnerable. It frightens me not to have complete control."

"You aren't weak-minded," he assured her, covering her fingers briefly. "You just have an

Achilles heel and have only been given silly sandals to wear over it. As soon as we get you some sensible shoes, you'll be fine."

Cyra smiled slightly at the analogy, then the image of this man's "sensible shoes." She thought of the sturdy black things her mother always wore. The woman had certainly not worshipped the god—or goddess—of fashion.

"And I promise not to take advantage of you again. At least, I won't until you get some sensible footwear," Thomas added. "After that, all bets are off."

"Are you flirting with me?" Cyra asked, intrigued by the notion.

"Yes, I believe I am. I think maybe I am still a little bit under the influence of that goblin drug." Thomas spoke his admission so mildly that he almost distracted Cyra from the fact that he looked a bit like some sort of predator. With his dark hair slicked back he resembled a large, wet panther—though she had never seen a panther with such flat gold eyes.

Of course, what he really resembles is a dragon, she thought, looking at the faint pattern on Thomas's skin exposed by the vee of his pleated shirt. And dragons have eyes of gold.

Cyra blinked twice.

"No way," she muttered, but took another quick look.

"Thomas?" she started to ask. "You never said what kind of fey you are. You aren't really—"

"No more questions right now," he interrupted, rising easily to his feet. His sinewy arms slid away from her fingertips in one smooth motion. "What we need more than anything else is something to eat, and then to rest."

Reminded of her body's needs, Cyra realized that she was ravenous. Her body was, in point of fact, starving. She hadn't eaten for—she thought back—five days! She'd only had water.

"I don't suppose this place runs to pizza?" she asked. "I'd commit murder for a pepperoni pizza with extra cheese and olives."

Thomas gave his half smile, his eyes golden, gleaming pools in the chamber's soft light. "I shouldn't think so—but with a *tomhnafurach*, one never knows."

Chapter Four

"What I have not been able to figure out is why they ever decided to store all this nuclear waste near a volcano. It seems so idiotic," Cyra mumbled around a mouthful of fruit. She was only nibbling now on the bright seedless berries Thomas had found for them. Her terrible hunger had abated quickly after she took her first few bites of the fruit. She dined now out of pleasure at the foreign taste and the slight euphoria it caused.

"The goblins arranged to have it brought there, of course. Plenty of rational people raised objections to storing nuclear waste in a region with energetic volcanic activity. But it isn't a heavily populated state—at least, not heavily populated by humans—and money talks, especially in Washington. In the end, the lutins got their way."

"I hadn't thought a lot about the goblins before this thing happened at Bracebridge, but now . . . are these creatures really 'goblins'? They don't seem much like the ones in fairy tales. Those goblins—at least in the stories *I* read—seemed almost benevolent . . . like brownies. These . . . I've come to think of them as thinking insects."

"It isn't an easy question to answer, if you're asking for a genetic analysis. We know little about these goblins pre-twentieth century, and the rest is just fanciful speculation."

"Tell me anyway. They weren't ever human, were they?" Cyra took another berry and stretched out her legs. She and Thomas were sitting near the rath, water that ringed a nearby tiny, flowered island like a moat. It was soothing to both eye and ear, the dancing waters' sound somehow intervening whenever her thoughts became too agitated, a sort of white noise that helped her remain calm. She had half an urge to lay her ear against the glassy floor and see if she could make out just what this fairy mound was whispering. It was strange to think that a place, rather than a person, could have this influence on her. Perhaps later she would be alarmed by it, but right now she was grateful to both Thomas and the shian for helping her re-gather her thoughts.

"Human?" Thomas repeated. "No. To get an answer about goblin heritage, we must enter the realm of myth and legend, science not yet wholly able to explain what they evolved from. The fossil remains of their American hives pre-date human civilization, so it is unlikely they are some rogue branch of the human family tree." Thomas's voice became deep and dreamy.

"I should hope not! I'd hate to think there was *any* relationship." Cyra settled in to learn as much as she could. "But go on."

"Some of our legends say that goblins are part Deev, and it is this which causes them to vie in ugliness of body and soul with the devil himself."

"Deev? You mean, the devil? But I can't imagine feys believe in Christian constructs!"

"We don't. The devil does not belong exclusively to Christians. And he exists. In other cultures he is known as Iblees. Also Azazeel. Oh yes, all cultures acknowledge that there is evil. Most give it a name, an identity. We call it Deev."

Cyra nodded. "Okay, I'll buy that. Go on with the story about these devil-spawn, then. They are the same as the ones in fairy tales?"

"Well, not the friendly ones. From the beginning of human existence, lutins were the enemy of man. It is thought that once they were *peries*—"

"Peries?"

"Yes. The fairest creation of the poetical imagination. Peries are beings made of light and thought, but these peries were different—darker and harder."

"Bad fairies, huh?" Cyra said.

"Yes. Bad fairies." Thomas smiled briefly. "These peries defied the goddess who demanded they share the earth with men and other lesser fey. They said to her: *'We are made of stone and beautiful black water and icy nights. We are as old as time. What is man but poorly shaped clay, and the other faeries but constructs of air and light? They are breakable. They are nothing.'*"

"How arrogant of them."

"Very." Thomas smiled again. "There was finally a war between the species, and the goddess banished them underground until they would make peace with those of earth and air. But these peries did not make peace. Soon, hatred and jealousy and all kinds of evil deeds transformed them. Their souls warped first, and then their bodies. But, rather than feel

63

shame at what they had become, they embraced it. They haughtily rejected the goddess and turned to other evil masters. That is when they must have bred with—"

"Is this really what happened?" Cyra interrupted. "I've never heard anything about this. It certainly wasn't in the Brothers Grimm."

Thomas shrugged, an oddly modern gesture that conflicted with his old-fashioned style of storytelling.

"Who can say if it is true? All the old ones who remember are gone now. But whatever their beginning, these creatures we call goblins have unquestionably bred themselves with demons and other evil beings. They have gotten larger and more magically powerful than the old European legends. And it isn't natural magick that they've chosen, so many of the pure elements—the sea and air especially—have rejected them.

"For this, they hate us, we other feys who stayed loyal to the goddess and are still filled with her pure power. And they hate humans because humans have science and technology to protect them. But more than either of these individually, the goblins especially hate those who possess both science and magic—for we who walk in both worlds are the greatest threat to them."

Cyra swallowed. "And that would include me?"

"Yes. The fact that you are part selkie would especially make them hate you, for though they need water to live, the greatest of waters, the sea, your people's mother, rejects them. Do you know anything of your people? The selkies, unlike many other fey, did not die off entirely during the Solar Event. Living deep beneath the sea, they were protected from much of the solar pollution. They still live and worship in the old ways. Of course, I suspect that you may have other blood in you as well. You have a certain elf-sheen. *Jure que plus belle este que fee.*"

Not sure why, Cyra felt herself smile. "What does that mean?"

"It means '*you are as fair as an elf woman.*' "

"Oh." Cyra looked down.

"I didn't mention this to embarrass you. It is simply fact."

"I'm not embarrassed," she lied. But of course she was—partly because there was still a lingering feeling that being fey was *bad*, and partly because Thomas thought she was pretty.

Of course, it was likely he knew her true feelings because he was still in her brain—a brain she didn't know very well, as it turned out. In a lot of ways, she was very human. Her everyday world hadn't prepared her for a journey through the arcane, and she didn't know how to react now that she was part of the magic of the world. Never had her common sense said: Here lie dragons, or, Beware of elves. If she had inner maps to the realms of magic, they were hidden deep in her psyche. Yet, the time had come for her to navigate this foreign land. Hopefully she would find something to guide her before she made too large a fool of herself.

Thomas smiled slightly, knowing her thoughts. Cyra rushed into speech, trying to distract both of them from her Achilles heel. "I've never been certain about the difference between elves and fairies. Or even dwarves. Any of this bedtime-story stuff. Faeries have wings, right?"

"Some do. Elves and faeries are close kin, both lovers of poetry and music. Generally, elves are taller and tend to live in mounds rather than gardens or places of air. Both races are beautiful." Thomas paused, then said: "I noticed the slight trough you have on each side of your spine. That is an elven mark. They are sometimes called 'hollow men' because of this. Of course, it's a mistake made by humans because actually only the elf women have hollows in their backs."

He looked over at her, gauging her reaction to this bit of news.

"*Hm.* I didn't know that . . . about elves. Go on."

"But the dwarves . . . dwarves always were different. Especially politically. They never had a monarchy. And they also liked to live below the earth or deep inside mountains. Though they were not evil, it never bothered them to be kept from the light and air."

"Did any survive the Solar Event and the drought?"

"Maybe. But we haven't found them yet."

"We? Are there many more of . . . us?"

Thomas smiled. "Yes. And we surviving feys are slowly organizing. We have been accepted by the human world, but . . . As of yet we have no system of governance, but since most of us consider ourselves American, we will probably marry the new and old systems and eventually we will have a parliament of sorts. Our current leader is called Jack Frost. It wasn't in the papers, but Jack and his wife Io were the ones who took out the Detroit hive and killed the presidential nominee William Hamilton when they found out he was a goblin."

Cyra blinked. "Politics and magic. They seem strange bedfellows," she said.

"Indeed, but the pairing has always been there. And a confederacy among feys—whatever our specialties and loyalties—is needed if we magical beings are to survive. These are perilous times for those who remain. Since the Solar Event we were all forced to integrate with human. Cooperation is imperative."

"Integrate? Are we all *crossed*?" Cyra felt a little overwhelmed.

"We believe so. No pure-blooded feys have been found anywhere in the world, excepting the selkies. Those of us on land are all hybrids."

"So, I'm part selkie and maybe elf . . ." Cyra couldn't help it; she reached back and felt the shallow trough that edged her spine. The physical proof of her mixed blood made her shiver. "Thomas, what are you? Are you an elf, too? Is that why this place knew you?" She looked into his yellow eyes and waited.

Thomas again smiled slightly, and Cyra was certain that he felt her remaining discomfort and confusion at the earlier compliment, and that he was amused at her returning to the subject in spite of it. What could she say? She was more curious than embarrassed, and she really did want to know about him. Silence and lies had been the emotional currency of her past life, but it seemed to be the coin of the realm no longer. Thomas seemed willing to speak to her about many personal, magical things. She was ready to listen.

"Would you like the poetical answer?" he asked.

"We could start with that."

"I was made of two smokeless fires and partly of great beauty. I'm one part dragon, one part jinn, one part peri, one part human wizard. My father was Zobalah, my mother Triste. If you study fey history, you will learn about them. They were rather famous—or infamous. It depends which books you read." Thomas turned his head and looked out over the rolling water. His angular face held slashes of shadow from the flickering firelight. He didn't look cold or forbidding, but his expression was stern.

"I don't mean to upset you by being personal," Cyra explained softly. "But you do look a little like a dragon—in a nice way—and I wondered."

"This doesn't upset me," Thomas said. He turned back to her, and she wondered whether he was lying. Unfortunately, she couldn't see into his mind the way he could look into hers. He continued: "It does, however, sometimes bother other people. Especially those who try to get close to me. You see, there are no *nice* dragons."

"I can't imagine why they'd be bothered," Cyra said honestly, looking him over. "Your markings are beautiful—like lace. And you seem very nice to me."

Thomas hesitated, then said: "It is not my skin that bothers them. Other parts of the dragon's nature can manifest themselves at inconvenient moments. Humans especially tend to be disconcerted when this happens, and less than confident about my assurances that I keep that part of me on a very short leash."

"You don't breathe fire, do you?" Cyra asked before she could stop herself. The thought of him throwing back his head as he climaxed and exhaling a long moan of flame over a lover was appalling.

Thomas gave another half smile and shook his head, but he didn't explain exactly what did frighten people. "Just now I wish I had more of my mother's gifts," he told her finally. "She had knowledge of futurity."

"You mean precognition?" Cyra shook her head. "No thanks. From all I've heard about people with *the sight*, it's more of a curse than a blessing. I wouldn't want it. Imagine knowing when friends or family would die."

"She did not see individual deaths," Thomas answered. "She saw magical cataclysms. She saw the end of the pure feys. She warned them, but, of course, there was nothing that could be done. Even their combined magic could not stop the deadliness of the sun."

Cyra started to ask another question, but she got ambushed by a yawn. It shuddered up from her torso, shaking her entire body.

"And I think that is enough tales for one day," Thomas decided. "It's time for you to sleep. We will worry about dragons and goblin plots later."

"Are you going to sleep too?" Cyra asked. She looked dubiously at the pallet of stones he had earlier assured her was a bed.

"Soon. I need to find some things in the *tomhnafurach* before we leave."

"What things? Clothes?" Cyra yawned again. Against her will, her eyes began to close. "You know, I feel a little like those birds who get drunk on pyracantha berries. My head is light, but I feel like I'm flying."

"You look a bit like those birds too." Thomas drew her to her feet, holding her up when she had trouble making her knees work properly. "In fact, I think it might be best . . ."

He slid his arms around her and lifted her into the air. He began walking toward the rock bed.

"Careful, I'm slippery," she warned, knowing Thomas would understand what she couldn't explain.

"I won't drop you. I've carried sea fey before."

She nodded, pleased. After a moment she asked, "Thomas, are you good at poker?"

He arrived at the bed. "Very. When I can find someone dumb enough to play with me."

He laid her down on the stone bier and watched as the rocks quickly conformed to her shape, snugged in around her. The firelight obligingly dimmed, bringing twilight to the chamber. "See? Snug as a bug in a rug," he said.

"What kind of bug?" Cyra asked. But she was asleep before he could answer.

Thomas looked down at the sleeping Cyra, bedeviled.

"You are part selkie and part *what*?" he asked himself. "Not just elf. Something the goblins want, obviously. But what? And how badly do they want you?" He shook his head. "Cyra Delphin, strange baby fey, what on earth am I going to do about you?"

He would likely have to do something, and soon. Though it was dangerous to have her near him right now—really at any time—she plainly could not be left on her own. The goblins would take her, mind and body and perhaps even soul, if they got the chance.

He couldn't allow that. The dragon inside him

especially wouldn't allow it. The beast had been twitching for the last several hours, testing the strength of the place where Thomas had it imprisoned. It was part of the unfortunate nature of the beast, which he had mentioned so casually. Dragons hoarded. Once they considered something theirs, it was theirs forever. The dragon had been lonely and bored for a long time now, and Thomas had the feeling it had decided—without ever actually seeing her—that Cyra Delphin belonged to it. And it wanted out to play with her.

Or maybe it was something more sinister. Maybe, like the goblins, the dragon could sense something in Cyra that made her useful to it. The thought brought a frown. He didn't need this added distraction. It was never wise to fight a battle on two fronts—especially when the second battle was an internal one. He would have to hope the dragon was just being a dragon, and not making definite plans to use this pretty sea fey in some nefarious scheme of its own.

Chapter Five

Cyra dreamed. The dream did not show her anything at first. Instead, it was a voice whispering in her ear, reminding her of a poem she had read in college.

For walking with his fey, her to the rock
    he brought,
On which he oft before his necromancies
    wrought.
And going in thereat, his magics to have
    shown,
She stopt the cavern's mouth with an
    enchanted stone,
Whose cunning strongly crost, amazed
    while he did stand,
She captive him conveyed unto the Faerie-
    land.

Suddenly an image bloomed in her mind of a man—a knight who was also a wizard—clad in somber robes. Beside him stood a creature of intense beauty, a being seemingly made of light.

Neither of them spoke, nor gave any other clues as to their identity, but Cyra was certain that she was looking at two of Thomas's ancestors, The two people from whom he derived his peri and human parts.

The image faded away and was replaced by another. Cyra saw the mound as it had been when feys still inhabited the shian. It was beautiful, full of wondrous gardens and light— a beautiful light that was bright but kinder than the sun because it came from the magic within and around every being who lived in the *tomhnafurach*. Again, a voice whispered in her brain telling her with words and images that it had not been men who forced the faeries underground with their weapons of cold iron, but rather the sun itself had driven them beneath the planet's surface. And once separated, the rivalries and wars between the magical races had started.

Cyra stirred uneasily. She was fascinated, but also fearful. What if the shian showed her something about herself—something awful? Something bad inside of her that made her attractive to the goblins. She wasn't ready to face any more truths about herself.

She wanted Thomas to come back. She wouldn't be frightened if he was with her. Her hand reached out, stretching for her savior.

Rising out of smoke, he appeared before her. He was Thomas and yet not—because though it was Thomas's face that approached her, on his back was a pair of wings, and in his eyes there burned a red fire.

His hands reached for her, stripping away the virginal white gown she wore. He laid her down on a stone altar as though preparing her for a sacrifice. She looked up, unafraid and unresisting as he lowered himself onto her. She would not die. She was not a victim, not a weapon—she was a vessel.

"For us," he whispered. "That we may live."

His kiss was hard, an onslaught, but she did not resist it. And as her lips parted and their breath joined, something that was Thomas—his magic, his soul—was joined to the power that was in her and made her strong. It also filled her with a longing and need for completeness that was almost pain.

His hands were on her then. There was no time for her to respond even had she known what to say. Her legs were pushed apart roughly on the cold stone.

She made no sound as he pushed into her. Her breath was gone, all words taken—just as she was being taken.

The cords in his neck pulled tight, the muscles of his chest segmenting into ridges, his leathery wings stretching toward the sky.

She arched up to meet him, to receive, and was filled with fire. It was the same magical fires where the first feys were born.

Thomas paused to look at the beautiful illuminated manuscript. He figured that these days they probably wrote more poetry about love than about power, but he was willing to bet that power was much more often in human thoughts. He knew it was so with goblins.

Of course, he thought while moving on, love hadn't been on his own mind a lot lately either. Or sympathy, or compassion. Softer emotions weren't a help in his line of work. They weren't a help now.

Thomas was searching for weapons. Not knives or guns—though he would not have turned those down, either—but rather weapons of magic and knowledge. He would love to find an elf-book, the small folios elves gave humans when they wished them to be able to see magical creatures and even understand their language. Such a tome would be of immense aid to Cyra. Her ignorance of her strengths and weaknesses made her extremely vulnerable to goblin attack. If she had had the gift of elf-sight, she would have known that goblins were manipulating her.

Also, such a gift might help her overcome her feelings of shame at being alien. It would give her access to fey language, and then Thomas could explain what they both were and why she should be proud of her heritage. It was difficult to do in English because the non-magical language simply did not have words for all the miraculous concepts that could be realized when not limited by the five human senses and the three-dimensional Newtonian universe Cyra had been exiled to when her parents took her skin.

Cyra. What an odd turn events had taken. Who could have anticipated this? A week ago Thomas had been having fun in Sin City, playing with the goblins' finances and working toward seducing the horrid Lilith.

It had been easy to subjugate a couple of the goblin-troll cross breeds in accounting and get them to cough up passwords for their computers. The kinds of goblins with the sorts of brains that could deal with tech stuff were also unusually susceptible to mind control.

After that, it had been a breeze to mess with

their systems. During daylight hours when the goblins slept below ground, Thomas had begun sliding money down the wire at the speed of light, routing it through a series of dummy banks before distributing the goblins' wealth— about $123 million, in fact—among deserving causes. He'd also left enough evidence behind to interest any non-corrupt Fed agents who happened to audit Lilith's empire. Doubtless a banker could have improved on his larceny, but Thomas was just a hacker and had been forced to make do with stealing what he could before blowing the goblin accounting system to cyber smithereens.

In the course of his massive electronic theft, Thomas had run across some other interesting files and those he'd copied and smuggled out online. It had been a bit tricky because security around the *lutinempire* site was tight—or had been before he'd gotten to it. A brief investigation had shown him enough to know that he was on to something important. It seemed that the goblin queen had bought herself some high-powered FBI types and a general or two in the Pentagon. The compromised Feds probably had no idea that it wasn't only their morals they had sold, but access to their computer systems. The goblins had been making extensive use of them, and setting up the corrupted agents to take the fall if their villainy was ever uncovered.

It was there, hidden among the other nefarious projects, that Thomas had come across a reference to Yucca Mountain. A little extra digging had uncovered General Fornix's plot to steal the nuclear waste stored there and make a dirty bomb.

Thomas had tried to lift the details out without alerting anyone, but the encryption on that part of the site had been dense and tricky. He'd blundered into a trap and alarms had gone off.

Things deteriorated quickly after that. One could usually Swiss cheese a problem, punching holes in it until it was gone, but this wasn't an occasion for a slow, methodical approach to disarmament. He hadn't had enough time to uncover all the details of the plot and gather evidence before his financial traps were sprung and the goblins were alerted that he'd been in their system.

It didn't take them long to interview the programming staff and find out who had been placed under compulsion, then guess who had done it. Sin City attracted magical types, but he was the only dragon in town. In fact, as far as he knew, he was the only dragon left in the world. That was what had made him attractive to Lilith.

Thomas smiled, showing a lot of teeth, some of which were quite sharp. It wasn't the pleasant half smile Cyra was used to seeing.

What a pity the goblin queen's interest in him hadn't been enough to get her alone. He would have enjoyed breaking her fat neck, and would have actually let the dragon out to do it. But Lilith had made it plain that though she really wanted to take a dragon to bed, she did nothing without her faithful troll, Lancilotto. And though Thomas was fast and also good at mind control, he knew he couldn't take out both Lilith and her enormous bodyguard. They were both clever and vicious—and strong. Lilith personally strangled the two cross-breed accountants who had given Thomas their passwords. Their necks had been the size of dinner plates, but she had crushed them like they were jelly. Then Lancilotto had torn them apart and eaten them.

Thomas hadn't actually felt what happened to the programmers, but he'd still been in one of the panicked accountants' head when he saw his friend strangled, then consumed.

Recalled to the present by a small rumble, Thomas eyed the map that suddenly appeared on the stone table which had risen out of the floor on his arrival. It was a thing of beauty, supposedly written by The Most Powerful Of

All, but Thomas didn't touch it. The map had a glow about it, suggesting it was enchanted. The last thing he needed at the moment was to get bitten by a *geas*. He didn't need a treasure-quest compulsion dragging him away from his urgent problems while he searched for apocryphal gold.

The mound was trying to be helpful, one by one offering up items that had been popular with other visitors, but so much of the magic was useless, having no power outside of the shian. There had been the golden bridle that would allow its possessor to control enchanted beasts—handy if Thomas had planned on subduing kelpies. Or maybe Cyra. And the celestial planisphere certainly was lovely, but without his mother's gift of futurity, he could look in the crystal ball all day and still see nothing useful.

Thomas strolled around the room. The floor was different here. It looked like it might have once been laid out as a mosaic of some sort, but the various stones had melted into a blurred pattern that was dreamy rather than distinct. Perhaps the magic was just fading from the shian and it was unable to hold on to the patterns of the fey-made art.

The next offering on the table was a pot of yellow powder that could turn any metal rubbed with it into gold. There was very little metal to be had in the mound, though, and in any event, Thomas needed cold iron more than gold, so this metallurgical transformer was useless.

He supposed that it might amuse Cyra to drive the Honda into the shian and then buff it out with the powder, but a gold car would be heavy and the pistons would melt as soon as the engine was started. They had to be practical.

A wrought censer was the next offering. Again, it was beautiful, but there was nothing to burn in it, even if Thomas had been inclined to summon something from the underworld.

Ah, but the next item at the buffet was very useful. It was what they called a thousand-key. Basically, it was a magical lockpick. Thomas pocketed it. He knew basic lock-picking, but it wasn't one of his lifelong passions, and there were many locks he couldn't manage on his own.

The last piece of the supernatural smorgasbord was a pot of unguent. Thomas sniffed it carefully. Four-leaf clover balm. If you rubbed it in one eye, it would show you all the magical beasties and places that lurked nearby. Rubbed in two eyes, it would drive a human mad.

Thomas considered the item carefully. The

ointment would help Cyra spot any goblin traps, but it would also show her many alarming things she was probably not ready to see. There were too many quick-moving shadows inside the mound. They would probably scare her into immobility if he didn't keep firm control of her mind.

Of course, later on . . .

Thomas slipped the unguent into his pocket with the key.

"So, no elf-books?" he asked the mound.

The Shian's constant whispering paused. Thomas waited, but no book appeared.

"Well, damn. Thank you for the key and the unguent. *Tapadh leibh,*" he added in Gaelic. Then after repeating his thanks again in Elvish, he retreated back to the room where Cyra slept.

Cyra was having another dream. She was walking naked through the desert night when a bright moon appeared from behind a cloud. Its brilliant face smiled benignly. Down reached a silver beam and began winding itself about her. She wanted to run away—knew she should because her parents were calling to her with angry voices—but the light was so beautiful, so soft on her skin. And the moon loved her too, claimed her as its child. It told her that she was being reborn and today was her birthday. She didn't need her skin anymore because the moon had something better.

Thomas stopped in his tracks, his feet riveted to the floor by spikes of amazement as he stared at the still sleeping Cyra. He was used to the shian's ways and was not surprised that it would try to do something for Cyra, but he had not expected this gift. Spread over the sleeping woman's body was a silver cape. The liquid crystal garment spun of moonshine was the badge of the Kloka—the elven conjurers.

A conjurer! Could that be what she was? They were rare, born only every millennium, and only to certain elfin families.

Thomas forced himself to move closer to Cyra's bed.

A kloka. It was difficult to credit—like seeing a unicorn in downtown Manhattan. But it would explain why the goblins wanted her. If she *was* Kloka, and they could somehow gain control of her mind, they could use her to cause mass hallucinations and hysteria among the human populace. Depending on her degree of power and control, she could project an illusion to an entire city. Maybe even an entire state. Really powerful conjurers had enchanted whole nations.

And the greatest of them could conjure more than just illusions.

"Goddess, preserve us," he whispered to himself.

Could she truly be part Kloka? And would that cape offer her protection, or would it only make her more vulnerable to the goblins? Maybe he should take it away, hide it until she had learned—

Cyra's eyes fluttered open. She smiled at him, her expression both sleepy and sweet as a Kewpie doll as she held out her arms.

"Isn't it pretty?" she asked, her voice a dreamy murmur. "The moon gave it to me, Thomas. Today is my new birthday. Have you brought me a present too?"

Chapter Six

The tunnels tended to look very much alike, but Cyra somehow realized that they were leaving the shian by a different route than they had entered. When she asked Thomas why, he explained that the first door had been sealed completely in case the goblin hunters had managed to track them.

"But what about my car? Won't they have trashed it?"

"Don't worry about the car. It was hidden. We'll still be able to use it."

"But how? Who . . . ?"

"Life is different here. Such things are arranged. Try not to put too much pressure on yourself by worrying about mundane matters. I'll let you know if we're in trouble."

Cyra snorted. "Don't put pressure on myself?" she repeated. She stopped in a light well and looked up at the opaque ceiling of glass— or something—that let a moderate amount of failing daylight into the chamber, allowing the various flowering vines to bask happily. "The goblins are getting ready to loose the Apocalypse on the western U.S. We have goblin hunters after us and may be stranded in the desert without transportation. We— What's that?"

Cyra peered into the shadows under a particularly dense tangle of red-flowering cane. It seemed to her that one of the shadows beneath it was moving, perhaps even staring at her with gray eyes.

"It's a dust bunny," Thomas said. "Don't worry about them. They're everywhere. You can see them now because of the unguent you rubbed in your eye." He sounded slightly disapproving.

Of course, he hadn't seemed happy to return from his last bath in the healing waters to discover her experimenting with the *gifts* he had handed over when she'd asked if he had brought her any presents. Perhaps he felt that she'd caused herself undue stress. But why had he given her the unguent if he didn't want her to use it?

"You must relax," he said. "We are not

stranded. We have food and water—and other things on our side."

"Relax? Right. You think maybe Moses tried that one on his fleeing people right before he began parting the Red Sea?"

"Probably, and to as little avail," Thomas sighed. "Come along, ye of little faith. No one has to part the sea, just the mountains."

"No one understood Pandora either," Cyra muttered to herself, feeling persecuted for her curiosity.

Thomas walked toward what looked like a blank red stone wall. "Oh, we all understood her. We just wished she had kept her hands to herself. Amateur!"

Cyra, surprisingly, felt hurt by this remark—and for being called an amateur—less for the word than the tone in which it was uttered. Thomas had been short with her ever since she woke up and showed him her cloak. His irritation was like sand trapped in the shell of her brain. She tried to think of something light to say, but couldn't.

The pause that followed was what one might call pregnant—except Cyra never used that word. Pregnant was a forbidden word, totally *verboten.* Children were absolutely out of the question for her because she was alien, unnatural, and no man would ever want—

"Stop that at once!" Thomas spun about and glared at her. "That is old programming from your parents. Erase it. You are fey, not the plague. Goddess, protect the innocent and stupid! It's no wonder the goblins got to you, Cyra. You've been brainwashed from birth. Isn't it bad enough that the drought and solar pollution killed off most of our kind? Should we be denied even the chance to repopulate?"

Suddenly, feeling Cyra's shocked pain like a whip across his shoulders, Thomas took two steps back and wrapped her in his arms. Remorse and apologies poured over her.

"I'm sorry," he began.

"No." Cyra interrupted him, wrapping her arms around his waist and accepting his gesture of comfort for what it was. "You're right. I have all this horrible stuff in my head and I—"

"You'll deal with it in time," Thomas assured her. "I am sorry for being so cross. That damned cloak has just opened up a whole new world of possibility and danger for us. It also makes it harder for me to . . ."

"To control me?"

"No, but to monitor—"

"It's okay, Thomas. You don't have to dress it up. I know that I'm probably a danger to you— to *us*—as I am. And I'm sorry. I am doing my best to learn everything as fast as I can." She rested her head on his chest. Then, hearing twin but slightly offset beats, she looked back up. "Thomas, do you have two hearts?"

"Yes." He paused then added: "One for the human, and one for the dragon. Though, if the right circumstances ever arise, I'll be able to send the dragon away and still live."

"The dragon needs his own heart?" Cyra asked, fascinated by the idea. She laid a hand on Thomas's breast, trying to feel where both hearts were. She added with growing excitement: "Your internal physiology must be absolutely fascinating!"

Thomas's lips twisted into a half smile, but there was no amusement in his reply. "The dragon needs his own everything. He's a dragon. He doesn't share well."

"But what about the jinn?"

"It's different. Besides, they don't have hearts." Thomas sounded suddenly sad.

Above them, the light changed from orange to gray, underlining his somber reply. He added in businesslike tones: "It's almost dark now. We should go. We need every minute of darkness for our travels. The day weakens us. And now that you are no longer under compulsion by the goblins you will feel the loss of the sea keenly during daylight hours." He ran his hands down her back a last time and then reluctantly stepped away from her.

Determined not to be a further burden, Cyra assumed an equally businesslike demeanor and stepped over to the wall, which she began examining with care.

"What are you looking for?" Thomas asked. He watched her run her hands over the rough stone and peer into cracks.

"The secret lever," Cyra answered, squatting down to feel the stone near the floor. "It has to be here someplace. Usually I am pretty good at finding things. I have a sort of gift for it."

"I see. But what makes you think there is some secret here?"

Detecting the amusement in his voice, Cyra stopped hunting and turned to face him. "There was always a secret entrance in Nancy Drew," she said. "And all the rest of this is like a bedtime story. . . ."

Thomas laughed. The sound was low and caressing to the ears.

Cyra stood again. She was glad that Thomas wasn't looking angry anymore, but she didn't especially like looking foolish. Again. "There's no hidden lever, no concealed trap door?"

"No. Not exactly." Thomas said something in a foreign tongue.

Behind Cyra there came a sound of crumbling rock. She turned quickly but was too late to see how the door appeared.

"What did you say? Was that a spell?" she demanded, thinking about Thomas's wizard grandfather that she'd seen in her dream.

"No. I simply asked the shian to please open the passage. Don't worry. When we have time I'll teach you to speak Elvish." Then Thomas stepped past her and went out into the night.

Cyra started after him, but paused. "I don't know if you can understand English," she said, addressing the room at large. "But I want to thank you for everything you've done."

A sudden soft breeze rose up and caressed her face with invisible fingers. *We'll be in touch, daughter,* said some other voice that spoke with thought and not with a tongue. *Our gift goes with you for now.*

Shaken by the final proof that the shian was truly alive, and wondering if the "touch" mentioned was literal, Cyra retreated down the short passage and out into the bright desert night.

Thomas insisted they approach the Panamint Mountains by a circuitous route. Cyra didn't argue the plan. They had managed to avoid any coyotes or bears on their journey so far, and she was more than content to have it remain that way.

Furnace Creek was unpleasantly warm as they passed through it, but not as hot as Bad Water had been. Thomas explained the extreme temperatures by pointing out that Bad Water was actually 200 feet below sea level. Once the heat settled into the airless depression, there was nothing to move it out.

"This is one of the driest places on earth," Thomas said, satisfaction clear in his voice. "The humidity rarely rises above five percent. The goblins can't live here. They'd desiccate like a mummy in half a day."

"I don't think selkies can live here either," Cyra muttered.

"Wait and see," was all Thomas said.

Soon after that, he directed them out onto the salt flats and toward the mountains. Though there was no road of any kind, somehow he managed to guide them into the foothills and then deep into the Panamint range.

"Stop here," Thomas said as they approached what looked like a blank cliff wall. "We must wait for moonset."

Cyra shut off the Honda's exhausted engine and climbed out of the car. Thomas joined her, turning to look with narrowed eyes out at the valley they'd left behind. He didn't seem to be exactly lost in appreciation of the view, but Cyra didn't interrupt his careful inspection.

She could certainly understand his lack of aesthetic appreciation. The brown and yellow valley was silvery in the moonlight, but there were no trees to break up the monotony of endless miles of low brown scrub. It was boring. The Nevada desert differed from the dry lands of Arizona and New Mexico. It wasn't red, it wasn't landscaped with giant striated stones, and it had no water. At least, none that Cyra could see.

"The moon is setting," Thomas said and turned to the cliff face. "Watch now. There."

He was right. In the last moments of silvery light, the outline of a door appeared. Thomas walked up to it and said something soft and musical in what Cyra assumed was yet another fey language. As had happened at the other shian, there was a sound of crumbling rock and the stones seemed to fold back on themselves, leaving a way open into a rough tunnel.

"That is so awesome," Cyra whispered. "You couldn't get a hole that deep even with dynamite. The whole mountain would cave in."

"Magic is often preferable to brute force," Thomas agreed. "You might remember that rule. Given the time, always ask permission. Magical things can be forced and manipulated, but there is always a high price for doing so." He looked at her. "Okay, let's go."

They climbed back into the Honda, and Cyra coaxed it once more to life. She turned on the car's fading headlights. She was getting tired, but Thomas had explained that it was her will holding the car together, that without her behind the wheel, the Honda would give up and die.

"We just drive in?" she asked, looking first at the tunnel and then at Thomas.

"Yes, just drive in."

"Okay." Cyra slipped the car in gear and started into the tunnel. She didn't look back when she heard the stones closing behind them.

It wasn't that she was afraid, she assured herself. But she had always been a little claustrophobic, so there was no need to risk upsetting herself by looking back at the wall now sealed behind them. Sudden awareness of the weight of the mountain overhead was quite disturbing enough.

The tunnel seemed to go on forever. Cyra kept looking at the odometer, wondering how far into the blackness they would have to go. Finally, at twenty miles, Thomas again told her to stop.

"We leave the car here," he said, climbing out.

Cyra joined him, this time pulling on her cloak. It made her feel slightly more protected.

Thomas frowned at the silver cape but didn't tell her to leave it behind. "This way," he said, stepping up to a blank wall and addressing it in a foreign tongue. A much smaller tunnel obligingly appeared. He turned and waited for Cyra.

Swallowing her uneasiness, she stepped into the narrow stone hall.

Her instincts had been right. She was entering a foreign world. The first chamber they encountered was peopled by the eight-foot forms of withered mummies. The creatures wore armbands of gold and carried spears that looked vaguely Mayan. They had disproportionately large heads that tilted forward so chins rested on broad chests. Cyra expected the room to smell musty, but the atmosphere was wholesome, dry and airy.

"What are they?" she asked, slightly revolted.

"Giants. We've left them here because we don't know anything about their burial rituals, and disturbing them does not seem wise." Thomas took her hand and squeezed it soothingly. "Don't be frightened. I won't let anything get you."

Surprised, Cyra looked up at him. "I'm all right," she assured him. "I was just a little surprised to see mummies. The other shian didn't have them."

"I know you are all right. It's just . . ." Thomas shrugged. "I hope you'll like it here. It is difficult that your first exposure to magic should come during such troubled times."

It didn't seem the right moment to make jokes about being gentle with a virgin, but Cyra didn't know what to say except: "I hope I'll like it here too."

Thomas nodded, then turned away.

They passed several chambers filled with gemstones and bricks of gold. The chambers were lit by small flames of blue and orange that bled out of the cracked walls. Seeing her amazement, Thomas explained.

"It's the giants' horde."

"It's real?"

"Yep. Real enough. But it can't be moved outside of the mountain. The giants laid some sort of spell on it, which so far no one has been able to crack. I gather the Paihute Indians tried, and a couple of men who stumbled into this place back in the '30s. But none of them had any luck bringing treasure out, so their tales were largely disbelieved—thank the goddess. We'd be buried under treasure hunters right now if the tale were widely accepted."

Cyra closed her enchanted eye. The one without the unguent saw only a room filled with cold, flickering shades of gloom. When she looked in with her magicked eye, she saw something more. There were tiny creatures with massive teeth and claws dancing in the shadows near the flames.

"And the fire? It's not . . . magical?"

"Natural gas. The giants' labyrinth is very clever. It doesn't go deep into the mountain, but everywhere they dwelled is filled with this fire. No one has been able to extinguish it either." Thomas touched her. "We will come back later so you can explore. It is almost dawn now. We need to go on."

The tunnel opened into a second chamber, this one fitted out with an enormous carved and polished table that looked a bit like the reception desk in a hotel lobby. Cyra half expected that they would have to sign some guest book before being allowed any farther.

When she mentioned this to Thomas, she got another of his half smiles. He said: "In a sense, you are right. This is a reception chamber." He raised his hand and rapped sharply on the table. Instead of speaking in Gaelic or Elvish, he crooned: "Little pigs, little pigs, let me come in. Or I'll huff and I'll puff and I'll—"

"There's no need for that, you windbag," a soft, amused voice interrupted. A tall man with

99

silvered hair and eyes stepped into the room. "Thomas, my quiet friend, we had just about abandoned all hope of seeing you again. We got your encrypted e-files and then nothing."

Thomas went to the man and they embraced. Cyra noted that while the silvery man was taller than Thomas, the half dragon-man had him in breadth of shoulders.

"I was pretty close to the end," Thomas admitted. "The goblins poisoned me and sent their hunters to chase me into the desert. But, as always, the goddess provided. Jack, meet my very own miracle."

Both men turned Cyra. She found herself blushing under the scrutiny of their beautiful, metallic eyes.

"This is Cyra Delphin of the selkie, and a kloka," Thomas said by way of introduction. "Cyra, this is Jack Frost."

Jack Frost? Cyra blinked but held her tongue against asking any questions. Jack frightened her a little bit. He seemed surrounded by an air of power, a will, which could at any moment snuff out her life like a breeze could a match's delicate flame. He was a different sort of fey, not like Thomas.

"It is a pleasure," Jack Frost answered, his tone warm and inviting—and completely at odds with his hard eyes, which studied her cloak.

"The pleasure is mine," Cyra lied, hiding her unease behind a serene mask. It earned her another half smile from Thomas.

"Let's go inside," Jack said finally, turning back to a narrow door. "Io will want to see you both."

Thomas took Cyra's arm, again offering unspoken reassurance.

"How are Zayn and Chloe?" he asked the other man.

"Good. Chloe and Io are both close to their time now." Jack's voice didn't change, but Cyra knew instinctively that he was anxious about something.

"All will be well," Thomas assured, apparently also sensing Jack's unease. "Feys can withstand almost anything."

"Except giving birth," Jack said quietly. "And Chloe isn't fey."

Cyra concentrated, forming her question clearly and then attempting to send it straight into Thomas's mind.

"What is he?"

Thomas blinked and looked down at her. He was apparently accustomed to seeing images in her head and feeling her emotions, but not receiving clearly structured requests for information.

"He is a death fey. Where did you learn to mind speak?"

"I've been practicing, talking to the shian," Cyra thought back, allowing her satisfaction to color her message.

Though the tunnel they traveled was enclosed, Cyra had the sense that they were passing over a bridge of some sort, leaving one magicked place and entering another. The change was invisible but nevertheless felt. The largest difference was the lifting of the oppressive weight that had seemed to press down all around them in the outer chambers.

Cyra began listening for the whispering that had been constantly in the background at the other shian. A murmuring was here, but the language, the tone was different. This place sounded distinctly feminine.

"What kind of place is this? It is not like the other one."

This time, Thomas looked truly surprised. *"This place was lived in mainly by faeries and demi-feys. The other was home to the elves. But how could you tell?"*

"The voices," she answered.

"You can hear them?"

"Yes, can't you?"

"Only when I really listen."

"Oh. I hear them all the time."

Jack opened a gate of delicately wrought silver, ushering them into a chamber filled with early dawn light. Once again, the *tomhnafurach* was making use of a light well and a crystal ceiling to capture and reflect the beautiful pink and gold hues that were the birth of a desert day.

"Welcome to *Cadalach.*" Jack's tone was formal. He gestured at the striking gardens. "Enter, all ye of the rainbow, and be at peace here."

A soft breeze scented with all the wonders of happy, growing things reached for Cyra and touched her on the cheek.

Come, daughter of the elves and of the sea, it said.

Cyra answered with her own soft sigh and stepped into the garden. She might have reservations about Jack Frost, the death fey, but the shian truly welcomed her.

Chapter Seven

That there was such an Eden in the desert, let alone under a mountain, was a marvel. Cyra did mental and emotional homage as she wandered with wide eyes and opened mind.

The garden's denizens were obviously real, yet somehow not something that belonged to reality. Reality was about the *now*, the fleeting moment. These gardens were timeless, seasonless, as close to eternal paradise as Cyra could imagine.

She walked through the bower, her senses overwhelmed. For the eyes and nose there were arrays of terraces, each buried under a waterfall of blossoms, flowers of unsubtle shades and less subtle fragrances. Yet not one color or scent or shape was something Cyra could name. It seemed as if she were taking in this garden with new eyes that were able to see things beyond the human spectrum of light, scenting things that had never been noticed when she limited herself to the human olfactory experience.

Had she really changed? Or had all this wonder—all this extrasensory ability—always been there while she walked around half blind and dumb? What a cripple she had been.

The garden didn't stop its sensual assault with what could be seen and smelled. It had treats for the ears; a soft sound of a phantom philomel; a familiar yet illusive whispering that rose up from the lavender-tinged water. And then there was that gentle breeze that slid over Cyra's bare skin in an invisible caress and showered her with a snowfall of faded petals as she passed beneath the heady vines that grew overhead.

This was a place that spoke coaxingly to the Cyra who had once been a happy child. It was a balm to her troubled heart. If she let herself, she knew that she could heal here. She could also become what she was meant to be.

She wanted to say something to Thomas about the stunning sensations bathing her senses, but . . . She shrugged helplessly. Some experiences could not be communicated with words. Or at least not with the words she had.

"I understand," he said softly, coming up behind her.

"It takes a lot of people that way," chimed in a soft, feminine voice.

Cyra turned and faced a small, dark fey with blue eyes that seemed lit from within. So bright were her irises that they seemed to have bled over into the whites of her eyes, staining them a softer shade of blue. It was probably startling enough to distract most people from noticing that she was pregnant.

"Cyra, this is Io," Thomas said, his voice warm with affection. "And the pretty shade behind her is Chloe. Chloe is Zayn's . . ."

"Wife," the slender creature supplied. She stepped out from behind Io and offered a fleeting smile. She was tiny, and delicately made of bruised flesh and shadows. There was a strange nervousness in her eyes, and her restless limbs looked like they needed to clutch at something. She, too, was obviously pregnant.

Cyra was hardly an expert, but she was fairly certain that though Chloe wasn't fey, some magic had been laid over her body and mind in an effort to save her life.

"Thomas, is she . . . ?"

"Human. She was attacked by gargoyles and is still not recovered. There may also be something wrong with the baby."

106

"Your cloak is very pretty," Chloe said.

"Thank you. It . . . was a birthday gift," Cyra answered. She knew her explanation was incomplete but felt unwilling to grope for the words that might explain how the moon had spun out this present while she was sleeping.

"And here is Zayn."

Cyra shifted her gaze to where Io was gesturing. A moment later the shadows pulled themselves together and a fey man appeared in the empty space.

"We have company, Zayn," Io said unnecessarily. "Thomas made it out of Sin City after all!"

"Thomas!" Zayn did not come forward to embrace the other man, but his voice and face proclaimed his happiness. "We'd all but given up on you!"

"Reports of my death have been greatly exaggerated," Thomas quipped.

"I'm sure they were—but not by much." Zayn looked down at Chloe, a quick glance that held worry. His face was exceptionally expressive. The fey tried for raillery, but his voice was hollow. "Leave it to you to find a pretty girl while you were going about it too."

"It's all in the wrist action," Thomas responded, doing a better job of sounding at ease. "This is Cyra Delphin. She's from California."

"I bet there's a story behind that too," Zayn remarked absently. "Welcome, Cyra."

"You'll have to tell us about your adventure later," Io ordered Thomas. "Right now, Cyra is probably tired and desperate for a bath."

Io's words were warm and truthful, but Cyra sensed that the woman was more concerned with Chloe's feelings than the state of Cyra's travel-weary body. Clearly, no one wanted the pregnant girl to hear whatever it was that Thomas had to say about Sin City.

Cyra could understand Jack's uneasiness with her pregnancy. Chloe didn't look strong enough for the rigors of giving birth. Magic was holding her outsides together, but inside she was still broken.

"Io's right. The story of how I met Cyra can wait for later," Thomas said, also looking at Chloe's averted face. "It's a long tale and I'm sure you all can guess the general outline anyway."

"Well, I for one am not interested in playing guessing games before breaking my fast. Come with me, Cyra," Io said. "We'll get you changed and then to the table for a meal. Chloe makes an awesome cup of coffee."

"Oh! Damn." Cyra clapped a hand to her head. "I left my suitcase in the car."

"Don't worry," Io answered. "It will be along

shortly. We have our very own invisible Jeeves to handle things for us."

They sounded like they were reading lines in a Noel Coward play, Cyra thought—or maybe one by Lewis Carroll. It was a different kind of unreality from the garden, and not one that she entirely trusted.

She looked at Thomas, asking if she should go. He nodded once. The council of war was about to get underway, and females weren't wanted at the table. Some things never changed—fey or human.

Cyra barely resisted the urge to stick her tongue out at him.

Io touched her on the arm. She looked vaguely amused.

"Ready?"

"Coffee sounds ambrosial," Cyra said, turning her attention to her hostess. She spoke her next lines without stumbling. "And bed even more so. We've been driving all night, and on some of the ghastliest roads ever *not* paved. In fact, *I* think this state has a lot of nerve even putting some of those goat trails on a map."

Chloe fell into step beside Cyra and Io as they went through a curtain made of some lacy vine and into another tunnel. Cyra tried not stare at her, but it was difficult because of the woman's collection of scars that covered her head to foot.

109

Her body looked as though a fat cobweb had been laid over her in a shroud. The gargoyle claws must have nearly shredded her to pieces.

They passed by a series of empty chambers whose original functions could only be guessed at. Cyra didn't ask any questions about her surroundings, and Io didn't offer any explanations.

Chloe didn't offer anything at all, and when they got to one chamber, obviously a bedroom, she left them.

"Are you the only ones living here now?" Cyra asked Io. Her question was a bit abrupt, but her curiosity would not be contained now that the other woman was gone.

"Yes, at least for right now. Not that there were hordes of us to begin with, you understand. But lately all the goblin hives have been extremely active, and we've had to send people to watch them."

"There are other feys in Sin City?"

"No. Thomas was the only one there. Believe it or not, it wasn't seen as the greatest threat. We have people in New Orleans, Los Angeles, San Francisco, New York and Chicago. As soon as Chloe and I give birth, Zayn will leave for Boston. But he can't go yet. Zayn is a healer and . . . and we may need him."

"And Jack?" Cyra asked.

"As soon as I give birth, he'll leave for Philadelphia. Unless things are very bad in Sin City . . . ? I still have a friend in Humans Under Ground who sometimes talks to me, and I gather that they are concerned."

Cyra hesitated. Chloe wasn't the only pregnant one, and Jack had been worried about his wife.

Io interrupted her thoughts: "It's okay. I'm not Chloe. You can tell me the truth."

"It's bad," Cyra answered. Then, finally realizing the full scope of what the goblins were planning, and how many people would die if they succeeded—among them her few remaining friends at Bracebridge—she added: "It's very, very bad. I think Thomas and I are going to have to go back. Soon."

Io stared at her, her expression and even her eyes growing bleak. Their glow dimmed.

"I'm sorry." Cyra spread her hands.

"Well, suffice it unto the day the trouble therein . . . Jack will probably have some ideas. He and Thomas have worked together many times before, and they are very good at foiling goblin plots," Io said. "At the very least, you'll leave here better equipped now that we understand the threat and can arm you."

"We're gonna need one awesome plan," Cyra

muttered. " 'Cause the goblins' plan's a real son of a bitch."

Io looked amused. "Jack and Thomas don't do mundane. Well, here is your room. Thomas said to put you here." She paused at a door. The panel was thick and aged to near-blackness. "There are two beds, if you need them."

"Um," Cyra began, feeling embarrassed, but Io just kept talking.

"There is also a pool for bathing. The other facilities are down that corridor. It's a bit rustic, I'm afraid. Have you ever used a bidet?"

"Uh . . . yes."

"Good. It is rather a similar setup here. Well, then, I guess there's no putting it off. Here is . . . Thomas's room." Io reached for the latch and pushed open the door. She stood aside so Cyra could see in.

"Oh my."

The light in the room was dim, being supplied only by a half dozen vases filled with luminescent water, but it was enough to see that the bedsteads that occupied the center of the chamber were ancient—over-carved, over-polished, over-draped—matching his and hers monarch beds. They were, depending on one's taste, either majestic or hideous. Looking more closely at the serpents coiled about the posters,

Cyra decided that hideous came closer to her choice.

She looked next at the walls. At least, she assumed there were walls under all the faded tapestries. There were dozens of those. And paintings too. Sculptures, friezes, plaques—a tombstone?

"I know that it's all a bit . . ." Io hesitated as she searched for a word. "Grand."

"Absolutely splendorous," Cyra agreed, stepping into the room. Her feet sank into the thick pelts that covered the floor. "Did Thomas choose this all by himself? Or did Hammer Horror Films help him with the decorating?"

Io grinned.

"They're family heirlooms, I gather. And a part of him likes to collect things."

The dragon in him probably would hoard art, Cyra thought, as Io went on: "But the beds *are* comfortable. And those velvet coverlets are thick as fur and twice as soft."

"Well, they must have *something* going for them. I've always been more of a minimalist myself," Cyra remarked.

Io laughed softly. "I'll leave you to your bath. Come next door when you are done and we'll have some breakfast."

"Okay, assuming I can find the bath." Cyra yawned suddenly.

"It's there, that pool behind the ivory screen. The one with the elephants and tigers."

"Ah! Well, thank you."

"My pleasure," Io assured her. "We are always glad to welcome another of our kind."

Cyra was still not certain how she felt about being one of Io's *kind*, but she appreciated the warmth in the woman's voice.

"And if you would rather sleep first, that is all right too," Io said. "I imagine that, after your last few days, you might need it. Deserts are wonderful because they keep goblins away, but they are not easy on feys either."

Especially selkies.

Cyra yawned again. She really should eat. Of course, she really should find Thomas and insist on being let in on their council of war. It was her right if she was going to make this her fight. And she already had, hadn't she?

As the door closed softly behind Io, Cyra turned and looked at the bed.

Tempting. But not without a bath.

Cyra slipped off her cloak, laying it out with care. Then she began to undress as she walked toward the murmuring water.

Chapter Eight

Jack, Zayn and Thomas took seats at the stone table. They had full goblets before them, but the delicate wine remained untouched. They would not drink until a decision was made.

"I realize that the timing is bad, what with all the strain between us and Humans Under Ground. They never did like us magical beings, and after you two flouted their leader in Detroit . . . But the situation in Sin City cannot wait," Thomas said. "I have to go back. Soon."

"I agree. But what about your Cyra?" Zayn asked. "She needs immediate help too. I can see that there is some injury to her, a vulnerability—probably her missing skin. You cannot mean to take her with you. It's too dangerous."

"I am all too aware of the danger. Have I not already paid for—" Thomas stopped, shocked by his own tone. He never thought about his wife. He never talked about her. *Never.* "But what can reasonably be done?"

"Leave Cyra here with Io," Jack suggested. "We can continue to educate her, if that's what she wishes. She can't be so attached to you in this short amount of time."

Thomas considered the suggestion, ignoring the voice in his head that said leaving Cyra behind would not be an easy thing for either him or her.

"She won't like being left out of this. Her thirst for revenge was very nearly at bloodlust level when I found her," he warned Jack. "You'd have your hands full with her."

"I didn't think she would be happy with the suggestion, but the need for revenge usually isn't enough to overwhelm *all* reason. At least, it isn't here. Cadalach has a soothing effect on newcomers. You know this." Jack looked into Thomas's eyes. "Enough with logic. What does your heart say?"

"I'm uneasy." Truthfully, he didn't like leaving Cyra at all, but he knew it was for the best. It likely would be a long time, if ever, before she would be strong enough—ruthless enough—to cope with the sort of work he did. And until she was ready—trained physically, mentally and magically—the kindest thing he could do was stay away from her. He stifled a sigh. "But I am certain that you are, as always, correct. Leaving her seems the lesser of evils, if she will agree."

"Make her agree," Zayn said. His face was tense, and Thomas knew that he was thinking about how Chloe had very nearly died under a gargoyle's claws. He understood Zayn's fear. Thomas himself had seen his wife die at the hands of trolls. It wasn't an experience one ever forgot. "Force her. It's for her own good," Zayn continued. "Look what happened to Chloe when goblins got her. By the goddess, that's why we had to get her out of Detroit. Io nearly died there, too."

Thomas looked at Jack. "Jack?"

The death fey shook his head. "You can try to erase her memory, but the magic in her is strong. I have a feeling that the more you try to push her in one direction, the stiffer her resistance will be. Maybe you should just go, leave her here. Or . . . try reasoning with her first. We don't want to lose her over this."

"Reasoning." Thomas nodded gloomily. "I'm getting better at that." He paused. "Just tell me one thing: Could you have managed to take out the goblin hive in Detroit without Io's help?"

"Truly?" Jack said. "I don't know. But she and I were lovers by then. Magic had mated

117

us—mingled our powers as it does. That isn't the case with you, is it?"

"No." Not yet.

"Okay, then. Let's move on to something simpler. Tell me about this General Fornix and how he's connected to Lilith."

"I suspect they are hive-mates. They wouldn't work together if they weren't, I don't think. As you know, goblins generally won't cooperate outside their own hive. One thing is for sure, we'll have to not only bring down the mountain to protect the nuclear material, but we'll have to get Fornix and Lilith as well." Thomas's voice was hard.

"I concur. Lilith has to go. She and her general."

"Get rid of the perps and you get rid of the problem," Zayn added. They were all in agreement.

Cyra was half asleep when Thomas arrived in their room. He came stalking into the chamber, feet hitting the ground like he intended to punish something by stomping it to death. He managed to walk noisily, his body expressing its anger even as he crossed over the piles of furs.

Cyra's eyes cracked open and she watched as he moved about the dim chamber with minimally controlled violence. He seemed on the verge of smashing something until he saw that she was sleeping. He paused then, for a moment, and when he resumed moving it was with a quiet tread.

Cyra's eyes drifted closed again, but she was aware that he leaned over her and smoothed her hair back with a light hand.

"Little fey, what am I to do with you? How can I protect you when there is no time for you to learn all you must? I hate to do it, but I'm going to have to leave you behind. Jack and Io will take care of you." He sighed, then turned toward the bathing pool.

His words were unsettling, and Cyra was tempted to push heavy sleep away long enough to watch Thomas undress, but her body would not cooperate. Exhausted after its long night of travel, it drew Morpheus's shroud up over her head and returned her to Nod. A part of her knew that she'd never be strong again if she did not sleep, and so she did not struggle against it.

She was dimly aware when Thomas also lay down for a nap. The sound of velvet covers being pulled aside was a caress to the ears that made her smile inside. Nevertheless, when he climbed into the other bed, she did not open her heavy eyes or try to elude sleep's soft comfort to coax him to her side. She didn't attempt to leave the healing sleep that cocooned her until Thomas began to dream—until she dreamed his nightmare with him.

The underworld was bathed in a sickly green. Ever after, the ghastly color would remind him of goblins, of hate, of loss.

"What is your name, quiet man?" the ancient goblin asked again, the voice so gravelly it was almost impossible to understand.

The crack of a whip filled the air behind him. Thomas did not allow himself to flinch or break eye contact with his young wife, even when the force of the blow knocked him forward and made the manacles bite deeper into his bloodied wrists.

Fire. The broad leather flayer braided with iron cut deeply, sawing through muscle and down to the bone. Thomas's brain was trying to send him into oblivion, but he couldn't look away from his wife—couldn't. Couldn't speak, couldn't blink, couldn't lose consciousness. He couldn't, or his wife would awake to this nightmare and start screaming. If she did that, she was doomed. Fear only made trolls more brutal. She was still alive because she was quiet.

But even this might not be enough to save her. Annissa's passivity was beginning to enrage Haarkon. He had brought her here to see her terrified reaction to her husband's torture and murder. He didn't understand how she could stand so still and indifferent, and what he didn't understand, he didn't like.

Thomas was afraid that Haarkon would soon figure out what he was doing and either kill him outright to end his mind control over his wife, or else have the trolls start carving up Annissa's body in order to get some reaction from him.

Annissa!

It was his fault! All his fault. She was an orphan of the first western drought, an innocent who hadn't even known that she was fey until he'd told her the truth of her nature. Then she had been frightened, bewildered. She had clung to him, asking for comfort, for help. He shouldn't have touched her, married her, not with his occupation. Hadn't his father always told him not to give hostages to fortune?

But he had been so lonely. And she was so beautiful and pure, and she needed him. And she had such potential power. He had been certain that he could teach her to use her magic. That she would eventually be able to defend herself and be the consort he had dreamed of. . . .

But she had never been able to control her power, to use it against others. He had tried to teach her, but it simply wasn't in her nature to—

The vicious whine of the whip came again. And then the bite, the pain that carved into his muscles and bones.

Nine. That was the ninth blow.

Blood and sweat poured down his brow, but Thomas kept his eyes wide. He would not let Annissa suffer for his mistakes.

Cyra opened her eyes and mouth and tried to scream, but Thomas wouldn't let her. He would not let either of them speak, or blink, or move because of Annissa.

Desperately, she tried to fight her way out of the bloody nightmare, tried vainly to take Thomas with her. But he wouldn't leave, not while Annissa lived. He'd stay there until it killed him.

"Tie the bitch up," Haarkon ordered, shoving the blank-faced Annissa at the giant, blood-spattered Malik. "Let's see if she takes being flayed herself with the same kind of calm."

No!

Thomas struggled back upright, forcing himself to ignore his dislocated shoulders and the spreading pool of blood beneath his feet.

Haarkon laughed, a dry hissing noise that

betrayed his mother's serpent bloodlines.

"Oh, the quiet man doesn't like this, does he? But let's do it anyway. Just for fun."

Cyra finally broke out of the dream, alone, but she could not entirely escape the effects of the vision. She still carried Thomas's pain with her, telling her he was locked inside the nightmare, being tortured—bleeding—dying.

Nauseated, she rolled onto her feet and lurched for Thomas's bed.

"Thomas! Wake up!"

Thomas let Annissa fall forward under the first deep blow and made her eyes close, praying the goblins would think she had fainted and would stop the flaying until she revived. But the trolls, Malik and Manvil, didn't care. The blood craze was on them. All they wanted was to wade in gore and feed. Not even Haarkon could stop them now.

Nothing could stop them except—except a larger, hungrier monster. . . . And there was one in the room. Hidden. Dangerous. A killer extraordinaire.

O Goddess, no! He couldn't. He shouldn't. It would eat him—destroy him body, mind and soul! He'd never let it out before. But Annissa . . . *Goddess!* He had no choice.

Despairing, Thomas finally looked deep inside. He had always feared the dragon and kept it buried, chained in the deepest wells of his psyche, but the beast, once aroused by thought and the smell of Annissa's blood, would be restrained no more. It lunged for the real world, where blood perfumed the air.

Let me free.

Thomas struggled for a moment longer, trying to put some constraints on the beast, but the dragon wouldn't stop and Thomas could no longer recall why he shouldn't give himself over to it. He had mainly fought to keep the monster from Annissa for fear it would frighten her. But now that didn't matter. Annissa wouldn't see anything.

Pleased with the capitulation of its host, the dragon roared to life and began clambering out of its mental prison.

No one will take Annissa away, it promised Thomas. *No one. I'll see them dead. I'll see her mercifully dead before I will allow Haarkon to take her, to hurt her any more.*

Thomas looked at the river of blood cascading from his wife's broken body and despaired. Feys could recover from terrible injury, but this had gone too far. He couldn't find her mind anymore. She was dying. She was probably already dead.

Do what you want, Thomas whispered to the beast, his vision blurring, the pain and grief at last taking his mind. *Hurt them. Kill them.*

I shall. They'll pay, Thomas.

The monster stretched and began pushing outward, fully manifesting itself for the first time. Thomas screamed aloud as the change happened, and the last bits of the skin on his body were pierced through with dragon scales.

Thomas was subordinated by the beast for the first time in his life, and he didn't care.

The dragon blinked its eyes and assessed its body as it surveyed the world. It had never known just what form it was carried in, had never been allowed to possess it, to use it. He found that he was small, like a man, and did not have the proper trachea—could not spit fire. But he had observed with other senses from his place in the darkness through the long years he had been held captive, and he knew the creature, Thomas, had other useful gifts. The sorcerer side of him could, with the dragon's help, probably reach inside the trolls' brains and make them burn with another kind of fire.

Oh, the quiet man would be quiet no more. But the dragon needed help to do this magic. The dragon made the grief-crazed Thomas

125

wake up and show him how to take a brain.

Thomas, no longer caring, did as the dragon asked. He started the compulsion spell that would allow the dragon to take the trolls' minds. But, before the spell was completed, he heard a voice calling to him from far away.

"Thomas!"

"What?"

"Thomas, come back!"

Cyra? But wasn't she dead? No! No, that was Annissa!

Thomas began to struggle, attempting to take back his mind and will. He called to the dragon. *Cyra is still alive. Stop!*

No! the dragon cried. *Not yet! They have to pay. They have to burn.*

Stop it! Thomas screamed back, trying to wake from the nightmare now that he realized what had happened. *It isn't Haarkon. That's Cyra! We're dreaming. You must stop!*

Dreaming? The dragon turned the thought over, examining the concept of his experience not being reality.

Yes. This is only a dream—it isn't real. And you'll hurt Cyra if you use this spell. Remember! This already happened—long ago. It isn't real, just memory.

Cyra? The dragon asked. *Yes, you thought of*

126

*her before. You want her, don't you? Show me
Cyra. I want to see.*

Thomas struggled against this suggestion,
but the dragon was adamant.

Cyra threw herself on Thomas.

"Wake up!" she sobbed. "Thomas! Come
back—"

Thomas's eyes popped open, but it was not
the man she knew who stared at her. The eyes
were gold but shot with red, and the pupils
were slitted. The creature who looked at her
had a gaze that opened into hell.

She was lying upon a dragon.

"Thomas," she whispered, not looking away
from the beast's terrifying eyes. "It's Cyra.
Come back to me. Wake up. Please."

"Cyra." The voice was a rasp and did not belong to Thomas. "I see."

A shudder traveled through Thomas's body,
a quaking of flesh that nearly dislodged her and
made Thomas screw up his face as though in
pain. His bloodied irises rolled back in his
head. Cyra was on the verge of calling for help,
fearing that he was having some form of seizure
when Thomas again opened his eyes and focused on her.

"Wait," he ordered, his voice still a rasp but

sounding closer to his own. "Don't move. He's going. I—"

It took another long minute, but the wracking tremors finally subsided. Cyra realized that Thomas truly was back in control when the last of the pain faded from her own body and the awful hellbroth of rage and guilt drained from her mind.

"Oh, Thomas." She sighed, collapsing on his chest. They were both coated in sweat: Thomas's a fine gold mist and Cyra's a gleaming liquid silver. "I was so frightened! I thought I'd lost you to the trolls."

"I'm sorry," he whispered. "I don't know how that happened. I never think of her anymore. It's been more than a century. It's just that she . . . she was . . ."

"It's okay. I know," Cyra whispered back, placing the softest of kisses at the side of his throat. She tried to comfort him physically because there were no words that could ever come close to expressing her compassion and horror at what he had lived through. "You don't have to talk. I was there with you. I know."

"You saw . . . ?" Thomas was unable to finish his question.

"Saw. Felt. Thomas, I still feel horrible," Cyra said, finally rising up so she could look into his beautiful tear-filled eyes. "It's my fault you dreamed, isn't it? It's because you think I'm like her—weak and helpless. Being with me has reminded you of it all. I feel so guilty that I've done this to you."

"No," Thomas denied, a tear rolling unnoticed from one eye. "The guilt is mine, and it is this that haunts me. It was all a mistake. I should never have married her. Soldiers and spies who fight goblins should never love ones who cannot care for themselves. I knew that. I knew it!"

"Never? But, Thomas, you said it yourself: We are all soldiers now. And would you have denied yourself the chance of a child? What of all that talk of repopulation?"

"No. Some feys cannot be soldiers. It isn't in their nature. It wasn't in hers. I doubt it's in yours."

His words hurt Cyra, putting something cold and indigestible in her stomach and something heavy in her heart. She reached out with a finger to brush his tear away.

She strove for some of the clinical detachment she had used in her job. Sometimes she had needed to ignore that her research was not just abstract figures, but rooted in people with mental problems that caused immeasurable anguish.

Problems she had helped cause?

Cyra pushed the thought away and tried to dissect Thomas's agony, taking it in small pieces so she would not be overwhelmed as she explored.

"The guilt belongs to that monster, Haarkon," she said, "who I sincerely hope is dead."

"Very dead. The dragon kept his word. But it didn't help," Thomas answered. He did not say what the dragon had done to him. Instead, a second tear rolled down his cheek. "Revenge didn't help."

"Revenge kept Haarkon from ever doing that again. And I'm glad he's dead. I hope your dragon was merciless," Cyra answered. "I hope he burned down their entire city and ate those trolls feet first."

"He did that and then some. The dragon was thorough. He began in their labyrinth and then moved up top. His rampage lasted for hours. There was nothing left when he was done—not one building or tree or goblin." Thomas paused to swallow. A third tear slipped from his eyes and mingled with the golden perspiration that dewed his skin.

Cyra chased this tear down, also, leaving a small silvery mark behind where she touched him. "Good. Though I don't understand exactly how he could do that without being able to breathe fire," she said. She didn't come out and

130

ask Thomas to explain. She couldn't, not if it would hurt him to remember.

"He couldn't breathe fire, but he could make others set them. He could make anyone he mind-controlled do . . . well, anything, and to anyone."

Anything. Thomas and his beast had that kind of power.

Cyra shivered. She should be afraid. She *was* afraid. Though he had taken control of her mind, she hadn't feared him because he was in complete control of himself. Until Thomas had looked at her with the beast's eyes, she hadn't understood what he meant about being part dragon, about the beast being *unpredictable.* Now she did.

"He only stopped when he realized I was dying and had to get to a healer." A fourth tear tracked down his cheek. Cyra, feeling a strange compulsion, leaned down and kissed it away.

Thomas closed his eyes and sighed, relaxing slightly.

"The healer had a hard time of it. I didn't want to come back, you see. And the dragon didn't want to go . . . Strange. You know, I didn't think that really worked," he murmured.

"What?"

"Kissing someone to make it better. But it does work. I feel . . . less dead now. More peaceful. Maybe you're magical or something." He tried to smile.

"Or something." Cyra really did smile. She was beginning to feel better, too, almost euphoric. Maybe it was relief, but her fear melted away and a quiet but fierce elation was beginning to burn inside her. "Mothers' magic is probably the oldest on earth," she pointed out, bending down to retrieve a fifth tear.

"That must be it. Though you are nothing like my mother." Thomas sounded better, his body calm and relaxed, yet a sixth tear leaked from his eye.

Cyra chased that one down too.

"You like my eyes?" Thomas asked. His arms settled around her waist. His hands lightly, reverently traced the curve of her hips.

"Yes," she answered. "They're beautiful. I hate to see them crying."

"Crying? But I can't cry," Thomas objected.

"Too macho for it?" Cyra asked, amused. She was feeling extraordinarily good—giddy even.

"No, but jinn and peries do not weep. And my magician forebear sold his tears—and his children's—for power. I have none to shed."

"Well, someone is crying," Cyra pointed out, bending down to take his last tear on the tip of her tongue.

"*Last tear? What . . . ?*" Cyra sat back up at

Thomas's confused thought, propping herself with her elbows as she met his eyes.

"But that isn't possible," he said. "Only the dragon can cry, and he'd only do that if . . ." Thomas stopped, his expression arrested.

"What?" Shaken a bit from her giddy mood, Cyra sat back even farther, where she could clearly see his face. "Thomas? Why would a dragon cry?"

His answer was to raise his hands and stare at them. The palms and fingertips were sheened with silver. "You're selkie. I forgot," he said, his voice stunned. Then urgently: "How many tears did he cry?"

"Seven," she answered promptly, and then frowned. Somehow this answer sounded significant. The fact that she remembered the number also made her nervous. "Thomas, what's wrong? What does this mean?"

"That sonofabitch did a selkie summoning ritual." Thomas's body began to tauten as new tension tightened his muscles.

Cyra was suddenly aware that she was sitting astride a naked man in nothing but her panties and a camisole, an old bit of cotton that was so thin and tight that merely breathing looked like a sexual advance. She looked down at her body and Thomas's; both of which were smeared with silvery sweat now drying to a powder.

"What is this stuff?" she asked, trying to brush the drying sweat away.

"Selkie brine. Your magic has betrayed you too." Thomas's voice was grim.

"What do you mean? Thomas . . ." Alarmed, she began to tremble. "What's happening?"

"Cyra, don't! You have to stay calm. I daren't go into your mind right now. Not with the dragon so close. You have to control yourself. Please."

His words were like a glass of cold water thrown in her face. She fought against the first tendrils of hysteria trying to invade her mind. She would not be like Annissa.

"But, what do you mean my magic betrayed me? I don't have 'magic.' Do I?"

"Jack warned me about this. Damn it! He told me that the moment he and Io thought of separating, the magic intervened. It had him bonded to Io before either of them knew what was happening. Our magic is probably playing games with us right now because it knows I have to leave. I should never have doubted that it would have its way."

"Bonded them," Cyra repeated. She tried to sit very still, but it was difficult with her growing awareness of Thomas lying beneath her.

Their body temperatures were climbing. She could feel their hearts beginning to sync, was able to count the pulses where their bodies met. "I don't understand. Games?"

"Your sweat. Cyra, that is selkie brine. It's an aphrodisiac that selkies use to seduce their lovers."

"But . . . Thomas, I wasn't trying to seduce you. You were having a nightmare—"

"I know. It wasn't *you*. It was . . . it was the magic in you—in *us*! And all around us."

"But I've *never* had this happen. I swear—"

"No, it wouldn't have. Out in the world we can control it. Human will is ascendant. But when we get close to magical places, sources of power, then the magic inside becomes . . . restless. Hungry. It starts seeking its own kind. It looks to mate. It's sly. It can take us unaware, even in our sleep, and make us do its will."

It sounded like Thomas was warning her that any erotic dreams she'd soon have would come with very serious consequences.

"Well, I apologize for sliming you," Cyra said, feeling color rise to her cheeks. It wasn't the thought of her lack of control that was making her flush, but rather her growing desire to lie back down on Thomas and . . . She shuddered. "I think I should be getting off—I mean—um, I should be going now."

"No!" Thomas's hands shot out and grabbed her waist, pulling her back against him. He rocked his hips once beneath her and then he blinked, surprised.

"Thomas?"

"Sorry." He immediately dropped his hands. "That was . . . that was *him.*"

"Him . . . ? Thomas, is there really a 'him'? I mean, isn't this dragon just a part of you? Maybe a part of you that is dark and violent and you'd rather not claim?" Cyra really, really wanted him to say yes to this. The idea of an independently willed dragon in him frightened her badly.

"Yes, there is a dragon." His answer was fast and given in a flat voice. "No, I only wish it was some part of me."

"Damn it. It's bad enough wanting you. How can I feel this attraction if there are two of you in there? How can I want you when I know he's in there, watching?"

"I know. It's . . . it's untenable. I've always felt this way. I've had to keep him locked away. But this time *he* called you."

"Well . . . does *he* at least have a name?"

"Yes, I gave him a name when he wouldn't tell me his, but it wouldn't be wise to use it."

Thomas shifted. Cyra believed the move to be uncalculated, but it pressed his groin against hers. The thin barrier of her cotton panties might as well have been missing. They both shuddered.

Cyra told herself to get down, but she didn't stir for fear that if she moved, it wouldn't be to get *off* Thomas.

"Why not use his name?" she asked. Then she remembered what Thomas had done to her when she spoke his name. "Oh. Mind control?"

"Yes, he can use it now. He learned how that day when Annissa died. Saying his name is like a summoning. Especially at present."

"Why now? Because of this . . . *brine*?"

"No. That is your power to use as you choose."

"My power? You mean, I can decide whether to um . . ."

"Seduce me. Yes."

Cyra didn't want to think about that. She was in no state to be making that sort of decision—was she?

Something fluttered in her abdomen, making muscles clench. Of course she could have Thomas. Didn't she want to?

"If not the brine, then what is it that makes the dragon so dangerous right now?" she asked. She tried to keep from giving in to the distraction of the heat growing between them.

Thomas exhaled, looking suddenly annoyed.

Cyra had an insane urge to laugh, but suppressed it, realizing it was incipient hysteria lingering in the back of her brain, waiting for a chance to manifest itself.

"The sneaky sonofabitch performed a summoning ritual."

"You said that. But what do you mean? He summoned what?"

"The tears. Those seven tears. That is the old way to call a selkie. How many of them did you touch with your lips?"

Cyra thought back. "Four."

"Well, that isn't as bad as it might be. But you have to be careful from here on out, Cyra. Never kiss—never *touch*—his tears again."

Thomas's words seemed to hurt the dragon. It snorted a reproach, and because she was now connected to the beast, they made Cyra feel terrible too. Suddenly she was aching, so alone that she thought she would die. Thomas didn't understand the dragon. She had to make him understand that the dragon meant no harm, that *she* meant no harm.

"Oh, Thomas." Her own tears began to fall, raining down on his beautifully patterned chest.

Thomas's face softened. "Sweetheart, don't cry. It's the dragon, Cyra. He's trying to trick

138

you. Those aren't true feelings. He doesn't think and feel the way we do."

"No." Cyra shook her head. She leaned down so that her lips hovered over Thomas's mouth. Slow silvery tears continued to flow from her eyes, wetting his lips. "He isn't pretending. He was crying because you can't. And he's just lonely. He lost Annissa, too. He . . . he *wants*. You want too. I can tell this—feel it."

"Don't! Please don't," Thomas begged. "I am covered in brine. I don't know if I can fight you and him. You don't want this, Cyra. Truly you don't. It's too soon. You are too vulnerable to face a union like this. Think! A few minutes ago you were afraid of the dragon. And this isn't just sex. Our magic is trying to bond us. Forever."

"But I do want this," she heard herself murmur. Her tears continued to fall. The words shocked some part of the old Cyra, but she ignored the slight twinge of protest. This was *right*. It was what she *needed*.

She'd even dreamed it the night she had been given her cloak. And the dragon hadn't hurt her then, had he?

"No. Even if you do want this, it's too soon. You don't understand who you are—what I am!" Thomas touched a hand to his damp cheek, staring at the tears that wetted his fingertips. He whispered, amazed: "They burn like quicksilver. Cyra, this is madness. It's more magic manipulating us. Stop. You must stop."

"You are afraid because you think I am like Annissa," Cyra whispered persuasively. "But I'm not. Thomas, I am strong. And I'm getting stronger with every passing minute. We don't need to be afraid. I can take care of myself. I know I can."

Thomas shuddered, his entire body flushing and growing hard. The tracery of scales on his skin began to darken. The pulse in his neck throbbed.

"You're wrong, but goddess help us, we're in for it anyway. These are conjurer's tears. I don't know if anyone could fight them. Even if they were in full possession of their will and senses."

"Yes, it's magic," she answered, realizing at some level that Thomas was right. It was something magical pouring from her eyes and binding him to her. "But it's a good thing."

"And you believe that this is what you want? That you are acting of your own free will?" His eyes were bleak as he asked her.

"Yes," she whispered, even though she knew her answer would upset him. Even though she knew the answer might not be true. "It's just a kiss, Thomas. Just one . . ."

"I think you are wrong. This isn't *just* anything, but so must it be," he whispered back, his voice resigned. His arms stole around her and he pulled her down for a kiss. "Okay, Cyra. Let's see if we can touch the fire and not get burned."

The goddess medallion that Thomas had given her for protection swung down between them, and Cyra was certain that she saw the golden lips smile. The deity's expression was no longer entirely benign.

Chapter Nine

Time seemed to stop, the moment when they lay so still and breathless expanding into a timeless eternity that shut out everything but desire.

Yet, even as she kissed the reluctant Thomas, Cyra knew his warning was true. She wasn't just taking a risk with her body, but also with her mind and heart. She was groping her way toward something as a newly blind person might, lost in a jungle of fresh sensation without any compass or guideposts. She should have been terrified—and maybe part of her was. But overwhelming any fear was a feeling of purpose and elation. It was liberating, exhilarating. And gone, at least temporarily, was the horrible burden of shame at what she was, the thing that had grown so heavy in her mind that it had slowly been alienating her from her own senses. She no longer had to deny what she was.

Her other, fiercer, primal emotions were new to her too. The last few days had blasted open some fresh pathways in her brain, and torrents of new feelings were flooding down them: awe, wonder, joyousness. They brought life to a part of her that had lain arid and desolate. And she could thank Thomas for this.

Thomas Marr—

She stopped, the half name reverberating like a klaxon in her brain. It still had power over her, and she didn't want that.

She frowned. This thought, or memory, did not belong inside their moment of wonder. She wouldn't think about it right now, wouldn't let it ruin her time with Thomas.

Far more pleasurable was the examination of these new places in her mind, these parts of her nature that had been closed off to her. It was as if the seeds of a particular new emotion had finally germinated and begun to develop inside her. Its flowers, much like the ones in the impossible garden that grew inside the shian, were different from anything she had ever known.

Were those seeds to some form of forbidden fruit? asked a distant voice from outside the moment, begging her to be cautious. *Most blooms went from bud to blossom to fruit without any conscious intent. But things were different here. Emotions like this surely did not happen by accident.*

But, if there was a design, then there had to be a designer, didn't there?

The thought might have been worth pursuing—part of Cyra said it was—but Thomas wrapped his long fingers over the sharp curve where her neck and shoulder met, and caressed her dancing pulse with his beautiful, clever fingers. Sensation and want of a kind and strength Cyra had never known blotted out all other thoughts and questions. Desire drew a velvet curtain between emotion and cold, logical reason.

Her hands kneaded the muscles beneath them, pleased at the heat and strength they found there. Thomas was different—*so* different—from anyone she had ever known.

Hungry now for other things, Cyra slid her lips from his mouth and down to the pulse in his throat. The small smear of silvered brine showed her where she had touched him before.

Yes, this was what she wanted—to taste, to feel. Perhaps if she touched him this way enough, she wouldn't need anything more.

Cyra sank her hands into Thomas's pitch-black hair, loving the way it felt trapped between her fingers: sleek, smooth, cool like silk.

Thomas moaned, but he did not stop her as she laved the skin above his pulse. Perhaps he was distracted by battle with his dragon. Perhaps he'd simply fallen into the same blinding enchantment that summoned her own wild needs. And maybe he just needed this as badly as she did. Maybe he hadn't known this pleasure either. Perhaps, like her, he was realizing that all other unions had been pale precursors to this event. How could she have ever considered Larry her lover? How could she even have contemplated calling what they had known *love*? This was magic. This was healing. It might even be salvation.

"Thomas?"

"Yes." His voice grated like sandpaper.

Cyra lifted her head and looked into Thomas's eyes. They were bright, a hammered gold lit by midnight torches, but they were still Thomas's eyes. Though it was not the beast staring out at her, there was a strange heat in Thomas's usually temperate gaze, something alien, something otherworldly. If she'd had any doubts about Thomas being something more than human, they would be forever gone.

She wondered briefly what she herself looked like. Was she as alien?

"I had forgotten that this could happen. A century has passed and I didn't think there was anything strong enough in this world to entice me again. Yet, here you sit, dressed in silver, tempting me. I can hear your thoughts." Thomas spoke, his voice low and rough. "It's in your eyes, too, selkie. There are oceans of desire in them. '*Come into the sea*,' they say. '*Come deeper, deeper. Come with me and we'll drown*.' But you don't know what you are asking of me—or us!"

Cyra shuddered. "Yes. Thomas, I do. I want to drown—with you. Please, please come with me. I don't know why, but I want this so very much."

Thomas reached around her and rolled, suddenly pulling her beneath him. He pinned her down with his body as though expecting some wild tide to rush in and tear her from his arms. Yet when he spoke, his words were completely contrary to his actions.

"You ask this of me and it seems I have no choice if you will it. Command me, and into the sea we go. But it would be far better for you to tell me to leave. For your sake and for mine. Tell me to leave you, Cyra, because I also want you so very badly and do not have the strength to leave on my own."

"But why send you away? Do you truly *want* to leave me, Thomas?"

"No. I want more than anything—more than I want my next breath, or even my life—to have you. But it's wrong. Dangerous. You saw what happened before. It could happen again. Easily."

Cyra frowned. He said he wanted her, but his words didn't sound at all joyous of this discovery. And he spoke sincerely of danger. . . . She waited, in a sort of pain, wanting nothing so much as to wrap herself around the hard length of his body, to pull herself into him until they were one. She could compel him, force him—

But she wouldn't. She *wouldn't!*

"Please, Thomas. Come with me," she coaxed a second time, pressing against him, unable to compel him but unable to leave him either. "I'm not forcing you. But I want you. You want me too. It feels right. Pre-ordained. Please say you'll come."

"Your words give me no help to do what is right." His tone was almost angry. "And you've asked me twice. Don't ask a third time."

"I am giving you a choice," Cyra protested. "I am not forcing you."

"Only with your words do you give me a choice. Not with your heart, not with your

147

mind. Think about this! Now. Before it is too late. Some part of you must still be capable of thought. Some part of you must recognize the danger. You know what I must do in Sin City— what the beast and I must do—and you know what danger you will be in if you are my lover. Did you learn nothing from my dreams? Those near me die. Always."

"Yes, I believe all this. But I know that I must help you too. None of this can be allowed to matter. I want you. I *need* you."

"And do you also want the dragon? What if he decides that he wants you too—that he will not remain quiescent? What will you do then?"

"I . . . I don't know." Frustration had Cyra near tears.

"But you should know. The beast is close. He's right under my skin." He looked down, veiling his eyes, and reached beneath her worn camisole to tear through the thin fabric with his fingers. She watched, fascinated and also shocked, as he shredded it with invisible claws. "The beast is not gentle. He has no scruples. He might not kill you, but he probably won't just kiss you either. And he won't stop just because you ask him to."

"Thomas?"

His head dropped, and with a low growl he turned his face to her breasts, her heart.

The die was cast. Not wanting to see who might be looking out of his eyes now if he turned her way, Cyra closed her own eyelids and twined about him.

His lips closed over one of her nipples—softly, gently. But she was well aware of the teeth that lay just behind them. His hand reached for her other breast and she remembered the claws that had destroyed her shirt. Excitement, and perhaps a bit of fear made her breath catch and her heartbeat double. Thomas had likely overstated things—she hoped—but the beast inside him *was* probably hungry, and who could know what true appetites it had? Could Thomas control it? Could she? Thomas was right. Just because the dragon had retreated once without harming her, didn't mean it would again.

Thomas's hands smoothed down her body, caressing, savoring, speaking of desire and praise and intended delight in the language of touch. Down he went, moving from one smooth curve to another, exploring her pale flesh with soft breaths, soft lips, soft hands.

Cyra forced herself to loosen the grip she had in Thomas's hair. She would trust. She might as well. Her small hands were no match for his strength if he turned the dragon loose upon her.

Thomas shuddered, as though hearing her decision to place her trust him, and finding it both exquisitely pleasurable and yet also horrifying.

"You've seen the beast, you know he's there, but still you come to me. It seems miraculous." His voice was so low that she almost couldn't hear it. "But is this salvation, or damnation? Or just trickery, the magic seducing us both for its own ends?"

"I don't know," she whispered. "I don't care. Heaven or hell or enchantment, all I know is that I want you. Please," she said for a third time.

Thomas paused, apparently still struggling with doubt.

Seeing his effort, and knowing that there must be cause, Cyra tried to shut off the desire. But tendrils of need crept through her body, unstoppable. From her very core they spread outward their need. Desire pushed against her skin, making her want to scream in frustration.

But she would not compel Thomas—she would not! If he wanted to leave, she would let him.

"But how much easier it is now that you *did* compel me," Thomas whispered. "This way, I share the responsibility, the blame, and maybe later the guilt. If I'm very unlucky, I'll share your death. And you mine. But you've asked three times. I cannot refuse you now."

He ran his hands over the length of her body and rocked against her. He was on fire. Lit by a fever, his skin almost glowed.

"Thomas, are you ill?" Cyra asked, touching his neck and face and frowning at his abnormally hot skin.

He laughed. "Ill? No, I burn. You started this fire, Cyra. Pray the ocean you seek will put this blaze out." He turned to look at her, eyes so bright they illuminated the velvet covers around them. He added in anger and disbelief: "Why do you look at me with soft eyes? I could devour you—and you'd let me. You must fight back!"

Cyra shivered and answered: "No, I won't fight you. That would only arouse the beast. I want *you.*"

Thomas groaned and sat up. He reached for her ankle, shackling it for a moment with his long fingers. Then he traced the inside of her thigh, urging her legs to part, for her to lie undefended.

Cyra made a breathless sound at the trail of fire he left on her skin, but she gave him what he wanted, let herself be made vulnerable.

He paused over the last scrap of material between them, as though giving her a final chance to refute her desires. All she could think of, all she could feel, was his touch, burning her as though the fragile barrier of her panties wasn't there.

And then it wasn't. With a low growl those, too, were shredded and cast aside.

Thomas lay down between her legs, his head above her belly.

A small part of Cyra wondered whether she should protest this, but modesty, shame and social teaching had all been shut out as unwelcome guests at this feast of the flesh, and so she said nothing.

She did gasp, though, as Thomas rubbed a cheek against the soft skin of her inner thigh and turned his face toward the heart of her. Fingers and tongue touched her together, a penetration that melted through any lingering resistance her muscles or will might have had.

Unable to endure so much sensual data flooding into her brain and down her nerves, Cyra closed her eyes, closed off her ears, and gave herself over to feeling. Thomas's touch seared, but the sweetest of pleasures was gathering. Her skin, her muscles, every fiber of her body shivered, waiting. It was sublime.

It was insane.

Thomas pulled back from her.

"Yes, it's true madness you've called," he

whispered. His voice reached her even as she willed it away. "But so very sweet. And even if it kills us both, I cannot stop it now."

He moved up her body and pressed against her, his muscles strung tight like piano wire. He throbbed. He burned. She could feel his need as plainly as her own, and it made her dizzy. Her own lust inched higher in her body, the sea in which she wished to drown lapping at her with inviting waves, telling her that all desires could be quenched there if she just grabbed hold of Thomas and pulled him down with her.

"Say no," Thomas urged. "Though you asked three times, it may not be too late if you bend all your will to refusing me." But despite his words, he fitted his body against hers. He spoke again, incongruously to his actions: "Send me away. Refuse this, Cyra. Now—before it's too late."

Refuse this. He meant more than the act of love, but Cyra refused to examine his intentions. She was in torment enough without opening herself to his anguish.

"I can't. I can't! Don't ask it." The words were almost a sob.

"And neither can I. We are both weakened by the magic. Someday, it will be the death of me." His words were bitter and sad, and Cyra wept because her triumph was somehow a disaster.

Thomas's movements after that were swift and almost violent. He rose onto his knees, his stronger legs pushing hers apart. His hard, swollen shaft pressed into her, and being softer, she yielded.

Shudders wracked him and he sucked in his breath, the pleasure so keen it was excruciating. Instinct said he should ride her hard, but he refused. He was slow, savoring the pleasure as though he—and she—might never know such a moment again. And there was every chance that he would not, for Death stalked them. And Cyra realized all this because parts of their mind still touched, and she knew his thoughts.

"I'm sorry," she whispered. Then her breath caught, as the waters of fulfillment finally closed over her head. She began drowning in sensation. Her mind, newly sensitized to magic and unable to bear Thomas's unguarded regret at this union, pulled in on itself and left her body without a guide.

She fainted in the throes of her climax, Thomas's pleasure as well as hers exploding in her head like a hand grenade. But even as she lost consciousness, she knew that Thomas was still planning on leaving her, and part of her wept at this loss.

"I can't undo this act," Thomas said, his voice fading into the black that fogged her battered mind. "But I will somehow keep you safe. I swear this."

Chapter Ten

*The walls were wet with slimy green plaster
and some form of condensation that looked like
blood but smelled chemical and made the eyes
burn.*

Cyra stood outside the tunnel that plunged
into the earth like the entrails of some great
beast. A thick stench filled the air. She recognized it, the concentrated form of Larry's body
odor. Gagging, Cyra stared hard at the warning
Thomas had left scrawled by the entrance of
hell.

Labyrinthus, hic habitat Goblinus.

Yes, she could see—smell—that goblins lived
in this labyrinth. And she was frightened, still
maybe a marionette of Fate, but one no longer
controlled by Thomas or goblins. He had cut
the emotional strings he'd used to help her,

severed the vestiges of control the goblins had retained, he had set her free. It was terrifying to think of holding herself erect without his assistance as she ventured into the goblin lair, but Thomas—ruthless, reliable, overly responsible—had gone this way. And so must she. . . .

Cyra opened her eyes, unwilling to finish her dream by venturing into the goblin's realm, but finding little comfort in the world to which she awoke. The shade of Thomas's unhappiness lingered over the chamber like a shroud, making the dim cavity and its antique beds even more somber.

There was no delaying judgment about her actions either. Memory rose instantly to accuse her.

What have I done? What have I done to Thomas?

Guilt and shame, the familiar, savage monsters, began chewing on her. She knew what she had done. She could not hide from the knowledge, waking or sleeping.

"Oh goddess!" Her first vandalism had been to peel back the bandage that Thomas kept over his wounded and apparently unhealing past. That had been inadvertent, perhaps excusable because she had rushed to him in the throes of a nightmare with the intention of giving aid and comfort.

But then, once she was in his bed, she had attacked him in a moment of vulnerability and seduced him against his will. She and that sly, weeping dragon had double-teamed him, held him against the emotional ropes and taken him, in spite of his protests. . . . At best, it had been a thoughtless, mindless thing to do. At worst? At worst, it was the cruelest, most callous act she had ever committed or contemplated.

Cyra rubbed her eyes.

And she wasn't even certain if taking Thomas had been what she really wanted to do, or if he had been right about it all being some kind of magical manipulation. She would like to think it was that, because it somewhat excused her actions. But that raised other just as disturbing questions about the benevolence of the powers which dwelled in this shian.

Perhaps the magic inside this mound was not case sensitive. Maybe it had seen the two of them as a sort of straightforward equation that needed solving: Two feys, unattached and already attracted, should be brought together. Maybe it hadn't realized what scars were in Thomas's psyche. And her own.

Or perhaps she was giving the shian too

158

much credit. Maybe it didn't think, but was instead like a magnet that collected potential lovers the way a magpie gathered shiny objects, then matched them together willy-nilly when the moon was full or Jupiter collided with Mars.

But was Cyra ready to call the previous night a freak accident? To deny all she had felt? She thought back, recalling Thomas not just with her mind, but with her body.

No. No, she wasn't ready to dismiss the unlooked-for beauty of what had passed between them. For there had been beauty mixed with the pain. It wasn't all blind happenstance, unlucky ships passing in the night.

But what *did* she feel for Thomas? Last night she had named it love. But she probably couldn't know the true answer to this until she was away from Cadalach, away from anyone and anything that could influence her mind.

Knowing it was useless, Cyra still reached out with her senses, searching for Thomas, hoping her dream was wrong and that he was nearby. There came no answer, not even a whisper. He was gone, and if his earlier words about his nightmare were any indication of intent, he was headed back to Sin City to deal with the goblins there, a modern Theseus volunteering to risk his life to save the world by killing the beast of the labyrinth.

Only there wasn't one beast; there were thousands. Maybe millions.

Cyra shoved back the covers and got out of bed. Silver powder glistened all over her body, marred only by the prints left by Thomas's hands and mouth.

Her hands clenched and so did her heart at the proof of her unintentional coercion. She might not be completely clear about her feelings for Thomas on this morning after, but one thing was for certain: she owed him. She owed him for her freedom from goblin mind control, owed him for opening her up to the experience of being a fey, and she owed him recompense for the damage she had done last night. And for these reasons, let alone because of what she felt, she was *not* leaving him to fight the goblins without support. Thomas had saved her from a nightmare of mental manipulation by her enemies. She would not leave him fighting his demons alone. He might think he was getting away with playing brave Theseus off to slay the Minotaur, but she was no Ariadne to be stuck on some island and abandoned. She would be like swift Atalanta—only not so easily distracted by shiny objects along the road to Sin City.

Of course, if she were really going to be the captain of her soul and sail forth to Thomas's

side to join him in battle, she would have to
take all her burdensome preconceptions, piled
up through the years, and get rid of them. She'd
have to scrape the barnacles off the hull of her
brain before she set out to sea. She had great
power around her—*within* her—if she wasn't
afraid to use it. And she would need that power.
Thomas hadn't been exaggerating about what
the goblins could do to them, if they were
caught. She had to find the courage to make
use of the gifts she had been given.

The shian could have stopped her from leaving
if it had wanted to. It could have rearranged its
tunnels or dimensions, causing her spatial and
other sorts of confusion. But perhaps it also felt
guilt for what had been done to Thomas. Or
maybe it felt Cyra's resolve to embrace her
power and knew it was time for her to go. Or
maybe it felt that its work was done.

Whatever its reasons, it did not hinder her
when she chose to leave.

Cyra moved swiftly and surreptitiously, trying not to attract attention. She stopped only
long enough to say goodbye to the lovely garden. Today she had the luxury of not being sen-
sually bemused, and she really noticed the
splendorous plants that grew there. She more

appreciated their foreign perfumes and exotic shapes and colors.

One patch of green attracted her particularly. It was unusual because the dark, thorny canes had no blossoms.

"That's Annissa's rose," Jack said softly, appearing behind her without warning. "Thomas brought it here after she died. He didn't know if it could live *inside* the shian, but somehow it has survived."

Cyra slowly turned to look at the death fey who was Thomas's friend. He didn't frighten her anymore.

"It survives, but it has no flowers," she pointed out. "Without them, does it want to live?"

"It blooms, but only once a year. It flowers on her birthday. On that day, it is covered in snowy white blossoms that smell of the first spring. And there's always one red bloom, too, right there at the heart of the shrub."

Cyra looked at the bristling canes and felt a chill creep over her.

"Does he come for her birthday?" she asked quietly.

"Thomas? No, never. Not after that first time when he saw the blossoms as a reproach."

Cyra nodded, her throat growing tight at the further evidence of her one-time lover's unhealed wounds. Not that she blamed him for avoiding the reminders of what had happened. Hadn't she also been running from her past?

"He's gone to Sin City, hasn't he?" she asked abruptly, no longer able to look at the living, floral reminder of the goblins' brutality. "He's going into the labyrinth to somehow shut down the goblins' tunnels."

Jack studied her with a bland gaze, but he didn't answer.

"He probably told you to keep me here," Cyra continued, turning fully to face the death fey. "For my own good, of course."

"Probably," Jack admitted.

"Did he fox my car?" she asked.

Jack began to smile at her prescience. "Probably," he repeated. "I would have."

"The carburetor?"

Jack's smile grew, transforming his face into something breathtakingly lovely as amusement lit his eyes. "Probably. I would."

"Well, it's a good thing I have another in the trunk then, isn't it?" Cyra said, hefting her suitcase.

"Probably," Jack answered for a fourth time. "I would too if I drove your car."

The last thing Cyra had imagined happening that morning was sharing a light moment with Jack. She began to laugh.

Jack joined her for a second, then sobered. "You do understand how truly dangerous Sin City is?"

Cyra also lost her smile at the question. "Probably. Actually . . . probably not. At least, not all the way to the bone. But I've been warned in full, living Technicolor—and I'm going anyway."

Jack nodded, as though unsurprised, and took her suitcase from her. "Come on. I'll help you change the carburetor and see if we can tune the engine a bit." Seeing Cyra's surprised look, he added: "I like cars. Even old rattletraps like yours."

A while later, Jack wiped his white hands on an oily rag.

"He won't be going by the name of Malcolm Fayre this time," Jack said. "He didn't say what name he'd be using or where he was planning to stay. Finding him might be difficult."

"I know what name he's using," Cyra answered, realizing that what she said was true. "He'll be using Thomas Dracon."

Jack nodded slowly, seeming surprised. "I do believe you're right." He dropped his rag into the trunk, then slammed the lid tight. "There is one other thing I should inquire about before I let you go."

"Yes?" Cyra asked, growing wary.

"Is there any chance you might be pregnant?"

Probably. "Not a chance," she lied, meeting Jack's gaze steadily.

Jack nodded, but he knew she was lying. Cyra could tell.

"He'll die if I don't go," Cyra explained. Then: "And don't say '*probably*.' This isn't a joke."

"I won't, mainly because I know that you're right." Jack gave a half smile. "I also know that you are a lot stronger than Thomas realizes. I can feel the magic crawling all over you, through you. You lack discipline and training, and there *is* some sort of hole in your psyche— but you aren't weak. Thomas will see this too. Eventually."

"I hope he will. Because I *am* strong." *She was a lot stronger than she had ever imagined.* Her heritage had always seemed like a heavy pack strapped to her back, a shameful weight that held her down. But Thomas had shown her something else, offered her another reality. Her parents' magical legacy, though weighty and a burden, could also be unfolded into wings that would lift her up if she let them.

Where Thomas's vision fell short was in thinking that she hadn't the courage to use her wings now that she'd found them. But she would prove him—and the goblins—wrong.

Oh, yes. A kloka—a novice kloka, but still a conjurer—was coming to Sin City. She wasn't taking her inner child, Mommy's good little girl, with her either. This wasn't about winning one for the Gipper, team spirit, or doing it for the old alma mater. She wasn't even going to this goblin town to save the population of California. She was going to Sin City to save Thomas so *he* could rescue California—and thus save himself from the regret he felt at their union.

And she was going because those goblin bastards deserved to shell out big time for what they had done to her. This was payback.

"One last thing. Thomas had an e-mail account that hasn't been discovered was his, as far as we can tell. He was user1812@lutin-empire.com. You can reach him there in an emergency. But only use it if you have no choice, and be guarded in what you say. The e-mail inside Sin City is monitored by the goblins, so be discreet or you'll both be dead before you can say dot-com."

Cyra nodded. "Thanks."

166

GET TWO FREE* BOOKS!

SIGN UP FOR THE LOVE SPELL ROMANCE BOOK CLUB TODAY.

LOWEST PRICES EVER!

Every month, you will receive two of the newest Love Spell titles for the low price of $8.50,* **a $4.50 savings!**

As a book club member, not only do you save **35% off the retail price**, you will receive the following special benefits:

- **30% off** all orders through our website and telecenter (plus, you still get 1 book FREE for every 5 books you buy!)

- Exclusive access to dollar sales, special discounts, and offers you won't be able to find anywhere else.

- Information about contests, author signings, and more!

- Convenient home delivery of your favorite books every month.

- A 10-day examination period. If you aren't satisfied, just return any books you don't want to keep.

There is no minimum number of books to buy, and you may cancel membership at any time.

* Please include $2.00 for shipping and handling.

NAME:_____

ADDRESS:_____

_____

_____

TELEPHONE: _____

E-MAIL: _____

_____ I want to pay by credit card.

__ Visa   __ MasterCard   __ Discover

Account Number: _____

Expiration date: _____

SIGNATURE: _____

*Send this form, along with $2.00 shipping
and handling for your FREE books, to:*

Love Spell Romance Book Club
20 Academy Street
Norwalk, CT 06850-4032

*Or fax (must include credit card
information!) to: 610.995.9274.
You can also sign up on the Web
at www.dorchesterpub.com.*

Offer open to residents of the U.S. and
Canada only. Canadian residents, please
call 1.800.481.9191 for pricing information.

Chapter Eleven

Cyra was seemingly alone in the desert, but she still found traces of Thomas in her head—not his conscious thoughts, but rather an emotional shade: impalpable, invisible, but still unquestionably present. It was enough to have her turning her head periodically to check the seat beside her for a passenger. *The Two Musketeers Ride Again*. The title didn't inspire a lot of confidence, especially when one of the musketeers wasn't even there.

At first the roads away from the shian were bad, little more than deer paths hacked through by ravines that bared the desert's harsh geology. There was no way for Cyra or the Honda to be comfortable, especially while the sun was overhead. Still, the car was behaving better than it had on their journey in. Whatever

Jack had done to it had improved its capacity to tolerate heat and dust.

The freakish optics from before had begun to plague her again. Something would move at the corner of her eyesight—a shadow that looked like a giant coyote, sometimes on four legs, sometimes on two. And, as had happened before, when she turned her head to look at it fully, it melted into the other stony shadows and disappeared. Was it the goblin hunter, the coyote, or was it just her eyes playing tricks?

The old nursery rhyme popped into her head again:

The other day upon the stair
I met a man who wasn't there.
He wasn't there again today—
O how I wish he'd go away!

Cyra relaxed. She asked herself why, if the images were goblin hunters as Thomas claimed, they hadn't attacked her. Perhaps they were just fears attached to shadow, simply a sort of psychic scarecrow planted in the desert to frighten any bold intruder away. Such wasn't a new technique. The real goblin hunters couldn't be everywhere, so the goblins likely made the holograms of them and hoped most intruders would be too intimidated to examine them. Cyra had done some work in a related field, deconstructing "ghosts" to help those with minor psychic ability who thought they were being haunted. She had learned that death or intense emotion could leave an imprint in the place where a traumatic event happened, which could be sensed by a certain percentage of the populace. Her work had been intended to help people, but reversing the process wouldn't be hard. It was annoying to think that the goblins might have used some of her research at Bracebridge to create these bug-a-boos. She tried to tell herself that the coyote and the bear made a nice change from the usual Freudian images chosen by the subconscious, but she didn't believe it. Penis envy was relatively harmless; the goblin hunters were not.

It was also not beyond all possibility that the shadow coyote was real and deadly but not attacking her because she was headed in the direction the goblins wanted her to go. After all, Thomas had been convinced the goblins wanted her alive.

Thomas! She couldn't keep him out of her mind.

She arrived at the outskirts of Sin City just after sundown. The gaudy whore was decked out in her dazzling neon finery, trolling for new victims for the goblin mafia that was now her master.

New masters, same old whore, getting what she seeks by playing on equal parts of human hope and greed.

To people only casually acquainted with goblins, Sin City might seem like an unlikely spot for a stronghold. It lacked the chief goblin requirement of a nearby lake fed by its own source of underground water. But this goblin town had something that the creatures liked even more than water: money. And enough money could make any water problem go away indefinitely. Of course, if Thomas were right about the goblins making a move on California, then they would soon have no such problems at all. West of the Sierras was lush and green.

The reminder of the goblins' plans strengthened Cyra's resolve. She pulled into the parking lot at a crowded diner and parked in the back. She wished that she could take the Honda with her, but didn't dare. The goblins likely had her license plate number. Even if she switched plates, they might be looking for any female under thirty arriving in a red Honda Civic. She couldn't chance it.

Of course, abandoning the car meant abandoning her luggage. It wasn't something she wanted to do either, but all she really needed were her purse, the full money belt and her cloak.

Resolute, she unclipped her seatbelt and started rummaging in the backseat. It took only a moment to stuff the cloak in her over-size handbag, tuck her hair up under a baseball cap and scrawl an exaggerated set of lips around her mouth with a tube of lipstick. The color was a ghastly red that she had gotten as a sample in a department store and forgotten to throw away. Perfect!

Cyra climbed out of the car, locking it behind her. She felt conspicuous in her cap and jeans, but made herself join a crowd of polyester-clad jolly-holidayers climbing aboard one of the many charter buses in the giant lot.

Though she wasn't wearing her cloak, Cyra could feel it tucked under her arm, urging her to new strength in its powerful presence. She hadn't used the cloak's power—didn't even know if she could—but she made a stab at trying to conjure the impression that she was another of the seniors from the Finlandia Retirement Home on her way to a long-awaited weekend of an endless date with some hot slot machines.

Amazingly, it seemed to work. No one questioned the addition to their number. No one noticed Cyra at all as she perched on her aisle seat and peered with hard eyes around her companion at the window.

They had to disembark at the gates of the city. Cyra paused outside the iron gateway looking at the garish neon above. The buzzing sign should have read: ABANDON ALL HOPE YE WHO ENTER HERE. Instead the flashing lights said: VIVA SIN CITY.

Well, what was it to be? What was her plan? Who was she—Atalanta or Themis . . . or Persephone? Emerging from hell to bring back happiness to the world sounded really good to her, but not if it took six months and she had to go back every year. Especially not if Thomas couldn't come with her. And Themis was always portrayed as being blindfolded with the scales of justice. Cyra thought that maybe she should stick to her original plan and concentrate on being fast.

There were two trolls at the gate giving out the city's famous *lucky charms*. Most tourists loved them and kept them as souvenirs. Cyra had friends who swore that they won more often when they gambled with the charms tucked up against their skin. They maintained that they never got caught speeding or cheating on their taxes—or spouses.

No one had ever mentioned the fact that luck came in types: good, bad and blind. Nor did they seem to be aware that there was balance in the universe. For everything good that happened, somewhere else something bad was waiting. No one Cyra had ever known complained about their charms jinxing them, or ruining their lives . . . but maybe people with really bad luck were ashamed to talk about it. And maybe some of them never made it out of Sin City to complain.

One of the two giant and incurious trolls dropped a copper talisman in Cyra's outstretched hand with a grunted: *"Welcome to Sin City. May the luck be with you."*

Magic!

Cyra almost gasped at the sharp stinging of the charm. It hit with a jolt of power that numbed her arm from fingers to elbow. She managed to maintain her smile until she was well away from the gates, and then she discarded both her grimace and the burning copper talisman. The smile died on its own, the charm got dropped into one of her neighbors' gaping handbags.

She began to discreetly massage life back into her limb. There was no way to know for certain, but Cyra was willing to bet that the copper charms were some sort of magic marker, some kind of bug or maybe even a tracking device. She was also sure that just like the psychic scarecrows planted around the city, if that's what those shadows had been, these charms were booby traps designed to catch feys before they got inside.

Another bus pulled up in a cloud of gray fumes and disgorged its passengers. Cyra needed to leave the Finlandia group and get far away from that charm in case it had somehow marked her. It was a risk switching buses right under the guards' noses, but one she had to take.

Cyra mingled casually with the pedestrian throng, working her way closer to the new transportation. She kept her head down, fussing with her purse, tugging at an imaginary sticking zipper. When it was time to leave, she climbed aboard the van with the Optimists, the Sirs and their wives, willing herself to blend in with the aged crowd.

Just as before, no one challenged her right to be there.

Breathing rapidly, her fear using oxygen at an accelerated rate, she found her window soon misted. She didn't wipe the condensation away. Her image would appear quite ghostly to anyone watching from the outside.

She waited, knuckles white, until the bus passed unmolested through the gates.

So, what now?

The cloak whispered to her, snagging her wandering attention, telling Cyra what she needed to do to make herself safe so she could start her search for Thomas.

It took some effort, a forcing open of stubborn doors in her brain, but with the cloak's help Cyra was able to understand enough of what Thomas did to her when he took over her mind that she was able to begin mentally eavesdropping on the woman next to her. Cyra studied her from the corner of her eye as she slowly, slyly inserted herself into the woman's thoughts.

The sixty-two-year-old beside her was named Mary Silverman and she was the wife of retired car salesman, Henry Silverman. They lived in Arizona. She was staying at Illusions for five days. Originally she'd been planning to share a room with Henry, but he'd gotten an invitation to a prestigious golf tournament. She was on her own for the weekend and a little nervous, even though many of her friends were staying at the same hotel.

She's perfect. You can do this.

Yes, she could. But should she? Hadn't she decided that mind control was wrong?

Cyra swallowed. Her conscience squawked briefly about what she was going to attempt, but she told it to screw itself. They were in a war situation and new morals applied. It wasn't as if she were going to hurt the woman . . . probably. Thomas hadn't hurt her, had he? And she would be very careful, stop at the first sign of pain in her subject.

Cyra turned slowly to the woman beside her, caught her eye and strengthened her place in Mary's brain, letting her presence spread over the woman's mind like a shadow. She said softly: "I'm Cyra Delphin. Mary, say my name. Now."

When Cyra got off the bus, Mary went with her. They walked with the others past Illusions's thundering waterfalls and interconnecting lagoons, and the older woman obediently checked herself and her niece, Henrietta, into their rooms—*there must have been a mistake in the booking. It was Henrietta, not Henry. Of course they needed two rooms! Wasn't there anything available? A suite—certainly that was fine.*

Cyra waited patiently at Mary's side while the paperwork was seen to, practicing her newly learned art of being inconspicuous, and then she and Mary walked over to the concierge's desk and arranged for transportation. Cyra Delphin couldn't have afforded anything like the car Mary wanted, but then Cyra wasn't paying for it.

As Mary dithered over her selection, Cyra caught sight of a brochure on the desk. She felt a small trill of nerves and directed Mary to change her demand.

The older goblin behind the desk never blinked at Mary's sudden request for a Harley-Davidson *Screamin' Eagle Road King*—with a full face shield helmet. Most people came to Sin City because they wanted to play with dangerous things. There were plenty of bikers who wanted to ride the kind of hogs that didn't worry about conforming to EPA standards. As far as the goblin was concerned, Mary was just one more human with a taste for a possibly perilous kink, and he was only too happy to offer her any form of creative—and expensive—fulfillment.

Once the transaction was complete, Cyra and Mary went into the ladies' room and, in a corner not covered by the security cameras, Mary handed over the key to the suite and the paperwork for the motorcycle. She then went into one of the stalls and promptly forgot that she had acquired either a niece or a motorcycle.

Feeling dizzy and dangerously exhausted, Cyra stepped out into the breathless night and surrendered her paperwork to one of the goblins on duty. She breathed shallowly of the hot, dark air while she waited for the valets to bring her bike around. Behind her, she could hear the explosion of the volcano, which erupted like clockwork every half hour.

She didn't feel like going anywhere that night, except to bed, but she needed to start searching for Thomas. She also wanted the motorcycle moved somewhere safe and well away from Illusions, where someone might recall that silver-haired Mary Silverman had actually rented it. Another hotel parking lot would do fine. They all had excellent security.

Cyra needed a toothbrush too, because she'd forgotten hers. And clothes— *Damn it!* It all meant more delay before she could begin her hunt for Thomas.

A light mist began falling as the beautiful black and gold monster rumbled onto the pavement under the porte cochere. Cyra didn't care for the manufactured precipitation, but it made sense that the building would be outfitted with misters. Goblins hated dry air and began to desiccate when they were too long away from water. It was an odd weakness, considering they were not bothered by things like toxic chemicals or radiation, but when it came to needing regular doses of moisture, they were as delicate as any hothouse flower. *Any poisonous, man-eating hothouse flower*, Cyra amended.

She allowed herself a small smile as she accepted the helmet and keys from the young goblin who reluctantly hopped off the bike. This was exactly what she wanted: something fast, maneuverable and that wouldn't get trapped in traffic. It was beautiful, too, the ultimate forbidden fruit.

Thank goodness she was wearing jeans. A dress would have looked stupid with this bike.

Correctly interpreting her smile as appreciation of all that gleaming chrome and the powerful rumble of a thoroughbred machine, the valet hissed happily: "It'sss brand new. Thisss bike'sss got a bored and ssstroked twin-cam engine. The V-twin torquessss at thirty-five hundred RPMs. Thisss isss a real musssscle bike, a beauty in black armor. It'll blow anything off the road."

"That's what I'm counting on. After all, I'm not looking to drive my daddy's Oldsmobile," she answered, taking off her cap and opening one of the bike's compartments. Hat and purse were dropped inside. She had a pang at being separated from her cloak, but she couldn't very well ride and carry a purse.

"Mosssst girlsss are afraid of bikesss. They don't want to rule the road."

179

"I'm not most girls."

The misters shut off and immediately Cyra began to steam, white vapor rising around her as well as off of her clothes. It looked ghostly, like she was some sort of wraith, and it gave her the creeps.

"No, I can tell. Here." The goblin reached inside his jacket pocket that said *Orel* and pulled out a pair of Harley-Davidson shades. He offered them to her. "You'll need thessse to look really cool."

"Thank you." Cyra forgot to be cautious and looked full into the goblin's eyes, and with the magic from the unguent she saw more than she wanted to: a young enemy with an embarrassing speech impediment and a shared taste for power bikes. He also had an impulsive—and possibly generous—heart, and he wanted to impress a pretty girl. He was afraid that he would fail.

He wasn't just a spinal cord without a brain or a personality to guide him. He wasn't just a thinking cockroach.

Moved by a kind of sympathy, Cyra stupidly, recklessly, let herself say: "Would you like to go for a ride with me?"

The young gray-green face lit up for a moment and then fell again. "I can't. Not while I'm working. Sssorry. They're ssstrict here. And they keep track of everything. I have to clock you in and out."

"Too bad. But maybe tomorrow night," she said, relieved that he had refused. *What in the name of the goddess is wrong with me?* She must be more tired than she'd realized. Still, she had just made a friend with her offer, and that could be useful. She thought wryly that it was always handy to have resources like Mary and Orel to call on. "So, Orel, anyplace good around here to eat?"

"Sssure. They have a bunch of great placesss here at the hotel. Try the Famousss People Buffet. You've never had anything like it." His black eyes sparkled, but with pleasure or mischief she couldn't tell. And she didn't dare try using stronger magic on him because other goblins would likely be screening for that sort of thing if what Orel had said was true. "I promisss it'sss a tassste sssensssation."

Cyra repressed a shudder and wondered sickly if they meant that dishes were named after famous people, or if they actually had famous people *in* them. With goblins, you never knew.

"Okay. I'll check it out later." Cyra climbed on the idling bike and checked the balance. It was heavy for a woman, but she could handle it easily. She was selkie and strong. For the first time in her life, she was happy about that.

Cyra put on the helmet, leaving the face shield up. It was hard to flirt if you kept your eyes hidden. She was just careful not to look into any of the dozen security cameras. It was a tiring posture to hold and look natural, head down and turned slightly away, but she maintained it, even when her neck protested.

"You really look like you belong on that bike," her new friend told her. He stroked the leather seat beside her. "Sssooo sssexy."

"You know, I think I *do* belong on it." She revved the engine. The noise from the mechanical monster drowned out all conversation and music until she throttled back.

"Wow." All the goblin's pointy teeth showed when he smiled.

The other goblin valets were beginning to pay attention to them, so Cyra cut things short. "Sssee you around, Orel," she deliberately hissed at the goblin, getting a startled look, then a grin and a wave of his long, forked tongue in return.

"Sssee you, Mary."

It didn't escape Cyra's attention that he'd noted her name on the paperwork. No one here was being conveniently careless. Cyra really wanted to move the bike away from the goblin sentries, but didn't know now if she should. It might arouse all kinds of suspicions.

Cyra nodded once. She flipped down the face shield, waved carelessly, and pulled out onto the gleaming red way that was Sin City Boulevard.

What a tease—what a user, she thought angrily. She wasn't speaking of the goblin.

"Okay, Thomas Marrowbone, where in this glittering gulch are you?" she whispered, using both her mouth and mind to form the urgent question. "Come out, come out, wherever you are."

But only the bike answered. It replied with a happy scream of power as it leapt toward the heart of the neon metropolis.

Chapter Twelve

The night was hot, exhilarating, and dangerous. She could not forget that. At any moment,
Henrietta Silverman could be unmasked and
revealed as an imposter. And that would be bad
news—for Cyra, for Thomas and for California.
They had no human police force in Sin City—
no courts, no lawyers, no Miranda rights for the
accused. The state department would not rush
in to bail Cyra out. There were trolls with guns
who took care of simple problems.

Anything important went to Lilith. Cyra
didn't kid herself that she was any match for
the goblin queen. She preferred the trolls. They
were very big, and she now knew that the legends were right and they did eat people, but
they were also stupid and slow. Lilith was re-
putedly neither.

Speaking of the queen bitch, where in this bright city did the goblin underground begin— or end? It was probably everywhere beneath the city. And there were likely entrances to that hive in every hotel. Cyra just needed to find one that wasn't popular and heavily guarded. She wouldn't use it except as a last resort, but she was fairly certain that Thomas would be eventually down there somewhere, trying to find the goblins' path to Yucca Mountain, trying to figure out how to blow it up without setting off the world's largest earthquake and killing everyone in the western United States.

She had to slow down at Paradise Isle, where the crowds were gathering outside to watch the battle between the navy and goblin pirates. The navy always lost, but no one got tired of watching the ship sink in the lagoon.

The Carrefour, Starlight Grand, Nero's—the architectural marvels were all still there, all still deceptively beautiful. Cyra stared up at the beam from the Nile that shot into space like a giant light saber. It was the brightest light in the world. She'd read somewhere that it was forty billion candlepower and could be seen from Los Angeles on a clear night. And it all belonged to Lilith now. That meant Cyra couldn't stay at any of the hotels. She'd have to find someone else like Mary to arrange accommodations for her somewhere less popular.

Like the Sunrise Station. Cyra slowed to a crawl and turned into the rutted driveway. Faux Mediterranean, a little run down with a drive-through wedding chapel whose sign boasted: A NEW WEDDING EVERY FIVE MINUTES! A NEW DIVORCE EVERY FORTY-FIVE! It looked like the kind of place where guests minded their own nefarious business and where a person could move about undisturbed by the hotel's oblivious custodians.

Cyra parked the Harley in the crumbling lot and waited patiently for someone to wander over to admire it. Whoever took the bait, she would take their mind.

This time, her *friend* was a man. His name was Lloyd. He was fifty-one and he liked blondes. Cyra obliged him by making him believe she looked like Marilyn Monroe. He was only too happy to take some cash from Cyra and rent her a room for the week. He thought about keeping the extra money for himself, but decided that he would be honest and bring it and the room key back to the pretty platinum-blond lady on the Harley.

Ten minutes later, Lloyd went out for a beer and forgot all about the room, the bike and the imaginary blonde.

Cyra couldn't forget, though. She felt like she had brain pollution, and her head was throbbing. Apparently she was good at manipulating people, but the talent came with a physical price that she was sure Thomas never paid. Probably there was some rule about stealing another person's magic that said there had to be balance. Nowhere in the universe did you get something for free.

Cyra rubbed her forehead. Should she stay the night at the Sunrise Station? It was right here. She could lie down for a brief rest and she wouldn't need to travel another weary mile with her head pounding.

Yet the watchful eyes at Illusions might be waiting to see if Henrietta actually used her room. It was a suite, after all. And Mary had made a fuss about getting it for her niece. That might have gotten the room flagged.

It was awfully tempting to blow the hotel off, but Cyra was more likely to see Lilith there, should the need arise. It was better to keep her options open. Sunrise Station was just a fallback place, somewhere to go if Henrietta got in trouble.

However, Henrietta was going to need some things, enough to convince the maids that she was real. Normally, Cyra wouldn't have minded a spot of commerce, but she was feeling very tired and her headache was getting worse by the minute. Every so often, imaginary lightning flickered at the corners of her eyes, and she had a metallic taste growing in her mouth. The idea of braving the malls that offered 'round the clock neon *shoppertainment* was unpleasant.

Cyra chose a nearby strip mall and, mindful of the motorcycle's limited compartment space, she shopped lightly—aspirin, toothpaste, underwear, two dark t-shirts with long sleeves, an extra pair of jeans, one sundress out of crinkle cloth and a pair of flat sandals. All of this went into a modest duffel.

Last stop, and the one that threatened to split her head open like a dropped egg, was a pawn shop where Cyra found another *friend* to purchase a handgun and ammunition—no waiting period necessary since the gun was hot. The pistol was repulsive, covered in feelings of anger and evil intent, but she took it anyway. If there ever was a situation where she might need a weapon, this was it.

Night, never really able to embrace the city through its shroud of garish light, was giving way completely as Cyra arrived back at Illusions.

She changed her mind about parking the Harley elsewhere, because it might raise some suspicions if she returned to the hotel without it. And there was no doubt that Orel would be aware of the fact if she failed to come back that night.

She was also too tired to hunt for another parking spot and then walk back to the hotel.

The pretend volcano was erupting again when Cyra pulled under the porte cochere, spewing sulfur into the air. It was a relief to surrender the idling bike into Orel's loving care. The constant vibration had made her hands and arms numb. The human valets were already coming on duty, but the goblin had lingered into the gauzy predawn hour, waiting for her return, eager to find out how she had liked the bike.

"Hey, Orel." Cyra forced herself to smile even though her head throbbed like an athlete's heart at the end of a triathlon. It was painful to remove her helmet, which had served as a sort of pressure bandage. She took her ticket stub from the goblin. "Awesome bike. She really goes. I thought I'd get airborne out on the highway."

The goblin smiled happily, showing teeth and a tip of the tongue. "Ssshe's a goer. You going to eat now?" he asked, looking hopeful.

Eat? Cyra all but shuddered.

"Nah. I'm off to bed. I'm kind of a night-owl," she lied. "Don't care for mornings much."

Reminded of the hour, the goblin looked over at the lightening eastern sky. His face lost some of its animation. "Yeah, me too," he said regretfully. "Well, sssee you, Mary."

"Manana." Cyra got her purse and duffel bag out of the motorcycle's storage compartment and started for the hotel, being careful to hold her head as still as possible.

Illusions's interior was done in warm, elegant colors and textures. Cyra's suite had a marble entryway, a thick diamond-patterned rug on the floor that went on for yards because it included a living room, dining room, master suite and a pair of bathrooms. There were fresh flowers everywhere, a pair of tickets for Zeigfield and Roi on the desk—they were using gargoyles as well as white tigers in their show now—and she really couldn't complain about the view, even if she was one floor shy of the penthouse suites.

What she could complain about was the poor security and the man waiting behind her bedroom door. The moment she passed through the wide doorway, he clapped one hand over her mouth and the other around her throat.

"Hug bitch! Did you think we wouldn't know you were here?" he growled.

Cyra's education had not been in neurosurgery, but her work at Bracebridge had given her a fairly complete understanding of the physical workings of the human body and mind. When cranial nerves received sensory input from excited extereceptors, it caused a transmission of an impulse across the synapses. Neurotransmitters would then bind with postsynaptic receptors and immediately thereafter motor neurons would transmit a message to the somatic nervous system directing appropriate contractions of the skeletal muscles. Autonomic nerves would prompt the heart and adrenal glands to greater effort. In the right situation hormones would be released—say if she were nursing and needed to produce more milk and needed large breasts.

Of course, it wasn't larger breasts she needed right then. And her attacker probably wasn't looking for them either.

Her courses in anatomy had also taught her that the human larynx is made up of nine pieces of useful cartilage, which could be easily and permanently damaged. In the same general region was the even more valuable and fragile trachea. She had always suspected that her own anatomy varied slightly from the norm, having a somewhat longer, thicker neck, but it did not differ so greatly that she could ignore an assault on her throat. Both trachea and larynx would suffer lasting damage if the hands wrapped around her neck got any tighter.

Months of self-defense training kicked in, and unlike in the classroom where she had felt a need to be cautious of her strength, Cyra felt no need to hold back when she used her elbows in her assailant's diaphragm. She slammed backward with all her might, then spun about and applied a flat-handed jab to the nose. Just as her instructor had promised, her attacker fell on the floor with a last whoosh of conscious air.

Cyra stared at him with blurred eyes as she fought to regain her breath. He was tall, brown haired, wearing a suit that looked vaguely like a uniform. He also had bad skin and enormous feet. Maybe he was part troll.

Once again glad to have superior strength at her disposal, Cyra dragged the man's body to the hotel door. A quick look through his pockets revealed that he had a master roomkey and nothing else. That could mean anything. He might be a well-connected thief in hotel camouflage. He might also be a hotel employee who had lost his name badge.

He had said something funny: *Hug bitch?* That didn't make any sense, unless . . . he might have meant H.U.G.—Humans Under Ground. That wouldn't be good. But how the hell could they suspect the nonexistent person,

Henrietta Silverman, of being with Humans Under Ground? And who the hell were "*they*" anyway? The goblins? Someone else?

Using words her mother would never have approved of, Cyra pocketed the master key and shoved the unconscious troll-man into the hall, not bothering to arrange his limbs for comfort.

She hung a DO NOT DISTURB sign on the door-knob and slammed the door with inconsiderate force, flipping the deadbolt and security latch. She then forced herself to a telephone. Her hands trembled as she reached for the receiver. Cyra's head hurt so badly that she could barely focus enough to read the options menu. White lightning crackled at the back of her head and she could feel her gorge beginning to rise.

The front desk picked up the phone immediately. "Front desk. How can I help you?"

"This is Henrietta Silverman. I've just been assaulted in my suite." Cyra's voice was thin and a bit shrill. But that was fine. It added verisimilitude.

There was a gasp and then a hurried: "Let me get the manager."

The phone changed hands.

"Miss Silverman, this is Manvil at the front desk. You say that you were *assaulted*? Stay where you are. Our head of daytime security, M. Beene, is on your floor. He'll be right there.

He's a tall man, brown hair, blue blazer, black slacks—"

"—and big shoes. We've met. What the hell kind of hotel are you running—a half-way house for perverts?" Cyra forced anger into her voice. She discovered that she had a real streak of bitchiness when she heard herself adding: "Don't bother sending anyone else along. And you can assure Mr. Beene when he wakes up that my breasts are quite secure right where they are . . . and if I see him again or catch him near my aunt I'm gonna blow his ugly, miniaturized pecker off."

She slammed the phone down and wondered if the bluff worked. If the management had sent him to check her out, would they be convinced of her innocence with this direct complaint?

There was no way to know.

Should she stay, or should she go?

Her stomach answered with a ferocious heave and Cyra ran for the nearest bathroom. When it finally emptied itself of food, Cyra didn't have the energy to seek her bed. Still on her knees, she pulled the radiantly white bath towels off the wrought-iron rod and made a nest on the floor, then fell slowly into a deep, comalike sleep, her fevered cheek pressed into the blessedly cold tile floor.

"Thomas, where are you?" she whispered in

her head, feeling more wretched than she ever had in her life.

"Sleep, Cyra. I'll see you soon."

"Thomas, is that really you?"

"Yes, it's me. Sleep, baby fey."

About that, she had no choice. Her body shut down before she could answer.

Chapter Thirteen

Thomas frowned as another shaft of pain lanced through his head. Damn it! Cyra had been up to something magical—and dangerously taxing. Now she was ill. Damn it! He didn't want her timid about her powers, but he didn't want her reckless either. From the moment he'd seen the e-mail at user1812@lutin-empire.com he'd known what was coming. Jack wouldn't have written unless it was something important. The only thing of immediate importance was Cyra.

Well, Cyra and the fact that Thomas had managed to tap into the goblins' security system and hijack a couple of cameras in Lilith's underground quarters. He temporarily had a ringside seat to the skullduggery. Watching an unpleasant four-way with Lilith, Lancilotto, a frightened lutin female, and a human who turned out to be Fornix wasn't pleasant, but Thomas managed to glean some very useful information from the pillow-talk they shared after while reclining on the body of the now dead lutin girl. The threesome took a few moments out from plotting genocide to decide that the girl had been strangled by Lancilotto for *treason* not for fun.

There had been no mention of dates, but there was no longer any doubt about it. Lilith was planning on irradiating California with the nuclear waste provided by Fornix and, unwittingly, the U.S. government. They were also doubling security at the city borders in case Thomas—or the kloka—tried to get back inside. It didn't cheer him any to learn that the guards had been ordered to take him and Cyra alive and bring them to Lilith for questioning. The coyote and bear were also actively hunting for feys in the desert. Cyra had been lucky to avoid them.

Cyra. Everything seemed to lead back to her eventually. Thomas had already been feeling guilty about his craven flight. He should have stuck around to face the music instead of leaving her to deal with it solo. How could he have expected Cyra to control the magic that was so new to her when he himself had been unable to resist it? And though he had feared that a union with Cyra would bring out all sorts of dire memories, nothing had happened after all. The dragon had retired without a fuss once he was sure what was going to happen, there was no reproaching shade in his dreams to remind him of his dead wife, and all his memories of this occasion were sweet, passionate ones.

But now Cyra had come to Sin City looking for him. He was going to have to go see her, apologize from the bottom of his heart for being a cad, and then convince her to leave the city before she got seriously hurt.

Thinking unkind thoughts about Jack for not stopping Cyra from leaving Cadalach, even though he knew his expectations were unreasonable, Thomas closed his portable PC and went to put on some shoes. He didn't admit to himself that part of him was really looking forward to seeing Cyra Delphin again. Or that he hoped she would not be so angry that she never wanted to see, speak, or touch him again. The same part of him wondered nervously what she would make of his short, punk hair and muscle-T that showed off his dragon "*tattoos*." Actually, his entire outfit was a medley of trendy, offensive emblems. The only thing he lacked was a body piercing, and that was because feys didn't like prolonged contact with metal.

Thomas added a pair of onyx black sunglasses to the ensemble, narrow rectangles that wrapped around his eyes, hiding them completely. A glance in the mirror assured him that he looked a *chic* horror—which was perfect. Fastidious people didn't visit Sin City. The three safest things for a fey to do was make like a coffee grinder and blend, blend, blend.

Cyra hadn't meant to sleep the day away, but her body made plans for recovery without informing her mind. She woke up on the bathroom floor just before sundown. A towel was glued to the side of her face, and she felt like she was recovering from a bout of flu.

As she turned on the taps in the shower and attempted to massage away some of the stiffness in her limbs and back, Cyra took a mental inventory, hoping her brain wasn't as bruised as her body. The news was good. Borrowing Thomas's magic the way she had been doing, influencing people's minds and everything, was something she'd been doing intuitively and not too well. But though it had made her body ill, her brain was remarkably clear. There were no side effects from her ruthless head-hopping and identity-switching.

It was a little disconcerting to learn that she was rather a hydra, multi-headed; that there were so many aspects of her personality that she had never known existed—and many came with sharp teeth and a bad attitude—but Cyra suspected she was going to find several of these new facets of her nature to be very useful here.

Once out of the shower and dressed in clean clothes, she checked her telephone for messages. *Nothing.* No complaints from the management about her treatment of their head of security. It looked like her claim of sexual harassment had paid off. Even if they—the mysterious "*they*"—knew his purposes had not been sexual, it had to reassure them that she had thought so. Perhaps they were now convinced that she wasn't with H.U.G.

Next on her body's list of demands was food. Cyra thought about room service, but that was too slow. Anyway, she didn't really want anyone else in her room. If she was going to meet with paranoid enemies of H.U.G., she wanted to be in public, where there would be some minimal safety from witnesses. Also, it would be hard to slip anything nasty—well, anything nasty aimed specifically at her—into a buffet.

Cyra quickly put on her garish lipstick and tucked her hair back under her cap. The Harley-Davidson shades completed the look.

The elevator was empty and silent as the grave, but it delivered her speedily to The Famous People Buffet that Orel had recommended.

Cyra was prepared to believe the worst about Lilith and everything she owned, but catching sight of the dessert table loaded with chocolate in every liquid and solid form known to man, she decided that maybe—just maybe—Lilith had one redeeming feature. Not everyone was a good hotelier.

Cyra spoke quickly to a passing waiter and requested a latte be brought to her as soon as possible. Since the waiter was human, she reinforced the request with the tiniest of mental shoves. She then grabbed a plate from a refrigerated tray and quickly loaded it with plump, glossy éclairs, adding extra chocolate sauce for good measure.

She and her caloric treats retreated to a quiet corner table where they could enjoy getting acquainted in private. She didn't really want any witnesses once the vulgar gulping began. The waiter brought her latte, the smell of the coffee mingling seductively with the cream and chocolate. Not bothering with any gastronomic foreplay, as soon as the waiter retreated, she quickly cut off a generous bite of pastry and stuffed it into her mouth.

And spat it out again. She didn't like to leap to conclusions—especially not about anything as beautiful as her chocolate-smothered éclair—so she allowed herself a full ten seconds to deduce that she really was tasting something bad in the food. It was some form of faerie bane, and maybe something else.

"Fiends! Wretched, vicious fiends!" she whispered, disappointment and hunger making her so angry that she was ready to pound someone.

Alarmed at the resurgence of the blinding anger she had felt so often at Bracebridge, and aware of the cameras around her, Cyra put her clenched hands under the table and made an effort to calm herself.

Thomas looked at Cyra's mangled éclair, then at his lover's face. He couldn't help smiling at her expression of concentrated loathing.

"You look like you're ready to throw that dish at someone," he said softly.

Cyra looked up, startled. For one moment, she looked angry enough to try dislocating both of his shoulders and maybe his jaw. "I *would* like to throw this dish, and you might well be my first choice of targets since the waiter has disappeared."

Thomas's brow rose. "I might be. Only you're too happy to see me to do that, aren't you?"

"Happy?" Cyra laughed once, a sound almost a sob. Her expression wavered, sliding from one tense emotion to another. "How very inadequate a word. I've been looking for you, Thomas."

Thomas took a seat at the table. He was careful not to overtly demonstrated any pleasure at seeing her, but he didn't pull back when Cyra's foot nudged his under the white linen tablecloth. He watched with interest as she gathered herself, reeling in her emotions and regulating her breathing. She kept her face averted against the overhead cameras. Though upset and enraged, this Cyra Delphin was about one hundred times more collected than the woman he had left at Cadalach.

And he hadn't been around to witness the transformation.

"You haven't been taking very good care of yourself," he scolded. "And you are doing the same thing again today. Did you learn nothing yesterday about stealing my magic?"

"Well, I wouldn't call it stealing, but I have been taking your name in vain a bit, so to speak," she admitted, speaking softly. "Or my own."

"I know. I've felt you."

"There's not much to it," she told him, and then glared when he smiled in what he knew was a most patronizing manner. "I figured out how to do it right away."

"There's not much to it if you don't mind half-killing yourself," he agreed, then rose to his feet. "Let's get out of here. I know someplace that has good coffee and decent éclairs. You'll feel better after you've eaten."

Cyra stood too. She scrawled her room number and name on the check the waiter had left with her latte. "That sounds lovely. Do you have a car?"

"After a fashion. It's in the Paradise Isle parking garage."

"Ah, then let's take mine." A mischievous smile touched her lips. "My wheels go so well with that outfit."

Thomas looked at her Harley-Davidson sunglasses and began to grin. "You didn't, did you?" He was surprised, but also obscurely pleased at the show of spirit. He hadn't thought Cyra bold enough for such an adventuresome choice of transportation.

"No, *I* didn't. My *aunt* did." She kept her voice low as they worked their way toward the elevator. "And I figured if I was going to cheat on the Honda, it should be with something exotic. I guess these days I'm just into bad boys."

"Your *aunt*? Adoptive, I presume. You have

been reckless. I want a helmet if you're driving," he warned her.

Cyra nodded. "Orel will get one for you."

"Orel?"

"My new friend, the goblin valet."

Thomas looked down at Cyra and got a small jolt. He couldn't see her eyes behind the shades, but her lips were tilted up at the corners in that alluring Kewpie-doll smile. "Well, well. You have been a busy little kloka, haven't you? You didn't try to use magic on the goblin, did you?"

"You have no idea how busy I've been. And no, I did not use magic on the goblin. I've been very careful."

Thomas snorted.

Cyra ignored him. "By the way, everyone at the hotel thinks I'm Henrietta Silverman. Except Orel. He thinks I'm Mary Silverman."

Thomas stared at her. "Hm . . . I think you'd better begin telling me just what you've been up to."

"Gladly, just as soon as you do the same."

Thomas frowned at the snippy reply. "Cyra, I'm not kidding."

"Thomas, neither am I." She looked up then, and as she tilted her head, he saw the mostly healed bruises on her throat.

"What happened? What are these marks on

your neck? Those are human handprints! Or . . . a troll-cross?" Thomas had to work to keep rage out of his voice. He had known Cyra was in pain, but he had thought it solely a side effect of using his magic. "Who did this to you?"

"Mr. Beene, daytime head of security for the Illusions hotel. He mistook me for someone in Humans Under Ground. It looks like we may not be the only players here in Sin City set on destroying Lilith's fun. Fortunately, Mr. Beene is rather slow and stupid."

"And where is Mr. Slow-and-Stupid now?" Thomas asked softly. Some of his anger leaked into his words, in spite of his efforts to keep it contained. Hearing it, he buckled down his emotion twice as securely, not wanting the dragon to be roused by his rage. It had taken him several days and constant effort to lock up the beast securely again after the nightmare and making love to Cyra. The creature hadn't tried in any way to manifest itself, but he'd felt its curiosity and watchfulness. A dragon's curiosity was almost always unhealthy for someone.

"I don't know where Mr. Beene is," Cyra answered, stepping into the elevator. "I dumped his body in the hall and told the front desk to come collect it."

"You . . . He was *dead*?" Thomas was again startled.

"No, not when I left him there. But if the other trolls found him like that . . . Well, who knows? I haven't seen him since. Close your mouth, Thomas. It's uncool with those sunglasses—which are excellent, by the way. I'll have to get some."

Cyra took out her hotel key and shoved it into the slot. She then pushed the button for the lobby and held it down, forcing the elevators to bypass all other floors.

Thomas checked the mirrored wall of the elevator car to make sure he wasn't actually gaping, then said firmly: "Okay, enough with the jokes. I want to know what's been happening. I especially want to know everything you've heard about Humans Under Ground in Sin City."

"And I want food. I'm starved. Somehow, I never got around to eating yesterday. Watch out for the security cameras in the lobby. They have this area thoroughly covered." Cyra withdrew her key and dropped it in her bag. She strode out of the elevator as quickly as the doors opened.

Thomas had never thought of jeans and a purse as being power clothes, but somehow Cyra made them look like a three-piece suit with Rolex, custom-made loafers, briefcase, and silk tie. It had to have something to do with her posture. And the attitude. This was a woman who believed herself to be in complete control of her destiny. What had changed?

Cyra Delphin, who are you?

She didn't reply. Bemused, Thomas followed.

Chapter Fourteen

The milkshake was stubborn, so thick that Cyra's eyes almost crossed as she sucked on the straw. She had related her adventures to Thomas and figured that she was now entitled to enjoy her meal of chicken Caesar salad, garlic fries, Paul Bunyon Burger—with cheese, bacon and grilled onions—and espresso chocolate-chip milkshake without interruption. That included not paying any attention to Thomas's amusement at the size of her feast.

The only thing marring her dining pleasure was knowing she was going to have to yell at Thomas when the meal was done. He was not keeping up his end of the bargain, the part where he also gave a full disclosure of his activities and plans. She could feel it coming—the women-and-children-into-the-lifeboat speech.

"And so what now?" Cyra asked as she sucked up the very last of the rogue chocolate chips at the bottom of her glass.

"So now I take you to a night club and show you a bit of what we're up against," Thomas answered. "And then I hope to convince you to leave Sin City while I finish my job. It won't take that long, you know."

"I have seen the enemy—and it is lounge lizards?" she asked facetiously, refusing to get alarmed on a full stomach.

"In a sense," Thomas answered, throwing some money on the table. "Let's go. The place I want to show you is next door in the Two-Bit Lounge."

"It looks sleazy," Cyra said.

"It is," Thomas agreed.

"Will the Harley be okay?" she asked, glancing over at the bike. It was parked under a large neon coffee cup that made its chrome sparkle like a showgirl wearing too many sequins.

"Yes, I arranged some special hallucinogenic wards. No one will touch it and stay sane, much less be able to drive it away."

"Really?" Cyra made a note to sample the wards when they got back. She could sense her cloak rolled up in her purse, and it felt ready to try a fresh conjuration, ready to feed her power if she wanted to make magic.

"Remember," Thomas said quietly. "I'm in your thoughts again, but not controlling you. The important thing is to believe in your role. Don't break character when in public. In fact, try not to do it even in private. If they have a scanner working the floor, they'll be looking for mental inconsistencies."

Cyra nodded.

The Two-Bit Lounge was filled with smoke, some tobacco and some not. The atmosphere was repulsive and made her eyes water, but Cyra didn't complain as they walked through the lobby full of clanging, strobe-lit slot machines and paused outside a small theater stage set apart from the casino in a curtained alcove.

"Do we need tickets?" Cyra asked.

"No. This one is free."

A few moments of the stand-up comedian's routine explained why they didn't dare charge for the show. It also convinced Cyra that Thomas hadn't brought her here just to appreciate the artist's lack of craft. The routine was, in fact, unbelievably awful. So awful that it had to be some form of experiment.

"Someone bake my wife, please," the goblin said, voice deadpan into his microphone. Cyra was about to speak when, after a full second's pause, the audience erupted into loud guffaws of laughter that went on for almost five seconds before dying abruptly as lights in a power outage.

Every sense she had went on alert. She took a step closer to the stage and felt something cold and sly moving over her skin. She wondered for an instant if it was one of the security scanners Thomas had mentioned. It didn't feel like a psychic emanation—but maybe goblins were different.

"Careful," Thomas warned, his voice soft as a sigh. The fact that he didn't use mind speech warned Cyra they were near something which could detect their true natures. "Hold your breath if you go any closer."

The bored comic went on with his routine, his green face staring into the distance: "My wife was complaining that she wasn't sexually satisfied. I said, 'How can you say that when I've got fourteen inches right here just waiting to please you?' She said, 'Twelve inches don't count when they come in four dicks and two tongues.'"

The stand-up paused. Again, something crawled over Cyra's skin with slimy legs. Not a scanner. It was . . . something else. Cyra began counting. *One-one thousand . . .* Begin laughter. *One-one thousand, two-one thousand, three-one thousand, four-one thousand, five-one thousand.* The laughter stopped.

"Did *you* kill my wife, sir? No? It must have been me, then." Cyra counted again. The effect repeated.

"Do you think when the cops say *'put your hands up'* that they mean all of them?" The goblin raised his top set of arms into the air while the lower left hand continued to hold the mike. His lower right limb reached into his jacket pocket. He pulled out a realistic revolver and pointed it at a man in the audience. He slowly pulled back the hammer until it was cocked, then pulled the trigger. The gun went off and made Cyra flinch, but no one else reacted. Then, after a full second's delay, the audience started laughing.

"I don't believe it," Cyra whispered.

"Believe it."

Thomas pulled her away from the small stage and urged her back outside. It was all Cyra could do to hold her tongue until they were safely away from listening ears.

"Thomas, do you know what that was?" she demanded when they got to the Harley and Thomas began the discreet process of removing wards.

"Yes. That was mass mind control," he said. He handed her a helmet.

"But how was it done? Was it . . . goblin magic?"

"Of a sort. Mainly it's mass hypnotism. And maybe drugs."

"But how can they do that? It's a sham, you know, subliminal messages and those hypnotists who say they can put an entire audience under. No one can control a crowd that large."

"You could," Thomas answered. "A kloka could do that and more." Cyra swallowed and he went on: "You're right that it's usually a sham. But the goblins have almost perfected a system of subliminal instruction administered with drugs that they pump through the ventilation systems of their hotels and casinos. It's a nasty trick they picked up from the hive in Detroit before Jack and Io took it out. Unfortunately, it is fairly effective on humans. They haven't yet started experiments that force people to commit violent acts, but I have seen them convince whole groups—strangers, tourists from Des Moines—to have sex on stage."

"This is terrible." Cyra thought of her work at Bracebridge and was wracked by guilt and anger. This might well be her fault.

She had a sense of some dark destiny racing toward them—and it was huge, mountainous, not to be deterred, and now unavoidable. Well, so be it then. Thomas wouldn't scare her away.

If Fate was coming for them, it would find her on her feet and at Thomas's side.

"Yes," he agreed. "It's terrible and it's everywhere. They aren't so blatant at the larger hotels and casinos where the wealthy patrons stay. At least not yet. But you can bet they have their ventilation systems all set to go for the day when they perfect their subliminal cocktail. Or when they finally capture a magical being who can be forced into working for them. Think what they could do with all the high rollers who come through here. They'll use you, Cyra. If they find you, they'll tear your brain to shreds looking for the secret. You have no idea what these creatures can do."

It was a good point, but it didn't matter to her. It couldn't matter. She felt as certain as sunrise that if she left Sin City, Thomas would die. And then she would die too.

"But what is it they want?" she asked, frustrated and fearful even with her determination in place. "I thought they wanted California. Why bother with all this nonsense if they are after real estate? They'll be able to take what they want after they have the bomb."

"They want what tyrants always want—everything. They want it all. There will never be enough power, money, water—anything—to satisfy them. California is a whim. A stepping stone to other things." Thomas pulled on his helmet and climbed aboard the bike. He'd allowed her to drive on their way to the restaurant, but had made her agree to let him have a turn when they were done eating. "Keys," he said, holding out his hand.

Cyra handed them over and climbed on behind Thomas. In spite of the heat, she was suddenly feeling rather cold and was quite happy to lean into Thomas's warmth.

"So, are you ready to be sensible now and leave Goblin Town West?" he asked her.

"No," Cyra answered, shaking her head.

"And why not? Did Jack beat you with a stupid stick while I was gone?" Thomas's voice was exasperated. "You can see what's happening.

"Yes. But I have this personal problem, and it won't wait."

"Yeah?"

"Yeah. I came to this goblin town for a reconciliation with my lover . . . and, if it goes well, to get laid too. I'd like to try it again without magic clouding my judgment."

"I see." Thomas sounded nonplussed.

"You don't really expect me to leave yet, do you, with this hanging fire? Or is your motherboard short a couple of microchips?" There was a pause after this announcement, almost as long as the one in the stand-up's routine.

Cyra was beginning to feel nervous when Thomas began to laugh. It was a soft laugh, but his chest rumbled beneath her hands.

"Is this feminine prioritization at work? Okay, I'll buy it. Yes, we need to sort out our relationship. I know it's important. And I'm touched that you came looking for me. I know I don't deserve it."

"Good—I'm glad we understand one another. I don't mind guys who are a little slow, but I can't stand ones who are completely clueless."

"So, your place or mine? Mine has a king-size water bed, a mirrored ceiling, and the original red fake fur carpet installed in the sixties."

"By all means," Cyra said, "let's make it yours." Something fluttered in the pit of her stomach, but she wasn't sure if it was lust or fear. Her feeling of invulnerability and control began to slide away. "My place isn't anywhere near as exciting or historical. Hell, it doesn't even have a radio. Just don't forget that we still need to reconcile our differences of plans and opinions. I won't be put off, Thomas. And if you make love to me and then sneak out again, I'll never forgive you."

"I'll bear it in mind." Thomas had stopped laughing, but there was still a smile in his voice.

Chapter Fifteen

Science could explain many things. For instance, the internal chemical reaction that occurred in two attracted biological systems—in this case, a man and a woman. Laymen called it body chemistry, but that was only partly right. What happened between Cyra and Thomas was so much more than plain old biology or chemistry. Yes, the parasympathetic neurons stimulated blood flow in the usual manner. This potential for action caused the release of acetylcholine and stimulated muscles to contraction. Since the cardiac muscle was auto-rhythmic and the flood of adrenaline caused it to beat faster, blood rushed to the lips and erogenous—

"Cyra, I can hear you," Thomas complained over the growl of the engine. "Words like acetylcholine kind of ruin the mood. Couldn't you just feel me up and enjoy the ride?"

Cyra exhaled slowly. Shared intelligence and experience meant a greater capacity for sensation and understanding—a unique experience afforded to no other species that she knew. It also meant that Thomas could make her feel naked without even trying. Would she ever get used to someone peeping in her brain?

"Thomas?"

"Yes?"

"I'm nervous."

"The room isn't that tacky," he said after a moment, but released one handlebar of the bike long enough to squeeze the hands she had wrapped around his waist. Cyra would have liked to lean her head against him and breathe in his calming scent, but a helmet made that rather difficult.

What was wrong with her? Why the nerves? They were headed to a passionate reconciliation—reunion—whatever this was. And this time she was clear that it was what she truly wanted. Their attraction was obviously not only something that Cadalach had done to them.

But then, after this, there would be a fight over her remaining with Thomas. They would both hate that. And she wondered if they should just get the fight over with. That would be the brave, mature thing to do: sort out what they were doing *before* they went to bed.

"*Probably,*" Thomas agreed. "*But do you really want it in that order?*"

"I wouldn't mind if I thought it would clear the air. But I don't think we're getting through this fight that quickly," she shouted up at him through the wind. Shouting was less personal than mind-speak when she was feeling shy.

"*No?*"

"No!"

"*Well, we'll have to sort it out with some rapidity. I have plans that can't wait.*"

"I'm sure you do," Cyra answered. "And I'd like to hear all about them."

"*All in good time, my pretty. All in good time. Now relax,*" Thomas said and thought at her, and then laughed. "Hold tight. You'll enjoy this stretch."

Cyra had come to know the Harley, the quirks of its greater weight when it cornered, ways to coax the gears into higher than standard performance. But what Thomas made it do when they hit an open stretch of road was diabolical. The engine screamed, a noise that pierced her ears like spikes. He pushed the machine beyond anything the performance specs ever anticipated.

Cyra had a moment of fear, but it was almost

instantly absorbed by a surge of adrenaline from the fey part of her brain. Brakes and tires lost a lot of traction when the road was hot, and the constant gusts of hot wind could be disconcerting, but Thomas and this bike were in some sort of Zen place where man and machine were one. Cyra wouldn't have been shocked if he'd managed to take them into the clouds. Caution was chucked by her misbehaving nerves to be carried away by the slipstream trailing behind them, and she allowed herself to be filled with exaltation.

"Thomas! You are either very, very bad for me—or very, very good!" she shouted when the engine was throttled back.

"And maybe both."

This made her laugh a bit wildly. "Faster. I want to fly again."

"Oh, you will. I promise, you will."

They arrived at a hotel at the outskirts of town. Cyra memorized its name and features for future reference but didn't allow herself any visceral reactions to what most people would have called *a dive*. Her thoughts were only for Thomas. Their attraction—this time separate from whatever had happened in Cadalach—was rising up and their thoughts, never truly separated from the moment they met, were beginning to twine about one another, rubbing up

221

against each other in erotic ways. Arousal fed arousal, and soon they experienced their deepest emotions and hungers without personal borders. It left Cyra feeling a bit disoriented.

Common sense told her to be wary, but she wasn't prepared to listen to her wariness, or Thomas's if it manifested itself. Life had been so joyless, so pointless for so long—and now, thanks to the goblins, even that simple, flat existence could be taken from them at any moment.

So to hell with common sense. She was ready to welcome Thomas in to explore the new, fertile territory of her mind. And into her heart, if he would go there. It was time for something to bloom in those dry lands.

Sensing this new invitation, Thomas laughed as he picked her up and carried her over the threshold of his room. It was as tacky as he had promised, and it made her laugh too. Pleasure at the ridiculousness of their situation rose up, powerful but delicate as the bubbles in a glass of champagne.

"And here's the best part." He tossed her lightly onto the bed—and it sloshed. He smiled down at her bobbing form. "Ever made love in your natural element?"

"No, never."

"Me either. I'm willing to bet—*oh, practically*

anything—that I'll enjoy this. How about you?"

"There isn't a doubt in my mind." Cyra smiled and rolled to her knees. Keeping balance was easy for her. She reached for Thomas, pulling off his shirt with one smooth tug. "Your taste in clothing is deteriorating. You've gone from lounge lizard to muscle boy—though the body is, of course, still exquisite."

Thomas rolled gracefully onto the bed, kicking his slacks away. His legs, like the rest of his body, were marked with the same delicate tracery he had on his chest and back. Cyra hummed her approval and pulled off her own shirt, suddenly wanting only to press skin to skin.

A quick flash of heat hit her solar plexus and made her heart stutter. It spread quickly downward. She reached out to touch Thomas, needing. She sighed.

"Flattery will get you anywhere. You needn't even be coherent about it. Sighs, groans, general gestures or expressions of awe or pleasure will all work fine." He helped her pull off her jeans, which seemed determined to stick to her, first at the hips and then at the knees and finally at the shoes she had forgotten to untie. Once her legs were bare, he dropped a kiss on her thigh. The small touch left her aquiver. Her breaths grew short and shuddery, and suddenly the light seemed too bright.

"Top or bottom?" he asked.

"Oh, top definitely," she said, rolling onto him. Her flesh pressed against his flesh, hers smooth like satin, his a warmer velvet that made the nerve endings in her body riot everyplace the two of them touched. She felt a shiver deep inside, a small burst of exploding sun that softened her muscles and made her ready, and she wondered how his brain, wrapped with hers, translated such feminine feelings of desire . . . or if it even could.

But of course he could feel this. She felt his need blazing like a beacon, guiding her toward what he wanted so badly. This wasn't plain old desire. It was as though he were starving for contact with her. There was a saying that if you tried to starve a wolf, the wolf would starve last. This was likely true of most predators. But eventually even the wildest loner like Thomas or a wolf could reach the point when it had to have sustenance or die.

Faced with such overwhelming want, it made foreplay seem unnecessary, ridiculous even. And suddenly, Cyra didn't want the gentle swaying of the waterbed either. Her feelings, like Thomas's, were not temperate and tame. She needed earth, solid beneath them because she wanted to hold him down and do things to his body. And why not? He could take it. That was the utterly wonderful thing about Thomas. She couldn't hurt him if she tried.

Smiling wickedly, she grabbed Thomas with arms and legs, and using her strength, she rolled them onto the floor. He could have stopped her, but he didn't. She gloried in her exercise of power—physical and emotional—and he reveled with her, urging her on.

"I don't mind a concussion for a good cause," he assured her when she paused a moment, looking deep into his eyes and memorizing his face. This moment had import and she wanted to remember it. She wanted him to remember it, too.

"Good." Cyra slid her body over his. His sex was hard, swollen. She took him into her, all the while laughing inside. She was laughing for the joy they felt, for the freedom of mind she had been forced to journey through hell to find, but finally did possess. "This is nuts, you know."

"And here I thought it was just plain old fun."

"There is nothing plain about it," she told him. Then, moving more deeply into his brain while inviting him into hers, she began to rock her body against his.

Thomas, eyes closing as he enjoyed the exquisite and complex sensations of being ravished mind and body by Cyra, had to agree.

Cyra didn't give Thomas a concussion, but it wasn't for lack of enthusiasm in their coupling. And it never once occurred to her to look for the dragon in her lover's eyes.

It didn't occur to Thomas to watch for him either.

Thomas came up from his glorious wallow in the pleasures of the flesh and realized that although he was more or less back in his own mind and body, his personal, emotional boundaries were a still a little slushy, melting like ice cream in the warmth of new feeling. This rosy glow around everything was a pleasant aftereffect of what he and Cyra had just shared, but he still reluctantly set about trying to completely reclaim his brain from Cyra and return it to the task at hand.

A quick look at the alarm clock confirmed that he had to get going. The fate of the world, at least a good chunk of it, was in his hands. This was no time for being lighthearted and sappy. His habitual cold logic needed to be restored. Now.

He also needed to summon the strength to send Cyra away from Sin City. He had to. She had proven to be more resourceful than he'd anticipated, but she might still betray herself to the wrong person. And the goblins could so easily capture her if she stayed where she was. He would not make the same mistake he had with Annissa. He would never survive another loss like that one.

"They could also capture me if I try to leave," Cyra murmured, burying her face in his side. "If they already suspect I'm here, as I believe they do, they'll be watching the gates and the airport."

"*Hmph.*" She had a point.

"You know I'm right."

"I'll argue with you later." Thomas stroked a hand down her glossy hair. "First, dress. I can't be serious with a naked woman."

"Okay." Cyra yawned.

Thomas, also fighting the urge to sleep, closed his eyes and concentrated on regaining a cautiously alarmed state of mind. He realized, when his initial attempt at seriousness failed, that he was actually feeling a little goofy and was having something like first-love jitters: those strange fits that made you never want to let the one you loved out of your sight, and that caused reasonable people to make stupid declarations about dying for love and wanting to be buried in a single grave so they could be together for all eternity. Under its influence, people rushed out and had lovers' names tattooed on their bodies, or ran off to the nearest wedding chapel to have Elvis marry them. He managed not to take things that far, but he finally admitted that he wasn't going to be sending Cyra away from Sin City. At least not now.

So, okay, she could stay as long as things didn't get too sticky. That was safer anyway: having her around where he could keep an eye on her, where he could keep her from abusing his magic and making herself ill.

That compromise made, Thomas tried speaking sternly to himself about duty, but he still wasn't very convincing. At the end of the lecture he continued to feel goofy and wanted to spend the rest of the night—and tomorrow, and tomorrow night—wrapped in Cyra's arms and body, either on the fuzzy red carpet or sloshing around in the water bed.

"Damn." He was hopeless, all drive gone.

"That's okay. I feel goofy, too, Thomas," Cyra confessed, throwing her arms around him as he sat up to look for his clothes. She kissed his thigh and then glanced up. The kewpie doll was back, though looking a lot more mussed and carnal than the original ever had. "And I don't care how stupid it sounds," she continued, "I don't want to leave you either. I know that what we're doing here is important—critical even. And I . . . I . . ."

Thomas looked down into her face, and he saw that she was also slowly returning to her own mind, reclaiming her body and thoughts. Thomas could feel the final withdrawal and regretted it, even though he understood the necessity. Cyra's eyes were growing a little shy and, finally, after all that had passed between them, she blushed with embarrassment.

"Well, damn. Don't be upset," he said. He gave her a moment to regain her composure then added: "But, Cyra, we have to be sensible." He ran a finger over her warmed cheek and then her lips. *Sensible, right.*

"Not yet." She sat up and kissed his chest lightly. Stretching, she made an effort to look sober. It wasn't a very good effort because her hair was rumpled and her lips looked slightly bruised. "I will be sensible, but . . . I mean, I need to see the underground, to get used to it. Just in case something happens and I need to find you in a hurry. So I should go with you now. That's reasonable, isn't it? And I'd be safe while I'm with you, so you needn't worry."

Thomas's lips quirked as he returned her embrace. He shook his head but said: "Well, I'm glad you thought of a sensible reason for me to take you along tonight, because I couldn't think of a single one that would hold water. But Cyra, this is just a short reconnaissance trip. You are *never* to go into the hive alone. And when we are done, you have to go back to your hotel and I have to get on with breaking into the network and finding out what Lilith and Fornix are up to. I mean it. And we can't meet again until it's time to act. You can't be near me. I'm a target. You'd be in danger the entire time."

"Yes, Thomas—but that's all for later. One step at a time." Cyra, looking much happier, rolled away from him and reached for her jeans. Probably, she didn't think he meant what he was saying. And the hell of it was, he wasn't certain he did either. Common sense was on holiday. And he really, really did not want to let go of her.

"This is *folie à deux*. We are both deluded," Thomas muttered. He had a completely, unforgivably masculine thought as he glanced over at her heart-shaped rear end when she crawled away from him. He was far too old for this adolescent nonsense—wasn't he?

Maybe not. She was really beautiful, really passionate, and had the best ass he'd seen in two hundred years. He sighed and gave up trying to be grim and reasonable. He was just going to be goofy for a while longer. Maybe he'd recover more of his senses once she had her clothes on.

"Goddess, I hope not," she muttered, stuffing her long legs into the skin-tight denim and wiggling back into her jeans. "There's got to be more to it than that. It isn't like you get out of *my* sight and then drop from *my* mind. You're some sort of tattoo in my brain. Probably somewhere around the dorsal-lateral prefrontal cortex," she added with a chuckle. "That's where I've erected the scaffolding that holds up your strange magic. My own power is probably buried down farther in my brain. You know, I wish I could do an MRI while working magic. I'd love to see the scan. I bet the whole frontal cortex is lit up like the Strip. And I know the anterior-singulet is active too. I can *feel* it working."

"You sound like a doctor again. Are you getting nervous? Or is this a new game we can play?"

"Well, I am a doctor. Only, I'm a mad scientist instead of an M.D." She laughed again as she tied her shoes. "If we were being formal, you would have to call me Dr. Delphin. Of course, we never had the chance to be formal. Talk about instant intimacy! There wasn't even time for a handshake before you were wedged in my brain. Now it feels like you've been there forever. I almost can't imagine what it will be like when you're gone."

I almost can't imagine what it will be like when you're gone.

The words were as sobering as a right-cross to the jaw, knocking all playfulness out of Thomas. He didn't answer immediately, uncertain of what to say in the face of this assumption that he would eventually leave her. He knew he wouldn't be leaving. He couldn't because he . . .well, *because.*

Because why?

Just because. He knew there was more to their union than simple desire, or the after effect of prolonged mind control, but he wasn't certain how to explain what was happening to Cyra if she didn't feel it too. And this was just the emotional side of the bonds they shared. There were physical considerations too.

However, her earlier reaction to the thought of having children had been telling. He wasn't certain that this was the moment to explain to her that the magic had chosen their destiny for them, and that they were now bonded in the most permanent of ways. They were going to have a child soon, regardless of whether she— or he—was ready. And that child would always give him entrée to Cyra's thoughts and a reason to be in her life.

That, however, was a far from romantic thing to say, and he had enough sense left to realize it. Breaking the news of impending motherhood before saying anything about his feelings would be suicidal.

Of course, once he considered it, it didn't seem a good time to bring up the subject of love either. He wasn't *that* goofy and incautious. Their feelings were so new—and so affected by their circumstances—that it wasn't realistic to think that they could know whether their emotions were truly lasting or simply situational. He knew he cared for her. But she'd probably doubt him if he said anything about his alien, quixotic thoughts. Hell, he doubted himself most of the time these days. What a time to undertake a wooing!

"What are you thinking?" Cyra asked, smoothing her clothes back into place.

Thomas shrugged, feeling a bit helpless. He finally said: "I was just thinking that I should get you flowers."

"Wow. You *are* feeling goofy." Her smile was blinding. "I like day lilies—orange ones. What kind do you like? Bloodred roses? Or is that too mundane? Maybe orchids? Or golden iris to match your eyes?"

Thomas thought for a moment. No one had ever asked him this before. Spies and goblin fighters didn't think about flowers. Yet there was something—it was several seconds before the stunning memory burst open in his brain.

"I like buttercups," he said at last.

"Buttercups? Really?" She cocked her head.

Thomas explained: "My mother took me to see the daffodil hills in California one April. It was right before she died. There were a million buttercups there too. That sea of gold was the prettiest thing I'd ever seen."

"I wish I'd been there."

He remembered that dawn vividly. His mother had called the site Nymphsfield. A creature of light herself, Triste had waded in among the dew-gilded blooms and then knelt down to kiss a handful of the vivid flowers whose warm color had dyed the early spring air a bright gold. Thomas watched, fascinated, as deeper color sprang from each flower her lips touched.

And then she danced. Her joy in the moment had made the dawn shiver as its new light burst over her and her son. The day encompassed Thomas, and his mother's transcendental pleasure had made him want to reach for the sun and babble poetry and songs and other nonsensical things.

It was the way he felt now.

This was a private memory, intensely personal and one he kept locked in a treasure chest of rare, happy moments. He seldom examined these memories, fearing that familiarity would weaken their power to lift his spirits. And he never shared these thoughts with anyone else, lest they somehow become tainted by another's reactions. But this time, having no corporeal flowers to proffer, he plucked out the safe-kept memory of that glorious sunrise and offered it to Cyra.

He watched her intently as the memory unfolded for her, taking extra pleasure in the way Cyra's eyes widened and a soft smile touched her lips as she saw Triste whirl among the golden blooms.

"So beautiful . . ." she whispered, awed. Then: "Buttercups . . . I'll remember," Cyra promised. "Thank you."

Chapter Sixteen

The roughness of the cavern floor necessitated a cautious pace even with the use of flashlights. Cyra and Thomas were away from the hive proper and exploring some of the natural tunnels that the goblins had not yet put to use. It was night, and most of the goblins were above ground.

Uncertain of the dress code for goblin reconnaissance, and having had few options anyway, Cyra was dressed in jeans and a t-shirt. Perhaps because he didn't want her to feel under-dressed, Thomas was wearing the same. Or perhaps this was the correct uniform.

Thomas was used to goblin hives and had warned Cyra that the beasts' colonies had a certain smell. The filters in the breathers they wore could strain out a lot, but the taint of ammonia, rotting fruit, blood—and beneath all that, the reek of the goblins themselves—sometimes seemed to absorb straight through the skin.

This passage was even more poisonous than the goblin tunnels, however. The air around them was filled with something other than gloom and the usual bad lutin smells. The atmosphere was so thick that it discouraged normal breathing as well as physical speech. Even with nose filters and goggles in place, the toxic gases like hydrogen sulfide and carbon monoxide were thick enough to be bothersome. There were also tendrils of some mucuslike slime hanging down from the tunnel's ceiling and it occasionally dropped sulfuric acid down on them. Thomas kept a close eye on the chromatograph he was carrying.

"It's a pity we can't get some extra oxygen in here. Water would do. Combined with the hydrogen sulfide gas it might make an environment too hostile for even goblins," Thomas thought to her.

"I don't know, if bacteria can live in it, I think goblins can, too," Cyra answered, her ability to mind-speak coming very easily now. Thomas's brain was becoming more familiar to her with every passing moment. *"I don't like all this slime-dripping-through-the-cracks*

stuff. It makes me think the whole thing is going to collapse and I'll drown, then be eaten to the bone by acid."

"Don't worry. You're fey. There isn't that much acid in the whole mountain range. You're probably right about the goblins, though. Bad air won't stop them. We still have to find some other way of keeping Lilith out of Yucca Mountain. If the danger of setting off a cataclysmic earthquake and dropping California into the ocean didn't exist, I'd just wire this whole place with explosives and collapse the tunnels. But since it is all connected, I would probably set off the volcano and trip several intersecting fault lines. It could kill thousands. Even millions. I think we need another plan."

They paused to look around, hoping to find some obvious solution. The walls of the tunnel were being eaten away by bacteria and they could see the fissured gypsum was unstable. There were several recent falls of fresh stone showing whitely where minor temors had passed through on their way down the fault line, leaving their damage behind. There had to be some way to bring the tunnels down without destroying the western United States in the process.

"Two hundred and fifty million years ago we wouldn't have had this problem. This whole *area was covered by the sea. It's a pity we can't turn back time. A little biblical-style flooding would take care of the problem."*

Cyra blinked as a mental light bulb went on.

"Thomas, that might be just what we need." She turned to look at him, an idea forming, growing brighter.

"What? To turn back time?" He paused. *"Damn! Get back! I can feel it coming!"*

"Feel what? Goblins?"

"Worse. Earthquake!" Thomas grabbed her and flattened her against the wall. An instant later, something rolled through the tunnel beneath their feet, flinging stones aside and tossing the two puny beings inside its belly onto the ground. Sharp rocks spattered them and Cyra could feel small droplets of acid burning her exposed skin. She wanted to brush them off but felt paralyzed by the stony rain that pelted them with fist-size stones. More frightening still was the stony shriek that filled the air with its inhuman roar. She'd never heard an earthquake make that sort of sound. All she could do was freeze and try to make herself small and inconspicuous.

The heaving of the earth seemed to go on forever, though in reality, it lasted only for several seconds. Cyra was a veteran of many earthshakers, but she had never experienced one while underground and in danger of being buried alive.

When the tremor did not immediately let up, Cyra grabbed Thomas's medallion. She prayed fervently, if a bit incoherently, that she would never experience anything like it again.

The earth eventually calmed. Silence, too, returned to the tunnel. Thomas finally rolled off of her.

"Are you all right?"

"I think so." Cyra pulled her left arm out of the rubble and flexed her fingers, pleased that they moved. She tried other muscles and took joy in their continued function. Heart, seething brain, terror-stricken limbs—everything was working. Her body hurt, but given how close a call they'd had, this was cause for rejoicing. Pain meant she was alive.

"I'm good. You?"

"Yes, just a little stunned." Thomas stood, a darker shadow in the swirling white dust, and reached for the one functioning flashlight. The other was buried under new rock fall. He panned the beam up and down the tunnel. *"I don't see any sign of a fissure opening. This must have been a true earthquake and not the volcano trying to let loose. And, see? You didn't drown in acid. There's nothing to worry about."*

"Ha!" Recalled to her idea, Cyra said ur-

gently: *"Never mind acid. Thomas, what would happen if a lot of water suddenly washed through these caves? Would it reach all the way to Yucca Mountain? Could we flood the goblin tunnels and make them useless?"*

Thomas turned the flashlight beam in her direction. Much of the light was deflected because of the powdered gypsum in the air, but it was still bright enough to make her squint behind her goggles. Like all her senses, her eyesight was more sensitive now.

"Hey," she protested.

"Sorry." Thomas lowered the beam to the floor. He reached out a hand to help her to her feet. His grasp lingered a moment longer than necessary. The dreamy romantic feeling from earlier in the night was gone, but both of them needed the reassurance of touch that they truly were unharmed. *"You're thinking of the new pipeline, aren't you? The one from Lake Mead."*

"It looks huge and runs right overhead. Would that be enough water to do it? If we could get it down here somehow? Maybe route it through one of the casinos?"

There was a sharp crack and another bit of wall caved in. Cyra flinched.

"Yeah . . . maybe." Thomas began towing her back toward the goblin tunnels even as his brain started ticking over possibilities. He

241

didn't say anything, but Cyra knew he was worried about aftershocks collapsing the tunnel.

"It would also divert water from the city."

"And give the goblins something else to worry about while we made our escape," he concluded. *"I like it. But I have to do some research. Can we fracture the ground enough to let in the water, but not set off an earthquake? And the timing of the flood will be important. . . . I'll have to figure out flow rates."*

"Why?"

Thomas glanced at her. *"I hadn't gotten around to mentioning this yet, but both Lilith and General Fornix will be at Yucca Mountain this Tuesday for the dedication ceremony. If we time it right, we can take out the goblin queen and the traitor at the same time. I know it's an added complication, but we've learned the hard way that you have to get the hive leaders. Nothing else is very effective."*

Cyra digested the news, and the fact that Thomas had kept it from her. Of course, that was before their reconciliation and before she had any need to know. And he had also elected to share the information with her now, so . . . She decided to save being upset at his reticence for another occasion.

"The ceremony?" Of course there would be one. They'd had to fight the building of the

Yucca Mountain facility all the way through the courts as well as Congress. *"Do you think this is why H.U.G. is here? Are they going to try something?"*

"That would be a logical guess." Thomas continued to guide Cyra through the bewildering underground maze that was so unlike the shian. The air was clearing, but it was still a completely alien land. *"But whatever their plan is, it probably doesn't involve the goblin caves. Humans can't survive in here. The labyrinth befuddles them and the air is poisonous. Still, it would be handy to know what they are up to. The enemy of our enemy being our friend and all that. Wait!"* Thomas halted abruptly.

"What is it? Another earthquake?"

"No. Listen."

They were paused at the junction of the natural tunnel with the goblins' excavated cave. The chamber was still empty because dawn was yet an hour away, but both of them sensed something different in the air of the hive. Or in the walls.

Cyra stopped breathing and concentrated on the green gloom. Something was wrong. She couldn't see anything, but something alien was among them.

"Thomas?"

"Yeah, I feel it."

"Feel it?"

Cyra looked harder. It seemed like the air quivered. Was it just her body protesting its further disorientation by an earthquake in the underground? Or was the cave actually sending out atmospheric vibrations? And how could something inaudible and almost unnoticeable by the other senses still manage to suggest that there was some giant snake nearby, rubbing its dry skin over the rough stone floor? Cyra found the sensation to be a whole new level of discomfort and alienation.

"I thought this place was dead—not like the tomhnafurach."

"I thought it was too," Thomas answered uneasily. *"Maybe the earthquake woke something up. Can you understand what it—"*

"No. It wasn't speaking exactly. Just kind of muttering and breathing."

Both spaces, the tunnel and the cave, were equally silent, but the goblins' tunnel was . . . waiting. The quiet, as the ear measured it, was as absolute as any grave, but somehow not empty or dead. Something paused, listening, sensing that it was not alone, and that it was about to embark on an assignation with the intruders on its doorstep. This wasn't anything that the cave or the intruders had arranged, but both were being forced toward some fate that could lead to their destruction. And the presence was aware that they were also aware. The intruders were something new, and maybe dangerous.

It was wary.

So were they.

"It knows we're here."

"Yes."

"Will it hurt us?"

"It may try, if it's frightened. But we don't have any choice but to go on. We can't stay here. The goblins will start heading down soon from their work above ground and we can't be caught here."

"I know." Cyra swallowed. *"Let me try to talk to it. I felt something intelligent. Maybe it's like the* tomhnafurach *and sees the goblins as parasites. Or perhaps it's like the shian where the giants lived, and it won't mind us, as long as we don't do anything to hurt it."*

"Okay, try it. I've got your back."

"You mean my brain."

"Just so."

Thomas's presence suddenly strengthened in Cyra's head, boosting her powers and keeping her calm. Still slightly nervous, Cyra reached out slowly with her mind, doing her best to keep her thoughts neutral and unthreatening as she reached for the other. This time she had no pain as she worked.

The cave's presence didn't have speech or thoughts that she could decipher, not the way a shian did. The cavern did not seem to recognize what she was, and it was perplexed by her. Cyra got a quick impression of hurt and outrage that its lovely white chandeliers of crystal gypsum had been shorn off, its walls plastered with glowing goblin slime and that its interior was being used to house the goblins' offal. The earthquake had been an attempt to knock the goblin plaster off its walls and had not been directed at them. The cavern hadn't even been aware that they were there.

Cyra whispered a reassurance and then quickly withdrew.

"So, is it a go?" Thomas asked. "It's odd, but even linked with you, I still couldn't understand it."

"It has to be a go. I'll do my best to reassure it one more time, but just in case—"

"We'll run. Fast."

"Yes. I really don't want to do another earthquake today. Or ever."

"No argument here," Thomas agreed.

Shaken, and feeling her way carefully, Cyra again sent her thoughts to brush up against the presence in the cave. This time it didn't

quiver at her touch. Its visual message was
clearer. It was communicating plainly that it
wanted the intruders—all of them—out. There
could be no doubt now about what it was saying. This cave was not dead, and the rock all
around was the stony flesh of an unknown sen-
tience.

Cyra answered it with a flash of what she
hoped would be recognized as understanding,
then grabbed Thomas's hand. They dashed for
the exit.

The cave, though still frustrated and out-
raged, let them go.

"I thought it would crush us," Cyra whispered as Thomas laid his ear against the door
that led into his hotel's basement. "It's really
angry about what the goblins have done while
it was sleeping. I think it would bring the whole
thing down on them if it wasn't going to destroy
itself by doing so."

"Well, that's good." Thomas answered softly,
using his thousand-key to open the lock. "An
angry cave might be useful."

"Good and useful how?" Cyra whispered,
spitting and then wiping the dust from her face.
She was feeling her bruises and knew it had to
be worse for Thomas since he'd taken the brunt
of the rockslide on his back as he protected her.

"I think we are going to need the cave's cooperation to let the water through. The pipeline doesn't run all the way to Yucca Mountain. The water would trickle in, but we need a lot of it in the tunnels all at once, channeled and directed, if we are going to flood all the way to the storage facility and drown Lilith and Fornix." Thomas stepped into the dark basement and gestured for Cyra to follow.

"I see. And how are we going to get the cave's cooperation?" Cyra asked. She took Thomas's hand.

"You're going to ask for it." His voice was matter-of-fact.

"I was afraid you'd say that. But, Thomas, I don't know *how* to ask. I can't just walk up and say 'pretty please with sugar on top.' We don't actually speak to one another. It's just sort of sensing and some visions."

"Hey, you're the one burning to be useful here in Sin City. You're also the one who speaks cave. You'll figure something out. Turn around. You're as white as a blizzard." Thomas began dusting her off.

"I don't '*speak* cave.' That sounds so stupid. And truthfully, I don't *speak* to them, they just . . . well . . . *they* speak to *me*. Sometimes." Cyra sneezed violently. "This dust is awful. How am I ever going to get clean?"

Thomas ignored her question. "Call it whatever you like. We've just caught a break: You have a gift. We're going to use it." Thomas smiled down at her with his ghostly white face. "Welcome to the wild side of espionage, magic, and sabotage, baby fey. Now you're playing in the big leagues."

"My parents would be so proud," she grumbled, pulling out her breathing apparatus and shaking her hair.

Thomas smiled. "No, you're right. They probably wouldn't be. Not at first. Not if they had you ignore your heritage. They wouldn't approve until they understood what was at stake. But I am damned proud of you."

Cyra blinked, and Thomas continued: "Cyra, when you open up that cave, you're going to save the lives of every human and fey in California—and the cave's happiness too. That passage will become the river Styx, separating humanity from the goblins' destructive plan. Think about it. Lilith thought she was going to make you into a tool to destroy humankind, and you've just turned the tables on her—and on the whole goblin hive! And you did this without any training and after escaping the goblins messing with your head. I would never have guessed that you had this strength in you. I was wrong."

Cyra colored, not at all certain that she was

ready to accept Thomas's accolades. For one thing, it was premature to be celebrating their victory. Also, she just didn't feel like true heroine material.

At least, she hadn't been before meeting Thomas. But maybe now, with help. . . . Cyra straightened and tried to look heroic, a difficult task when she was standing in a dark, cluttered basement, covered in rock dust and feeling like an over-floured biscuit.

"This is all well and good, but, Thomas, you're forgetting something."

"What?"

"I'm not alone here. And I never would have escaped from the goblins if you hadn't found me in the desert. And I know nothing about blowing up pipelines or hacking into computers or . . . *anything*. You'll have to do all of this stuff. If California is saved, it will be because *we* saved it."

Thomas nodded. He liked the way she said *we*. "Okay, you're right. *We* will save it. Together."

"Okay, then." Cyra smiled up at him. "I'm glad I'm not flying solo here. I would be too frightened."

"Me, too," he agreed.

"We make a great team." She stood on tiptoes and kissed his cheek.

* * *

At her kiss, Thomas's heart rolled over and he suddenly realized he was more than halfway in love with Cyra. He had been thinking it was just adrenaline and lust—affection too—and some magic. That sounded stupid now, but he hadn't recognized what was happening to him at first. This love wasn't the tame and well-tended Eden he had expected, that he had once known. This was different. Cyra wasn't the sweet, docile Annissa. His and Cyra's paradise was overgrown and filled with hazards; its rivers were not all gentle. Its flora came with thorns. And there was a dragon they would have to face—but face it they could because Cyra was strong.

For the first time, Thomas was confident that they could overcome. The *we* on Cyra's tongue had more strength in it than he had ever imagined an English word could possess.

"Thomas? What's wrong? You look funny." Cyra's thought-speak probed him gently.

If only he could discover what she was feeling. He couldn't tell from mind-speak alone. That part of her mind, the center of emotions, was closed off to him, and he couldn't open it.

"Nothing," he said. Frustrated, he felt his own emotions retreating from Cyra, hiding behind a wall of privacy, where she couldn't discover them.

Sensing his retreat, Cyra withdrew from his mind.

"Okay. Shall we go?" she asked, ducking her head so he couldn't see her expression. Her averted face, her obvious displeasure made Thomas feel like swearing, but instead he took Cyra's hand and led her out of the basement full of packing crates.

Chapter Seventeen

Cyra showered at Thomas's place, giggling a bit at the mirrored bathroom tiles that distorted her figure to giraffe-like proportions, but even after she was scrubbed clean and kissed senseless, she still felt the effects of the hostile goblin underground. Her skin was slightly reddened everywhere it had been exposed to the dripping acid, and it was uncomfortably dry, as were her fingernails. Also, once her arousal had been sated, her body just plain hurt. She healed quickly, but those falling rocks had been hard and numerous. The thought of venturing back into that environment didn't thrill her.

Thomas, withdrawn from her mentally and watching her closely with his unblinking golden eyes, had offered to see her back to her hotel, or at least the vicinity, but she declined.

Their moment of selfish sappiness was over. She knew that he was eager to start work on plotting flow rates through the tunnels and to get word out to Jack about what he intended to do, in case the death fey had some new information or insights about the situation.

And Cyra had a job to do too. Instead of arguing with her about allowing him to do the chivalrous thing and send her away, Thomas had given her clear instructions about how to set up an e-mail account in one of the Internet cafes—just in case something happened and they weren't able to use mind-speak from across the city.

Since mind-speaking was somewhat tiring, and probably impossible if she was working magic on someone, Cyra reluctantly agreed.

"This is dangerous, though, isn't it?" she asked. "Jack warned me that I shouldn't contact you except in an emergency because the goblins monitor everything on the Net here."

"It's not dangerous if we're careful and use cutouts and shields. Now, don't worry about the name on your account. Take whatever default one is assigned. I'll find you as long as you use the key phrase. You'll know I've got you when you receive some spam from *Demonicus Italiano*. The restaurant is closed for repairs right now, but it shouldn't cause any flags to go up on the goblins' security grid. If I see anything suspicious, I'll warn you away. Okay?"

"Okay."

"And a couple of last words of warning: No booze until this is over. Magic and alcohol don't go well together. Keep your brain sharp so that I can find you."

"No problem. I've never been able to tolerate alcohol."

So that was how Cyra found herself walking alone through the shoppertainment haven called The Cathay Passage, erected with much fanfare next to the Ali-Baba Hotel. She was looking for moisturizer, possible entrances to the goblin underground and also an Internet cafe.

She had to give the goblins credit for knowing when to leave human creations alone. Their impulse was to meddle and distort anything they touched, but Lilith had managed to overcome her subjects' natural inclination.

The mall was impressive, laid out to recreate the ancient trade route from Europe to the Far East. The dining selection was impressive, too: Sages, Lombatto's—all the finest restaurants were there perfuming the air with their edibles. The high-end retailers were there *en force* too. It was eight stories of goblin-enriching venues, and all were doing a booming business at eight

A.M. as Cyra walked through the land of commerce.

The vaulted arcade in the new North Africa was lovely, though the red and black stones of the steep arches reminded her a bit of a poisonous coral snake waiting to drop on her head. The place was furnished with genuine artifacts and some impressive mosaic tiles featuring mythical beasts—at least, Cyra hoped they were mythical. The pale tans of Moorish architecture gracefully and gradually transformed into the rich scarlets and golds of farthest China—minus any hint of poverty, of course.

The painted sky above her looked almost real. Unfortunately, there were no doors on the walls conveniently marked GOBLIN UNDERGROUND. The smell of goblin was also very faint and not localized, so she couldn't track them that way.

She did very well at not succumbing to the mall's blandishments until she came to the indoor bay. It was hard to ignore the harbor that anchored a full-size clipper ship, and after a moment of internal battle, Cyra allowed herself to stop and admire it, the way any tourist would.

The fantasy construct was amazing and reminded her of Robert Louis Stevenson's poem,

"Block City." There was even a wave machine that sent gentle ripples through the dark water, which rocked the ship softly and set the mooring lines to creaking.

As Cyra stood there, the sky overhead began to cloud up in a realistic manner and a moment, later it started to rain over the bay. This happened at the quarter hour, every hour. Cyra didn't remove her sunglasses, even when they became spotted with droplets.

It was the perfect place for hydrophilics to have breakfast. Cyra wondered, for a short moment, how many of the "*people*" there were really modified goblins, sent to spy on the tourists. They all looked and smelled normal, but who could tell? Remove the lower arms, take off the scent glands, bleach the skin, and goblins looked almost human. Cyra could survey them to see who was human and who was not, but it would be a stupid thing to do when goblin security was so tight. They would notice her attention. She couldn't let the fantasy atmosphere of the place lull her into believing that she could relax her guard. This looked like Fantasyland, but it wasn't.

No, she couldn't trust anything here. The Fantasia empire had always seemed benevolent, but though the mal's owner was a huge multi-national company, it probably didn't have this much wealth naturally at its disposal. It also wouldn't hire man-eating trolls for its security force. Or it wouldn't have last time Cyra looked. The world was changing so quickly, perhaps this wasn't true anymore.

Paranoia threatened briefly, but Cyra fought it back. Instead of looking at her fellow shoppers with suspicious eyes, she stood at the dock, clutching her purse tightly, and tried to do the math, to calculate the money taken in at a place like Cathay Passage. But even excluding the casinos' income, she couldn't wrap her brain around the kind of lucre that built things like this. It wasn't just Cathay Passage either. There were huge fantasy malls at The Coliseum, The Rio Grand, Via Carrefour, and The Saint Germaine, all open around the clock to take in eager tourist dollars. Humans had created them, but they surely didn't own them now. How had the goblins first managed to wrest control away? There'd been no talk of corporate takeovers in the media, no rash of CEO deaths in the news, no plummeting stock prices.

Cyra suddenly thought of Larry. *Replicants. Of course!* Modified goblins had taken the human investors' places in a bloodless *coup*. With the right kinds of plastic surgery, goblins could be made to look like anyone. If they could get

to the presidential candidate, William Hamilton, the way Thomas said they had, they could
get anybody.

Shaking her head, Cyra turned away from
the fake harbor, tracing the man-made horizon
to remind herself that it was all a construct and
not real. It was then that she spotted it: an entrance to the underground. It was on the far
side of the harbor, located just above the wa-
terline. If she hadn't made out the thin platform
as a wave curled away from the scaffolding, she
never would have noticed the tiny seam in the
wall that marked the door.

"Well, damn." There was an awful lot of water
in the man-made bay. Not enough to flood
Yucca Mountain, but plenty to take out the hive
below The Ali-Baba if they needed to.

Satisfied, Cyra began looking for a cafe with
Internet access. It didn't take her long to find
one once she shooed away the team of contor-
tionists who wanted—seemingly passionately—
to perform for her, and then made it past the
belly dancers and snake charmers and the
herd of animatronic camels. She'd heard that
goblins didn't like animals and wondered if it
was that or camels' habit of biting that kept the
mall from using real beasts. Everything else,
from art to asps, was fairly authentic.

Yes, goblins were always brilliant at getting

people to spend money, and always made it easy to do so. That meant online shopping and gambling were available at any of the finer hotels for those who wanted to access those things while they dined. The goblins provided easy Internet access at all bistros, bars and cafes.

As Thomas had told her, Cyra found that she could open an account with a credit card, but the computers were also set up to take tokens. She removed one of the five-dollar pieces of brass Thomas had given her and fed it into the slot at the side of the PC. A gaudy screen for Lutin Empire came up immediately. Dazzling offerings of things expensive and illegal outside the Glitter Gulch—but very available here—were paraded before her eyes, including prostitutes and art that she was certain she had once seen hanging in the Metropolitan.

The website was fascinating and begged her to explore its shady entertainments, but following Thomas's instructions, Cyra looked up something harmless—moisturizers—and then chose one of the available stores to shop in. She called up a brand at random, then clicked on the query button. Investigation into the depths of the goblin black market would have to wait. It was Thomas's *forte* anyway.

When the PC came back asking for her e-mail

address, Cyra clicked the option of setting up a new e-mail account for the store to reply to. Asked if she would like to choose a name or be assigned one, she selected the default name and was given beauty2691@lutinempire.com. She submitted her question about sunscreen using the key phrase "keep me safe" that Thomas had selected, and then logged off.

She then strolled away as quickly as possible, not staying long enough to be approached by a waiter who might remember her as the woman who had applied for that address. Of course, during the day service personnel were likely to be human, and therefore able to be influenced if she sensed danger. But Cyra wanted to avoid using magic as much as possible since it made her feel ill without Thomas's help, and there was always the chance of being detected by any psychic goblin sentries nearby.

Her next stop was a small boutique on The Great Wall that carried cosmetics and palm-readers who could predict your love life and what skin-care regime you should follow in the coming season. Armed with a great deal of money that Jack had stolen from the goblins on his last visit, Cyra explained that she was an Aquarius and then splurged on an entire line of recommended European beauty products designed for those with birthdays in early February.

The clerk never blinked when she paid cash for her purchases. Lots of people had underground incomes and didn't like to leave paper trails behind them. No questions were asked. That could be useful, unless . . .

Cyra looked about casually and quickly spotted the security cameras. Of course, the place was wired. Cashiers didn't ask questions because the cameras knew everything that an eye or ear could tell them.

Cyra took a quick peep at the young cashier's mind to see if she was aware that she was being observed, and was amused to see that the woman thought her a high-priced call girl. The sooth-sayer in the chair in the corner wasn't thinking of anything but how much she wanted to go back to bed.

Mission accomplished, Cyra took her embroidered satin bag, stuffed with tissue-wrapped promises of youth in fancy bottles and jars, and sauntered toward the exit where she'd left her Harley.

She killed a little more time selecting a cocktail dress for that evening. If she was going to mingle with the high rollers, and eavesdrop on their minds in hopes of discovering how far along the goblins were with their mind-control techniques, then she needed to look the part. Her usual taste ran to something basic and black, but Sin City shops didn't subscribe to such sedate selections. Cyra chose the closest thing she could find: a Vivienne Hartwood frock in midnight blue. The price tag attached to the dress had entirely too many zeros, but knowing she was spending the goblins' money, Cyra bought it along with matching shoes that had mirrored heels. Doing so gave her a feeling of intense glee.

"What are you up to?" Thomas asked, startling her with how clear his words were, even from a distance. *"I worry when you have such obviously wicked thoughts and I'm nowhere around."*

"I'm shopping. The clerks think I'm a call girl. They also have no idea they are being watched by the goblins. We have an entrance to the hive in the harbor here in Cathay Passage. Can you say 'Noah's ark part two?' I don't know how much water is here, but it's a lot."

"You've been busy. Good work." Thomas's thoughts were warm. *"I don't know if we can actually destroy all the goblins' sources of water, but we'll take out as many as we can. Did you get an e-mail account?"*

"Yes, my new e-mail address is beauty2691@ lutinempire.com.*"*

263

"Hmm. I've got it. You are being spammed as we speak. Save Demonicus Italiano's e-mail address to reply. If you need to meet with me, send a note asking about restaurant hours. If it's urgent, ask about a time after midnight." There was a confused pause as Thomas sorted out what else he wanted to say. Finally he settled on a brisk: *"Have fun shopping. And take care."*

"I will. Bye." Cyra was careful not to sound wistful. She didn't mention that she missed him. *"Goddess be with you,"* she added as she reached into her shirt and touched Thomas's medallion.

"And also with you."

Chapter Eighteen

"Cyra?"

Thomas's voice was calm, but the fact that he was talking to her at all was not a good sign. Cyra's pulse picked up its already slightly accelerated pace. Her heart had begun to hammer the moment she realized that some sort of mind control was being used on the casino's main floor. The goblins hadn't used it before in public areas of the hotel—not that she had seen, at least.

"Time to swap your gladrags, sweetie. Our plans have just been changed. I heard from Jack. The schedule was moved up and Fornix will be at Yucca Mountain just before dawn this morning. I'm afraid we have to go in tonight."

"Oh, damn," Cyra thought.

"Don't worry. I have the explosives."

Cyra paused in front of a slot machine and pretended to read the instructions while Thomas outlined his altered plan. The people around Cyra were not paying much attention to anything but their gambling. She had, in fact, seen livelier entities floating belly-up in a goldfish bowl.

"I know you aren't ready to talk to the cave again," Thomas went on when she didn't answer, *"but it's that or steal an atom bomb. I have enough explosives to open the waterway, but only the cave can break the earth and give us the direct channel we need. We don't have time to rig a blast at the storage site and also one inside the mountain itself—"*

"I know. It isn't that. I just wish we had time to create a diversion. Once you start blowing things up, we're going to be targeted by every troll here. And they won't worry about being discreet anymore. A lot of people may get hurt."

"I know." Thomas didn't add that unfortunately there was no time for another plan. This was it. She was going on stage without a dress rehearsal. Of course, so was he. And he had to deal with explosives. All that was required of her was that she speak to a mountain.

"Okay, give me a minute to get changed," she thought at him.

"You have about two hours. There's no—"

"Hang on. Thomas, I feel something . . . close."

"What is it?"

"I'm not sure."

Cyra's eyes locked on the man facing her across the slot machines. There was something about him, a sense of purpose that wasn't stirring in the others. He wasn't feeding coins into the machine in front of him with the same blank concentration of the surrounding people. Knowing it was a dreadful risk, Cyra reached out and touched him. It was a mental caress lighter than Christmas snow, and he was distracted by ordering a club soda and lime from a passing cocktail waitress.

"What are you doing?" Thomas asked.

Cyra inhaled. Peter Grant, in the dust-colored suit, didn't look like a saboteur—but he was. He worked for H.U.G. Of course, a good saboteur wouldn't look like one. If Cyra hadn't encountered a stray thought hanging in the air, she never would have known that this soft-spoken man with the monotonous voice and dull gray eyes was planning on blowing up Lilith's headquarters under Cathay Passage at almost the same time she and Thomas were going to take out the rest of the labyrinth. Peter was also planning on taking out Las Vegas's water supply.

It was a real pity that his plan wouldn't work. It would make for a fine diversion, just the kind they needed; but he was going to try and slip his briefcase of explosives past a security team of modified goblins that would smell the plastique at twenty yards. Cyra also knew from her trip underground that Peter had the wrong location marked for the big kaboom. He'd be blowing up a dung heap. Worse, he would likely anger the mountain and make her job impossible.

Well, hell. Peter was like a perverse gift from the gods. If only there were something she could do to redirect him without tipping her hand, some way to let him discover the deficiencies of his plot without exposing her own plans—

"Damn it, Cyra! Answer me. Whatever you are thinking, don't do it."

"Hang on."

But there *was* something she could use! The faerie unguent. It was risky, of course. Thomas had said that it could drive men insane. Of course, the saboteur would know he was up against supernatural beasties, and he had to have some magical resistance or he wouldn't be in Sin City, let alone wandering around in a casino that was using mass mind control on its patrons. And just a small dab of the unguent in one eye would allow Peter Grant to see the danger around him and avoid walking into a trap.

It would also let him see the hidden door in the harbor.

"Cyra, don't make me take you over. Answer me. What are you doing?" Thomas interrupted her thoughts, this time more forcefully. The man was like mental superglue now that they were getting close to the final hour.

"I'm helping H.U.G. create a diversion for us," she answered hastily.

"Helping H.U.G.? Why am I suddenly worried?" Thomas's thoughts were again calm, but Cyra knew him well. He was bothered, a bad state for him to be in when he was preparing explosives. *"You aren't going to try to mind control a H.U.G. operative in the middle of the casino, are you?"*

"No, nothing that dangerous. Don't be so nervous." Cyra reached into her purse and uncapped the unguent. She dipped the tip of her index finger into the cream and tried to blank out her mind so no one could read her intent. *"Be quiet now, Thomas. I have to be able to talk and act naturally."*

"Damn it." Thomas wanted to argue, to order Cyra not to take whatever risk she was contemplating, but he didn't once he sensed her in ac-

tion. He stayed back, the merest shadow in her mind, and held his peace. She was sure that she'd hear about this mad plan later, though— and she didn't blame Thomas a bit. It was insane—she knew that. But what choice did they have here in the eleventh hour? The dusty devil in the brown suit was a better alternative than drowning in the deep blue goblin sea.

Cyra pasted on her brightest smile and slipped up next to the H.U.G. operative. The man was slowly feeding coins into the nickel slot machine as he looked the room over with cool eyes. He smelled vaguely of mothballs. Cyra found him repellant. In the back of her mind, she could feel Thomas stiffen as he discovered Peter through her senses.

"Hi, Peter." Startled, the agent turned and looked full into her eyes. Locked stare to stare, Cyra could finally feel the total ruthlessness inside the man. He was dust alright—toxic dust. How had the goblins missed him coming through their gates? Probably because they screened for magic, not for psychopaths.

"Yes?" The voice was polite. The gaze was hard.

"Remember me? It's . . ." Damn! She couldn't use her real surname when there was any chance that goblins would hear. So much for using her name to give him a minor compulsion to cooperate with her. "It's Henrietta from California." Not giving him a chance to respond, she rushed on: "Oops. You have an eyelash about to get in your eye. Hold still, now."

She moved fast, leaving a tiny dab of unguent at the corner of his left eye. Peter blinked and then started to frown. His eyes darted back and forth before he focused on her again.

"What the—"

"There you go. If you're going to gamble, it's a good idea to see things clearly. Really."

The dull eyes slowly widened as the unguent melted and ran into the left orb. Peter's gaze scurried around the room, chasing scary shadows. It was difficult to tell in the cold blue light of the slots' flickering neon, but it seemed his face went ashen. Cyra could understand that reaction. He would be looking at the goblins around them, the ones he had thought were human, and he would be noticing for the first time where their faces had been seamed together during surgery, seeing where the patches of grafted flesh didn't match in tone because they came from more than one source. He would also be seeing the slitted pupils under the concealing contact lenses. There was an especially ugly quartet of security guards lounging by the exit that looked like a nasty version of the living dead in black bow ties.

Their dark suits were spattered with blood.

"Peter." Cyra spoke sharply, then waited until his alarmed gaze returned to her face. He had the look of a wild animal held at bay, and it took her aback. It would be very bad if he went feral on her now. She added more softly: "I'm a friend. And I want you to succeed in your undertaking. But you need to be cautious. Some things have changed."

"I don't know what—" he began. It was a risk, but Cyra sent him a quick mental flash of the hidden door in the mall's harbor near the Moroccan restaurant. Startled a second time, Peter sucked in a deep breath and quit talking.

"Have you lost your mind? He's a witch hunter! Quick! Tell him you're psychic," Thomas whispered urgently. *"H.U.G. sees almost all magical beings as enemies, but they do recruit psychics."*

"I'm kind of psychic about some things," Cyra said, giving Peter the suggested explanation for the vision. "Anyhow, my senses are telling me that this slot isn't going to pay off for you right now. If I were you, I'd go somewhere for a bite of dinner and try again later. I hear the Tradewinds Moroccan restaurant at Cathay Passage is wonderful."

"Well, I . . ." Peter rallied and pasted on a smile. The twisted lips did not improve his expression because his eyes remained cold and suspicious. "I'll certainly have to try it. Would you like to come along? We could catch up on things."

"I'd love to, but I have other plans this evening."

"You're damned right you do." Thomas sounded annoyed. *"Are you trying to give me thrombosis? Of all the reckless—"*

"Hush!"

"Maybe later. I'm sure we'll meet again," Cyra lied. Another heaven and another earth would come to pass before she'd see this man again. Something about him scared her almost as much as the goblins.

"Okay." Peter glanced around the room a second time. Now his gaze was less panicked. He had his breathing back under control. Yes, this one was cold, a cold son of a bitch. "Well, goodnight then."

"Tell him to go with God."

"Go with God," Cyra said.

Satisfied at the password, Peter nodded.

Cyra made her way toward the elevators, keeping her pace and breathing even, her eyes blank. She needed to change before she took out the Harley. She was not going to be like one of those stupid women in a disaster movie who had to outrun floods and monsters in a tight skirt and high heels.

Her nerves were a bit shaken after the encounter, but she was also pleased with what she had done.

"Why did you take the risk?" Thomas asked her. *"It was a mad thing to do."*

"Penis envy. That's what Freud would say," she answered crossly. *"Maybe I'm tired of you having all the fun."*

"Cyra—"

"It's insurance, okay? You need time to get away from the pipeline, and I just bought you some. And anyway, I couldn't let him walk into the trolls. You know they would have been there waiting, licking their chops and thinking: Yum-yum! Human, the other white meat."

"Cyra, I hate the trolls too. But this is a war. Undeclared war, but still war. You can't compromise the mission with compassion. Civilian casualties, especially among H.U.G.—"

"Look, I know H.U.G. isn't allied with us, but I just don't think it's right to feed anyone to the enemy, okay?" Though Peter Grant might be an exception. Pull off his skin and Cyra wasn't sure there was a real soul underneath. She added, practically: *"Especially not if they can be useful. Anyway, it's done. There's no point in chewing on past gristle, is there?"*

Thomas sighed. She couldn't hear it, but she could feel the long exhalation as she readied her stolen security key and pushed the elevator call button.

"You're right, of course. But you're turning my hair gray."

"You're two-hundred-something years old. You deserve some gray. Anyway—" The elevator opened in front of her and out walked an impatient Lilith and her entourage. *"Holy shit."*

A miasma of general hostility welled out around the queen of Sin City, adding to the goblin-scented air a new kind of chill. The effluvium surrounding the goblin queen was not visible, but Cyra registered with all her other senses the toxins, poisons and invisible rotting things that clung to Lilith's aura. This was a soul-eater, a connoisseur of black arts. And she had human blood on her, too, perhaps unnoticed by others because they thought she was wearing red nail polish.

"That'll teach the deadbeats. When you say you charge an arm and a leg in interest, you mean it," one of her flunkies said with a laugh.

Shaken, Cyra fell back. She had seen the John Collier painting of Lilith and had naively carried that image in her mind. But the goblin in front of her in no way resembled that beautiful creature on canvas.

Both Liliths were supposedly evil, but only one looked it. Unlike the other goblins who worked in the casino, the being before Cyra hadn't bothered with any modification. Her scent glands were intact and she had both sets of arms covered in porous goblin skin that could not displace heat, but oozed sweaty fluid. As she walked on bare feet, she left a thin slimy trail behind her.

If that wasn't repellant enough, she was also a shade of moldy gray-green and had a set of wiry hairs protruding from her upper lip like a waxed mustache. Small tusks curved out of her lower jaw.

"She looks like she bites the heads off live chickens for breakfast."

"No, not chickens." Thomas's thoughts were more subdued than usual. He seemed able to sense that Lilith was dripping with blood.

It said a lot for the queen's sheer ugliness that she managed to overshadow the giant troll beside her. He was the largest hobgoblin-cross Cyra had ever seen, a walking nightmare of scars and tattoos and curved, gilded tusks that had grown through his lower lip. As he breathed, a foul halitosis washed over her.

"Ugh! I feel sick."

"That's Lancilotto. Don't look either of them in the eye." Thomas's thoughts were urgent, like

nails grinding on a chalkboard. *"They have self-control issues and might take eye contact as an invitation. Lancilotto can kill at ten paces—and not with a gun. I mean it, Cyra. Don't look at them! I can't help you if they decide to take you someplace for some fun and games."*

Cyra knew what this stark admission cost Thomas. She shivered at the memory of what had happened to Annissa and carefully kept her eyes and surface thoughts unfocused as she slipped back through the dull-eyed crowd and headed for another elevator. She would have known even without Thomas's warning that these two were distilled evil, but his reminder of Annissa's fate brought the point home with the force of a crossbow bolt loosed at close range.

This wasn't a game.

Suddenly, Cyra knew it was time to leave Sin City. Now, before she was really frightened, before Lilith and Lancilotto and all the other goblins turned into some monolithically evil thing that grew in her imagination until it was a beast existing solely to eat her up, one nerve, one fear, one insecurity at a time. Her imagination could still grant her some clemency because the goblins had not yet annihilated her world. She didn't have nightmares every time she closed her eyes. She could function, live, love.

They'd damaged her, knocked her trust on end—though that was probably something she should be thankful for, considering whom she had chosen to trust—but they hadn't damaged her beyond repair. She wasn't Annissa or Chloe. Not yet.

"Oh, love," she whispered softly when the doors had closed on her, shutting her off from the evil in the casino. Suddenly she wanted Thomas near her—was dizzy with the need of him. But, of course, that wasn't possible. Heart squeezed tight, she went on: *"I'm sorry for all the worry I've caused you. I just . . ."*

"Don't be sorry." Thomas's voice was brusque, but she felt the emotion behind it, the worry. He was trying to prop her back up because he sensed her sudden fear and knew it was as dangerous as her recklessness had been. Or more so. *"Just be safe."*

"I shall. No more risks."

"Keep that promise. Please. I swear I'll be fine. I don't need a diversion. I have plenty of time and an escape hatch, okay?"

"I will keep this promise. Don't worry—I will."

"I'm sorry this touched you, Cyra. Sorry the ugliness came into your world."

"It's not your fault, Thomas. Fate had this all arranged."

Cyra looked at the flashing numbers on the

elevator and began to sweat. It wasn't the humid elevator air that triggered her nerves and sweat glands. It was fright. She decided that she didn't like intrigue after all.

She looked at her watch. *Countdown.* No more time for extracurricular goofing around—which was too bad because she suddenly and ardently wanted to have a T-bone steak with gorgonzola butter for dinner. But now she was too nervous to eat and shouldn't try and function on a full stomach.

"For breakfast," Thomas promised. *"And a banana split for dessert. We'll drive all the way to California to get it if we have to."*

"It's a date," she answered, making her thoughts sound brave. To herself she thought: Please, goddess, please! Let us live to eat another breakfast.

The elevator doors opened with a soft chime. Runners, take your mark she thought. It was time to go.

Chapter Nineteen

The elevator opened on the lower basement level and on Mr. Beene. Since his dawning expression was one of cold hostility, Cyra assumed that all had not been forgiven from their last meeting. She lashed out immediately.

Following the drill from her self-defense class, she kicked out sideways to Beene's kneecap and raked her heel down his shin. She finished her assault with a hard stomp to his arch. Next came a fist to the gut that bent him double and then an open-hand jab to the chin that snapped his head back. It was over in ten seconds. Once again, Mr. Beene was knocked out cold. She was getting really good at this. The thought didn't cheer her. In fact, it made her a little sick.

"Cyra? What happened?"

"Nothing," she said firmly. Cyra stepped over the body, looking around hurriedly. *"I'm just getting ready to head underground now."*

"And everything is okay?" Thomas's voice was distant and distracted. Cyra sought his mind and had a brief flash of colored wires and some sort of timing device.

"Just the same old, same old," she answered. *"You don't need to worry about a thing."*

And he didn't because she was worrying enough for both of them. She had her breather in place, but the smell of goblin was still thick in the air. She was slightly dizzy, and she knew that if she forgot and inhaled through her mouth, the scent would catch at the back of her throat and make her gag.

"Better than ipecac," she muttered, but was annoyed because her voice sounded so nervous.

She paused for a second, listening to the reassuring hum of the generators and the ticking of the ventilation systems. Normal. It all sounded perfectly fine. Other than Beene, there was no one in the underground. No little goblin officials ready to question her about her intentions or lack of a proper visa for Lilithland— *And the purpose of your business in the hive, kloka?*

"Business . . . and pleasure," she said to

281

herself. Except the goblin customs agent's accent should be French. He'd say in a snotty, high voice—what would he say?

"Thomas, how do you say, 'Do you have anything to declare?' in French?" she asked without thinking.

Thomas was slow to answer.

"Vouz n'avez rien à declarer? Why? Cyra, what's wrong?"

"Nothing. I just think I'd like to learn French someday. If I live," she added aloud.

"Uh, Cyra, are you really okay? 'Cause you sound a bit weirded out. Worried." Thomas definitely sounded worried, himself. Which was bad. Cyra had to stop bothering him. She had to get a grip on herself.

"Really, I'm fine. Just thinking about things to do later," she assured him. *"Wouldn't it be fun to take a vacation in Paris?"*

Liar, liar! She really wasn't entirely okay. Fear and anticipation were crawling all over her skin, making her itch.

"Paris. Uh-huh. And do you have anything to declare to me right now? Anything I need to know?"

"Only my brilliance." And that she loved him. Oh, how she loved him! But that was for later. Their love had no place in the underground. And it seemed like a jinx to mention it now.

Who knew which perverse divine being might be listening and decide to destroy them for daring to think of happiness?

Not that Cyra belonged in the underground either. She wasn't some damned mole—or goblin—who liked rooting around in a dank hive. This place was an affront to her senses, alien and ugly. She was of the sea and air, and something about the mountain's weight and vastness made her doubt whether she'd emerge again.

Of course, if she did, she'd come like Persephone with the seeds of spring clasped in her hands.

And if she didn't? a voice asked. *Who besides Thomas would know or care?* She was homeless, forgotten—

Stop that! She'd sprain a nerve if she wasn't careful. And she had so few nerves left. She needed every one of them screwed to the sticking point to do what she had to do. *Because, let's be honest here, the underground scares me.* More than goblins, more than trolls, this ancient, hostile pile of rocks that dripped acid and hated all invaders terrified her.

It was old. It was immense. And she had to convince it to harm itself.

Cyra stepped up to the giant door that separated the hotel basement from the actual goblin hive. As Thomas had predicted, it was unlocked and unguarded through either stupid arrogance or sublime confidence on the goblins' part. Yet how could she know if either was justified?

It took an effort to pull the door open because, despite the chill, Cyra's hands were slicked with sweat and her muscles simply didn't want to cooperate. They tried to sabotage her by making her weak and clumsy. *Please,* they sniveled. *We don't want to do this.*

Cyra took a small step and another. She was inside the hive, then, no longer in the realm of men but trespassing in the labyrinth of her enemies. She was alien, an intruder traveling into the belly of the beast.

Her ears hurt, they were straining so hard. The air around her was restless, apparently as disturbed as she. Cyra didn't like the vague sounds of movement down in the dark just beyond where her eyes could peer. Nothing in the underground was her friend, and she was walking into the lair of some very nasty predators: goblins, trolls . . . H.U.G. agents with bombs. And then there was the cave itself.

"Yes, we meet again. And so soon." So soon, and too late to turn back and come up with another plan—though Cyra wanted with all her heart to do just that. Her voice came out thin as she intoned: "Yea, though I walk through the valley of the shadow of death, I shall still fear evil, for this is one son of a bitch of a valley."

Cyra was just talking to herself. It wasn't so unusual a coping mechanism. Her comments were acerbic, almost playful. She'd be fine.

She had to be. Everything hinged on her being able to make the mountain do what they wanted. Thomas's job was to stop worrying and get the bomb wired.

He looked down and forced himself to concentrate. He had to bypass the conduit threaded into the main body of the device. It was a challenge—but absolutely critical—that he keep all dirt and sand out of the threads so the contact was clean and everything aligned. Without clear contacts, the touchy device was useless.

Goblins sure did stink. And the tunnel from the casino was unpleasantly breezier than the last time. It was like walking into a flatulent giant's bowels, and Cyra reckoned that she had gone about far enough up this particular intestine. She could feel the cave now, hear it. She was beyond where the goblins had plastered.

A large gust of air rushed down at her. Hearing the tell-tale dry rasp of stone chips, she flattened herself against the wall and turned her head away. Detritus whirled around her. She practically kissed the stone wall, hiding her eyes with her hands. The rock was bitter, hard, dusty, burning—but she kept her lips and face pressed tight against it and concentrated with all her will, focusing her message on the intelligence she sensed living in the searing stone.

"The air that has so lately kissed thee—Come on! Wake up, cave! Stop snoring. We need to talk."

As the wind died, Cyra risked a quick look at her watch. Though it felt like she had been underground for an eternity, time was left—but it was quickly running out. Fornix would have already arrived at Yucca Mountain. Lilith would be there too.

The cave didn't answer.

"Damn it." Cyra looked back the way she had come and closed her eyes against the green light oozing from the goblins' crumbling spackle. She tried to concentrate on the task at hand. The light was sly and stealthy, surreal. It confused. It lied. Cyra was already walking in an eerie wilderness of suspenseful emotion where the stark possibility of failure loomed too large. She didn't need visual deceit to distract her from her job, especially since she couldn't ask Thomas for help this time.

Instead of giving in to her building fear, Cyra called up her memories of every earthquake she had ever endured, every explosion, every eruption she had seen on TV and projected them at the geologic intelligence, thrust them at the wall like a javelin. And, though it was a slight lie, she blamed the goblins for everything.

Something enormous and alien shifted and brushed against her mind.

"Who's there? Go away."

Great. She finally had the cave's attention, but it wasn't happy. *"I can't."*

Annoyed, it stretched its muscles, shaking more plaster and rock loose and further degrading the air. It was hot and it itched, and it was ready for a cleansing of all parasites. But how? Maybe it should just crush them all, sacrifice some of itself and be done.

Tiring rapidly as the oxygen depleted, Cyra again projected what would happen to California if the goblins were allowed to carry out their plan, concentrating not on the human loss, but rather on geographic cataclysms.

"You again?" There came a sigh, and another gust of some poisoned wind that stung even as it clung. It stuck to Cyra's face like a wet veil and made her sinuses clammy even through her breather. She kept up the mental barrage

287

until she was sure that the cave understood.

"You can stop them, if you want," she told it. *"I can show you what you have to do to be clean again."*

The cave sighed once more, this time more gently.

Taking the reaction as a sign to go on, Cyra started explaining what she needed the cavern to do, emphasizing the fact that by doing this, it would finally be able to wash itself clean of the goblins' taint by wiping them out once and for all.

As she talked, she tried hard not to think of words like "murder" and "genocide." They didn't apply when you were at war with an enemy that wanted all of your kind dead. Even those goblins who weren't actually tunneling to steal nuclear waste would be aware of Lilith's plan and guilty of complicity with their silence and inaction. This was self-defense—and protection of millions of innocent human lives. So, maybe she was lying a little about what the goblins had done to this particular cave. In this case, the end definitely justified the means.

Thomas lifted the flange and stared at the gear train. Why, oh why couldn't he have found some dynamite on the black market? These

fussy bang-sticks were so much more bothersome. And dangerous.

Thomas shoved his hair back with an impatient hand and then paused while he regained
his composure. He was tired. Exhausted people
made mistakes. Just now, any mistake would
be fatal.

Well, he had been tired before and had managed. He just needed to work a little longer and
then it would be over. His war with the goblins
had gone on for years—a century even. And for
those hundred years he had plied his trade as
saboteur and spy without making a mistake.
This was a mission like any other.

A part of him argued back at this glib confidence. He hadn't minded the work in the old
days. He had, in fact, been consumed with the
need for revenge. His life simply didn't seem to
have any meaning or purpose beyond destroying goblins.

But things had changed. Now he was tired
from splitting his attention between his job and
Cyra, and he was probably being overly hesitant. After all, he once again had "hostages to
Fate," people he cared about. Down inside, he
felt that it was time to get out and start living
life as it should be lived—as it *would* be lived.

It was a good reason to be nervous. It was an
odd truth, but in this line of work, the moment

a man got hesitant he usually died.

But he had to stop thinking this way. Yes, he had more to lose now, but the best way not to lose it was to focus on the job at hand. He wasn't *that* tired.

"Just let me pull this one off and then I'm done. Cyra and I will make babies and help with the convocation of feys, and we'll work on the side of life instead of death. But, Goddess, you have to help me one more time because you know how I hate these damned things!" he muttered. He shifted so he was out of the thin dawnlight and not casting a shadow on the bomb.

It wasn't the best prayer he had ever offered. But for some reason, this time his deity answered. He felt her pass through him like an evening breeze creeping inland from the sea. The sweat on his brow dried and he felt his exhaustion lift. Thomas looked at his hands. They were steady, the fingers stained with lubricant, but they no longer trembled.

"Thank you."

Relieved, he began setting the pins. He needed a big bang—but not too big a bang. And the energy needed to be forced into the pipeline, not into the earth. It was critical that he do nothing to the cave that might be seen as an attack as long as Cyra was inside. There was no telling what sort of revenge it might take on her.

The sockets and springs of his bomb sounded almost musical as the tiny balls slipped home—Christmas sleigh bells, or maybe windchimes. The sound didn't accord well with the smell of silicone in the air.

Finally, all that was left was for Thomas to flip the lever on the timer, and then all of Lilith's madness would end. He looked at his watch. There was no time left for speeches or second-guessing of their decision.

"Bye-bye, bitch," he whispered. Then he threw the switch that started the bomb ticking down.

"I begin."

The voice was a sonic boom that hurt Cyra's head, and she was so exhausted that it took her a moment to understand what the words meant. When she finally recovered from the cave's subliminal buffeting and looked up, her legs went nerveless and she found herself sitting on the cave's filthy floor. Capillaries appeared in slow-motion on the ceiling and then broke open. They grew almost as fast as her alarm. There came a series of cracks that sounded all too much like a skull crunching, and then burning water began to rush into the cave.

Cyra stared at it stupidly. Trapped? She was trapped! The cave hadn't waited for her to get out.

I'm going to die.

Well, at least if she died down here she wouldn't end up in a coffin pumped full of orange formaldehyde, she thought fatalistically. And their plan was putting an end to Lilith's plundering and evil. The goblin queen wouldn't be hurting people anymore. She and Fornix wouldn't be irradiating the entire West Coast. Surely that was worth any sacrifice.

But Thomas—O, Goddess! What of Thomas?

"Get out, stupid one." The foreign rumble of thought hurt her head. *"Flee while you can!"*

"What?"

The ground bucked violently. There was a gasp, then what sounded like a flapping of wings. Bats? She hated bats!

"No! No! No!"

Her stress level finally topped out, and time began to speed up again. The left hemisphere of her brain began processing information and making survival decisions, since her right brain had gone comatose and suicidal. Among its first commands were that her limbs not be nerveless anymore. Cyra struggled to her feet and then fled back down the tunnels toward the hotel.

Once her right brain realized that she wasn't going to die, it began cooperating and she was able to reach out for Thomas.

"Thomas! It's happening!" she shouted.

Thomas didn't answer. He was there, she could feel him, but he was doing something or facing someone that he didn't want her to know about. All she could see were red flashing numbers, counting down at a rapid pace.

"Oh damn," she heard him say, then he disappeared completely.

"Thomas! Thomas, I'm coming! Don't you dare die!" She projected her thoughts at him, not certain if he could hear, but putting everything she had into the message anyway. *"Don't you dare die now! I love you!"*

98—97—96— Thomas looked up from the flashing timer and stared into the red, liquid eyes of the creature the goblins called the coyote.

Damn. He hadn't heard a thing. Not a sound! But the beast was there all the same. And the sneaky son of bitch was huge! He had never guessed that it would be so big. So very, very big.

Unbidden—and certainly unwanted—fear

rushed in on the heels of the first adrenaline surge. It was an understandable fear, what with the coyote's size, its thrusting muzzle full of curved teeth, its crimson eyes gleaming in its bony skull. This sort of fright could be managed—Thomas had faced it before.

But the fear grew the moment he looked into the monster's eyes and read in them the total assurance that he would die, that he would end his life in the belly of this beast. This red gaze held destiny.

"Thomas! It's happening. The cave is cracking." Cyra called, her tone both excited and terrified.

Thomas got to his feet slowly, reaching for the crowbar that he'd brought along and raising it above his head. *90—89—88—* The timer counted down. It would also destroy anything that was near it when it ticked down to *00* and began flooding the underground.

The coyote looked at Thomas's weapon and made a noise that sounded almost like a laugh.

Damn.

72—71—70— Thomas noted with detached interest that there was a sudden hollow place in his stomach, sweat on his palms and a chill on his skin that owed nothing to the pre-dawn hour. Nothing to worry about, he assured himself. It wasn't Fate putting a mark upon him; it was just adrenaline preparing him for a battle.

Snarling, the coyote finally sprang, maw opened impossibly wide as the lower jaw unhinged like a snake's. Thomas knew that if those teeth locked shut on him, they'd shear through bone.

The monster was preternaturally fast, and it was all Thomas could do to leap away in time. Even as he jumped, he swung the crowbar. He put his full strength into the blow, knowing he would only get one. A single strike would not kill the goblin hunter, but it wouldn't have to. It just had to buy him enough time to get to the van and away from the bomb. The explosion should take care of the coyote. It was going to be a big one since the blast was rigged to move upward and outward.

"Thomas, I'm coming. Don't you dare die," he heard. *"I'll be right there."* Thomas didn't answer Cyra even though her voice was frantic. He did his best to shut her off from what was happening.

He spared an instant—less than a second—to think of the woman who had graced him with her reluctant care and life. She was a less-than-gentle benediction, so unlike his first wife, but a divine blessing all the same. He wanted to have the chance to live a long, happy life with her. And he *would* have it. No damned goblin dog was going to deprive him of that. This time, the goblins wouldn't win.

Inside him, the dragon had woken. It roared with fury and lent its strength to Thomas's blow. The crowbar connected—but not before the coyote's curving fangs slashed through the flesh of Thomas's other arm and took some of it away.

Ignoring the pain, Thomas tore loose and ran for the van. Behind him, he heard the coyote scramble to its feet. In his mind's eye, he saw the counter clicking down: *30—29—28—*

Hell and damnation, he wasn't going to make it.

Something huge and clawed landed clumsily on his back. Argh! The stink! The thing wasn't decaying, but it certainly smelled rotten. Why did evil always smell so bad?

4—3—2— Okay, this worked for him. Hopefully the coyote would shield him from the worst of the shrapnel. *Go ahead, stand up tall, you bastar—*

00—

Boom!

Thomas's voice came to Cyra just as she escaped the last of the city traffic and kicked her Harley into high gear. It was almost sunrise. The goblins would be going back to their hive soon and discovering it was gone. Then they'd be out, patrolling the shadows with vengeance in their hearts.

"That's it, Cyra! We're done! H.U.G. blew the dam and who knows what else. Head for high ground. The whole plain is going to flood." Thomas's presence was weak but steady.

"At the speed of light," she agreed, forcing the bike to go even faster. She hadn't heard the explosion, but her ears were still ringing from the roaring in the cave. The long hour of persuasion and escape had left her a little dizzy.

She could sense beyond her own physical and psychic distress that Thomas was in pain, but obviously not anywhere near death. They *had* done it! They'd actually pulled it off! Her relief made her even dizzier. *"Just call us Persephone, Thomas! By the way, what happened to you? Where did you go? Why didn't you answer me? I've been scared half to death."*

"I was a little busy. I had to break a crowbar over a coyote's head."

"Oh. Well, good. You mean the *coyote?"* Cyra exhaled. The coyote. So, it had been real, not just some scarecrow the goblins planted in the desert to scare away feys and psychics. She was probably very lucky not to have had to fight it, herself. Obviously. *"Uh—is it dead?"*

"I really couldn't say. Part of the pipeline fell

on it. And it kept chasing me. Getting smashed by my van can't have helped it any. But don't worry. Just go like a bat out of hell and get to high ground."

"I am. Lucky thing they have no speed limits here. I've broken every highway safety rule in the book. Where are you?"

"Not far from our rendezvous point. But I have to change a tire. That damned coyote had a hard head. I hope there's a spare—I don't really feel like walking. Or swimming."

Cyra gave a small gasp of laughter.

"Okay, I won't worry. But damn it! Don't shut me out again. And take care. You scared me. We're almost home-free now, so don't do anything stupid."

"You know it." Thomas disappeared again.

Probably he was just tired. She certainly was. She had never been so tired in her life.

Thomas had lied a bit about the flat tire. His van had been caught in the tail of the explosion and the tires were melted. The entire right side of the vehicle had also buckled as though slammed by a giant's fists.

Fortunately, the motorcycle he had stashed in the back seemed unharmed. All he had to do was stop his arm from bleeding like a butchered hog and get the damned thing out of the smoking wreckage before the van blew up. Maybe there would be some kind of first aid kit in the glove compartment.

Thomas took a step toward the van and then—unbelievably—heard a growl.

He spun around quickly, facing his apparently unstoppable killer. The coyote was in tatters and burned black in many places, but it was still standing.

"Why don't you just give up and die?" Thomas said to it. "It would be the sportsman-like thing to do," he added.

The coyote snarled.

However, before either of them could move, the ground groaned beneath their feet and the cliff face above them slid sideways in the air, coming loose with an ear-splitting crack. A slab of stone as big as a house toppled toward them, chased by bits of burning rock propelled like buckshot from a gun.

Volcano? Geyser?

Whatever force was chucking mountains around, Thomas decided the coyote could face it. He himself knew when he was outclassed. He turned and fled, vaulting tumbling boulders as he went.

Cyra saw the lone goblin as she rounded the bend and recognized him instantly, though the sky was still dark. Behind his small form, a thin stream of white vapor rose into the air from an ancient Honda Civic, just like her old car, telling a familiar tale of overheated woe.

The goblin raised his hands, flagging her down as he looked urgently upward. There was some easing of the darkness, but dawn was several minutes away. Still, that was probably too close for comfort to a goblin stranded away from his hive.

"Damn." She couldn't leave Orel standing at the side of the road and looking so desperate, could she?

Don't be a fool! she scolded herself.

"Double damn." She shouldn't stop. She really shouldn't, she thought even as she downshifted. But if she didn't, he would probably drown. He would crawl down some crack to avoid the sun and get smothered when the flood came. She couldn't let that happen.

And maybe, a part of her thought, *saving Orel would atone for what she had done to his family, if he had one. After the flood, Orel would probably be an orphan.* .

"Hey, Orel," she greeted him as she brought the Harley to a halt. "You need a ride?"

"Thanksss, Mary." The goblin hopped up behind her. He didn't need to be told to hurry. Terror of the sunrise was sufficient inducement to speed. His tone was worried as he asked: "Where are you going?"

"Away from here," she muttered, then took the bike up to speed as quickly as she could. Louder, she added: "Don't worry, Orel. You'll be okay. I'll get you to some shelter."

Thomas looked at the newly arranged landscape and started to swear. The good news was, there wasn't a river of lava rushing toward him. The less happy news was, the road was completely blocked by a fall of giant stones. Cyra would never get through it on her motorcycle. She would have to climb over.

Also, unbelievably, the coyote was still alive under a huge pile of debris. He was buried under a ton of rock, but the damned thing was still trying to squirm its way out. It just didn't know when to give up. Maybe it couldn't. Some magic was powering it, forcing it to go on when it should be dead. Maybe . . .

Suddenly, it wailed, a call for help.

More bad news. Goddess, damn it! A moment later, Thomas heard the low, answering growl behind him.

There was one last obstacle that stood between her and freedom. Cyra estimated that they had twenty seconds before they reached the gates of Sin City. She glanced at her watch, but again lost track of the time when she looked away. She'd already looked at the watch half a dozen times. She supposed it didn't matter, exactly. The only real measure of time that mattered was the sun on the horizon. The sun would hurt Orel, and it would also force all the trolls inside. She'd been praying for it to rise.

She started counting: *Twenty, nineteen* . . . She and Orel were almost at the gates. The two troll guards saw them coming and lifted their weapons a few inches. They were probably nervous after the sounds of explosions, but they would also be reassured by the sight of a goblin on the back of this bike. They'd look and think: *Nothing suspicious here. Just a girl and her goblin out for a late night ride. Besides, the sun was almost up.* Maybe . . .

No. The sun wouldn't save her. And they were too close! They were still too near the gates, and she was losing speed as they climbed uphill. They'd try and stop her, and if they did they would sense her magic. It was crawling all over her— Damn it! Screw caution. So what if she blew her cover and made the goblins' Most Wanted list. It wasn't like she was ever coming back here.

Throwing all prudence to the wind, Cyra pushed out mentally, simultaneously shoving her magic at the guards and gunning the bike, making the tires shrill as they grabbed the pavement.

"Move, you bastards or I'll run you down—yes!" Either her magic or her speed made the trolls fall back from their post; their jaws slack, their weapons lowered. They looked dazed.

"Mary?" Orel shouted, sounding surprised as he peered around her shoulder. "Did you just use magic on those guards?"

"Yes, Orel, I did. The sun's almost up, and this really isn't the time for us to slow down," she shouted back. An explosion echoed through the canyon and punctuated her words. Thomas was right. H.U.G. was doing more than blowing up the dam and the lake in Cathay Passage. It sounded like the beginning of World War Three.

Or maybe the cavern had gotten carried away with its spring cleaning and set off a volcano.

"That sssounded like dynamite. Or a volcano." Orel shouted back, echoing her thoughts. Clearly he was getting really worried. She didn't blame him. If those trolls decided to shoot after all, it would be into his back—a bad end for an obedient little goblin.

"It did, didn't it?"

"Ssshould we go back and check it out?"

"No, I don't think so." She stopped talking,

303

then. The roar of water suddenly filled her ears, louder even than the Harley's engine. "Oh damn! They got the back-up reservoir too."

Go! Go! Go! She urged the Harley, not bothering to look back to see if the tide was gaining on her. Orel's arms tightened around her waist, and she was sure she heard him hissing *ssshhhhhiiit* as they started up the steep grade out of Sin City's canyon. White water licked at their heels.

Chapter Twenty

The sun rose like an explosion from the mouth of a black cannon. At first the light was beautiful, a gauzy pink streaked with fiery red that enchanted the eye. Ten minutes later, it was a crimson punishment.

Worried, Cyra looked down at the set of hands clasped about her waist. Orel hadn't complained, but she could see that his skin had already begun to cure in the dry heat. His shriveling fingers looked like empty gloves beginning to curl in on themselves. Only, gloves didn't have fingernails where the skin peeled away and the horny extrusions bled.

Appalled at his rapid deterioration even in this gentle morning light, Cyra brought the bike to a halt and quickly removed her helmet. The unfiltered sun was like ground glass in her eyes. She knew it had to be even worse for Orel.

"Let go," she ordered, shrugging off her coat. "Put this on. You're burning."

"You need it," Orel answered, careful not to whimper. "It hurtsss you too. I can tell."

"I don't need it as badly as you do." She swiveled around and added with a slight smile: "Don't make me get off this bike and stuff you in that jacket."

Something complicated and incomprehensible passed through the goblin's eyes, and then Orel smiled back as best he could with his graying, pained face. His dewlaps were withering, his lips cracking in tiny lines. The goblin swiftly pulled on Cyra's coat and then took her helmet. He pulled the jacket cuffs down over his damaged hands. His second set of arms were folded tightly against his body as they tried to escape the sun's cruel light. "Thanksss."

"We're almost to Red Rock Canyon. They'll have water there. You'll be okay." If they didn't drown—but surely they were above the flood line by now. And the cave would be sending the water mostly underground.

Cyra pulled out her sunglasses and put them on. They helped some, but the daylight was still like spikes in her eyes. Using magic had left her dangerously weak, but she reached out for Orel with her mind and tried to send him some mental painkillers.

The goblin shuddered and then relaxed slightly.

"Mary, I—" Orel was interrupted by a mad howl. The noise was distant, but it still made every hair on Cyra's body stiffen. It frightened the goblin too. He whispered: "The coyote."

"I thought it was dead," Cyra said blankly. "Thomas smashed it with a van. It has to be dead."

"No," the goblin answered, terror in his voice. "That *is* the coyote. And he's calling the pack."

"Come on!" Cyra urged as Orel fastened the strap on his helmet. "We have to go. They're after Thomas!"

"They?"

"Yes—the hunters. And if the coyote is there, the bear won't be far behind."

"The bear! Ssshit!" It didn't seem possible, but Orel's voice was even more frightened. Cyra was certain that if he weren't facing certain death from dehydration, he would jump off the bike and run away into the desert.

Cyra understood. That howl was like nothing she had ever heard. She was terrified, too, but she gunned the engine and the Harley obligingly tore at the road with its steel-belted claws. Then they were off to Thomas's rescue. The Two

Musketeers were at it again, although slightly different in—

"Here we go again."

"Thomas?"

"I'm a little busy right now. I'll have to get back to you."

Cyra had a wildly inappropriate urge to laugh but stifled it. It wouldn't do for Orel to think that she wasn't in control of herself. And maybe, if she didn't give in to hysteria, that would remain true.

The bear was huge, larger than any real bear Thomas had ever heard of. It stood almost twenty feet tall and had an elongated snout. It waved at him with forelegs armed with hooked claws, each hook longer than Thomas's hands. Those claws glinted in the sun. Its huge head snaked back and forth on an unnaturally long neck, like a cobra after its prey. Its mouth was full of equally long fangs.

Like the coyote, the bear didn't look the least bit frightened of Thomas or his crowbar.

"Here we go again."

"Thomas?"

"I'm a little busy right now. I'll have to get back to you."

* * *

Cyra miscalculated braking on the loose gravel and laid the bike down hard on its side. Fortunately, both she and Orel were thrown clear of the sparking metal as it skittered over the ground toward the mountain of debris blocking the road. The engine died as the bike smacked into the rockslide.

"Orel, are you okay?" But she needn't have asked. The tiny goblin was already scampering off for a dark crevasse. She couldn't blame him. His half-exposed hands had withered to mummified paws.

"It's time to rethink my donations to the World Wildlife Federation."

"Thomas?"

"Stay where you are, Cyra."

On the other side of the small red mountain there came a bellow that shook the very heavens. Battle was being joined.

"Thomas!"

There was no answer.

"Damn it!" Instinctively, Cyra reached into the messenger bag slung across her chest and pulled out her cloak. She dragged it on.

"Thomas!" she shouted, clawing at the pile of debris that blocked her way. It took a long, painful minute to scramble over the sharp, red stones. The unsteady pile shook with constant low-pitched vibration. The smell of baking rock was thick in the air.

She was breathing hard as she crested the hill, and Cyra stared down at a living nightmare of fur and bones and massive claws that confronted Thomas. "Oh, Goddess," she gasped.

Cognitive dissonance—that was what the condition was called. The brain expected to see one thing—a bear—but was confronted with something else. Expectation and reality collided in a dizzying rush.

"Thomas!" Cyra's breath stopped as the hideous face of a monster swiveled to look up at her. No, this wasn't a bear. To call this beast a bear was to compare a T-Rex to a gecko. She hadn't thought there could be anything viler than Lilith and her bodyguard—but she'd been wrong. This putrescent conglomeration of claws and drool and bones was much, much worse. And it was about the size of a two-story house.

"Cyra! Get out! I can handle him. I just need to get him under an overhang, and then I can bring the cliff down on him."

She really wanted to believe Thomas, but she didn't. There wasn't that much cliff in the whole of the park.

"Get real, Thomas. I'm not leaving," she shouted at him. But she couldn't think what to do. Fear and exhaustion had claimed her brain; she was paralyzed by the sight in front of her, shaken to the marrow of her freezing bones. But—and this was unexpected though welcome—Thomas didn't know how close to breaking she was. Pride was the bootstrap you hauled yourself up by when you didn't actually have boots. If her lover could face a grim reaper wrapped in bearskin and baring its dripping fangs, so could she. Somehow.

But how? What could she do? They needed a tank, or a cruise missile, or . . . a *dragon*. Of course! The dragon could fight the bear. The dragon probably *wanted* to fight the bear. But Thomas was likely afraid of the consequences— and he couldn't be.

"Thomas, release the dragon!" she shouted at him. "Let him out."

Surprisingly, he answered: "I can't. I tried already. Some weird magic is blocking it. He's finally ready to leave, but . . . I need another vessel for him."

The bear, tiring of their shouted conversation, turned to Thomas and began lumbering toward him.

Thomas yelled up at Cyra, "If you want to be useful, find a vessel for me! Something the dragon can possess. And make it something big."

"Thomas! Get away from there!" Cyra shouted, picking up rocks and hurling them down on the bear as it advanced. The stones mostly thumped off his hide with little effect, but the bear didn't seem to like getting hit in the face, so Cyra switched her aim to his head. All the while her brain chattered like a squirrel: *A vessel? A vessel! The dragon needs a vessel.*

Behind her there came a sharp crack and then another bit of cliff fell away, spattering Cyra with dust and rock and revealing something that looked like a hook.

"Use that, Cyra!" Thomas shouted, pointing above her just before he rolled clear of the bear's swinging claws. The beast wasn't especially fast, but one blow could cut Thomas in half.

Cyra turned and looked up at the wounded cliff where the rockslide had originated. It took her a moment to realize that she was staring at giant bones, the remains of a terrible lizard whose skeleton had turned to stone millions of years before. The skeleton was maybe fifteen feet long with snaggled teeth and badly twisted claws. It was also a tremendous archaeological discovery, as one had never been found in Nevada. But what was of more immediate import was the fact that the stone fangs and talons were as long and sharp as anything the bear

312

had, and would do terrible damage when used correctly. But how?

"Hurry, Cyra. The dragon wants out."

Suddenly she understood what Thomas and the dragon wanted—and agreed that it would make a formidable weapon, if she could wield it. She didn't know how it would be accomplished, but she had to somehow force those bones out of these petrified dunes and turn them back into living—*fighting*—flesh and bone.

"Why couldn't it have been a frozen *live* lizard?" she muttered to herself as she tried to marshal her thoughts and magic. *"What do I do?"*

"You're a conjurer. Call it." Thomas's thought was frantic.

"But I don't know . . ." She broke off as pictures came into her mind, impressions of great sorceries to be done. Was this her heritage, everything she'd denied herself up until now? It all seemed so simple.

Cyra followed her newfound instincts without hesitation, though the flood of information left her dizzy and with goose flesh crawling up her arms. She took a breath and focused her thoughts, trying to draw also on Thomas's will, and then she threw their gathered power at the skeleton.

It worked. Ancient stone trembled under the assault of their combined magic, began to fall away as though whacked off by a sculptor's invisible hammer. Soon the bones were mostly free.

"Now what?" she asked herself. Terror and exertion strained her lungs and made it hard to speak. It was all she could do to magically hold the heavy bones together and dodge the falling rockface. She turned to look down at Thomas.

"Now we make war," he answered.

The cruel sun shone down out of an otherwise empty sky. Every ripple of the shifting earth was lit with blinding fire, and Cyra did not see what happened next. Thomas managed to move without her knowledge. It seemed for an instant that he didn't cast a shadow; it just folded up and drew inside him. Then, as she watched, Thomas cast out a spirit, a dragon, that flew through the air and then disappeared into the bones she had freed.

Suddenly, those bones were alive and moving on their own, thrashing about as the stone beast tried to align the parts that had been twisted in its tomb.

"Do it, Cyra!" Thomas called hoarsely.

Cyra did what he asked, throwing in her whole will and using the cloak's added power to give the skeleton—the dragon—complete mobility. On her own, even with her newfound knowledge, she couldn't have done it, wouldn't have known how—but both Thomas and the dragon were helping her, guiding her. As fast as she could think it, muscles grew, blood vessels, organs, flesh. Ligaments reattached themselves to the ancient lizard skeleton. Somehow, it was working.

Yet, even with the aid from Thomas and the dragon, and with her cloak and its tap into some other source of power, Cyra could feel the strength bleeding out of her. This was sucking the magic from her, and the dragon was there, lapping it up.

So, too, was something else. And that something made her hair stand on end. Lilith. Somehow the goblin queen or her ghost was here with them, adding her power to the bear's.

"Thomas! I think Lilith is here!"

"That's impossible. She would have died when the pipeline burst."

"Then her ghost has come to play."

Cyra began to see phantom flashes of lightning, red and white fireworks exploding in her retinas, and feared that it wasn't an illusion, that she was truly losing her sight. Her tympanic membrane was rushing with blood, pulsing, on the verge of exploding. The pressure was enough to stop her lungs. She had to fight for every breath. She had to control her heart as well.

She took two deep breaths, trying to stem the tide of adrenaline before she blew a blood vessel in her brain, before the panic at what was happening overwhelmed her body and killed her. It could happen. One could die of stress and fear. If she were to stay on top of things, she would have to regain control of her body. She had to stop the magical hemorrhage too.

A part of her noted that her mouth was dry. She thought, *I could drink a lake*. And then she remembered that only minutes ago, in the tunnels below Sin City, she had feared drowning. An hour hadn't passed, but it felt like something that had happened in another life.

"Dragon, stop! Don't take any more from her." Thomas shouted at the beast, and Cyra felt it reluctantly ease back from her magical wound.

The other parasite did not. Lilith—it *was* the goblin green, wasn't it?—was trying to suck her dry.

Hot, she was so hot! Cyra crawled down the rest of the small mountain, trying to get out of the sun, hoping that the shade would stanch some of her magical bleeding. But she only managed to bruise herself, and tumbled to a stop at the bottom of the slope, fetched up against a giant boulder.

"Goddess," she croaked. She could not recall ever suffering this much pain. And something was still draining her. "Help me. Help us."

"Cyra, get away from there!"

"I can't."

"I'm not kidding! Move!"

Beside her, something began to shove its way out of the landslide. Startled, Cyra scrambled away from it, then watched in horror as a long, blackened snout appeared.

"No! No! *Noooo*—" she denied. But the coyote continued to struggle under the pile of rocks. Cyra whispered: "You're dead."

"Not dead enough," Thomas called. He was running about, still baiting the bear. "I can't seem to kill the damned thing! It's getting power from somewhere."

Cyra suddenly understood: It was getting power from her—enough to raise itself from the dead. Horrified, she realized that if she couldn't bandage her wounds, the beast would eventually recharge enough to free itself. And then it would rush in to help the bear.

She glanced over to her lover. Thomas had his hands full battling the one giant, clawed creature, and the dragon was trying to finish the resurrection that Cyra had started. Neither

317

could be spared to fight this goblin hellhound. Especially not since it had dined on her magic and might have read her mind—it might know their weaknesses. No, this beast was all hers to deal with.

She tried getting into its mind, but couldn't. It—maybe with Lilith's help—was using Cyra's magic against her to create a shield.

"Fine. There's always more than one way to skin a goblin hunter."

Recalling the gun in her bag, Cyra started digging. The man whom she'd bought the handgun from had told her that it was the most powerful weapon they had, that at point blank range it could punch through half a foot of tree stump and leave a really nasty hole. Cyra didn't know what it would do to an arcane coyote's skull, but it had to be helpful in her present predicament.

She tried not to be entirely distracted from the task of feeding some of her raw power to the dragon as he finished building his muscles and pulled an armored skin into place, but it was hard with the coyote's toothy snout becoming more and more free, inching ever closer to her with nostrils flaring wide as it drank in her scent and hunted for more of her magic.

She might not know how to kill the damn thing magically, but she was beginning to find it hard to ignore the powerful aura of evil that surrounded the human gun she'd bought. It called to her, dared her to use it.

"Cyra, what are you doing? Don't get near the coyote. It's an eye-biter. It'll bespell you!"

Oh, yeah? They'd just see about that. It probably wasn't cricket in this sort of situation—duels between magical creatures likely had rules—but hell, she was part human and she'd win any way she could.

The gun, reeking of concentrated human evil, slipped into her hand. Cyra let her heavy purse drop to the ground, kicked it away.

She'd never shot anything—never killed even an animal—but she knew what she had to do. She crawled closer to the hideous head that had shoved its way out of the debris, its ugly jaws snapping ferociously, and she unloaded the gun into its skull, sending shot after shot through its red eyes and into its murderous brain.

"Die! Just die! And take that goblin bitch with you," she whispered, adding punch to each bullet as she worked an informal death spell. Little by little, she felt the beast's magic crumble, and she finally saw into its mind. The sight was enough to make her recoil—hate and endless ravening hunger for other creatures' souls, that's all there was in the red ruin of its head.

The beast had been made to eat power and take it back to Lilith. Cyra whispered: "Never again. Never."

The reverberation from the discharges caused more rocks to break loose from their infirm walls, and Cyra had to roll backward to avoid being buried with the monster when another section of the cliff slowly tumbled down on them.

This time, the coyote didn't move under its stone pyre. She could feel that it was dead.

"Well damn, girl! Did Jack give you lessons on killing things?" Thomas thought fleetingly. Then he turned to strike out at the bear, trying again to draw it back from the wounded dragon who was struggling clumsily to his feet and pulling his tail out of the mountain. The dragon's muscles were still not entirely grown, and it moved in awkward jerks. It needed more magic, more power.

The bear suddenly realized that its companion was dead. Giving a terrible howl that pierced the ears like iron spikes, it seemed to swell in size. Cyra realized it was trying to drink its dead comrade's power, and she went in and pulled the magic away. Unwise or not, she took the corrupt power and funneled it toward the dragon.

"Thomas, look out!" The bear's lower jaw unhinged as it roared in rage and started to charge again.

Cyra struggled to her feet, not certain what to do but knowing she had to take action. If the bear was anything like the coyote, it would not tire; it would not cease the attack until they were all torn to bloody shreds and then eaten, their power swallowed up forever.

Suddenly, a fuselage of stones was loosed on the bear from above. Cyra looked up at their benefactor. Orel had come to their aid, distracting the monster and buying them a little more time.

The dragon called to her, reclaiming her attention and ruthlessly demanding that she find more energy. She'd given him everything the coyote had left, but it still wasn't enough. She had to help modify the dinosaur body. It wasn't large enough to fight the bear as it was. It needed wings. Mostly, it needed another stomach, like a cow had, a place to mix the incendiary chemicals it would need to make fire, and the body needed a better esophagus and a second trachea—one that could carry a conflagration out of his mouth.

Oh, yes. The dragon needed to make napalm. He needed to now, and Thomas couldn't give him any more energy and still stay on his feet.

Now what? She had nothing left to give.

The dragon's mind called to her. *"There's more. Find it somewhere. Take it from someone, if you have to. Take it from your little goblin."*

When she didn't immediately respond, the dragon reached inside her and started dragging her power out.

Cyra gasped with pain at the violation, then fell to her knees and onto her side. She felt like she was dying, her heart on the verge of stopping, but she didn't fight. Instead, she did what the dragon asked and poured herself into creating what he needed, pulling magic and chemicals out of the ground itself. She wouldn't have known what he needed, but Thomas did: lead oxide, sulfur, ammonium phosphate . . .

It hurt. The pain was like nothing she had ever known, but Cyra had no choice but to go on helping the dragon. It was obvious that Thomas could not defeat the bear; he was lucky to be still alive. The beast had some magical armor that no spells could penetrate. And since Cyra would not leave Thomas, they would both die if the dragon could not win this fight.

They could not lose. This evil creature would be invincible with their combined magics inside it.

"Cyra!" Thomas's voice was frantic as he felt her slipping away. Then to the dragon he called: "Damn you! Stop! Stop now, or I'll kill you myself!"

"No, Thomas. It's okay. Let him."

Not waiting for her to perfect his hide or construct a second trachea, the dragon turned its long neck and spit out a cloud of fire as soon as its belly was full of chemicals. It wasn't particularly large or strong, but it singed the bear's face and averted its charge at Thomas.

The bear turned back to the dragon, its jaws wide. But its distraction didn't last long; it sensed who was actually in control, and it shrewdly spun and ran back at Thomas.

"Cyra!" the dragon called. But she was now truly empty, nothing left but the low embers of her life itself.

Yet, she still had the gun. Somewhere . . .

Almost unable to see anymore, Cyra forced herself to crawl toward her purse. Her cloak lay on the ground, having fallen off in the melee. She gathered it to her. She noted that blood was running from her nose and eyes. Had she given so much of her life force away?

"What are you doing? Lie still!" Thomas shouted, even as he dodged another passing swipe from the bear's vicious claws.

"The gun," she thought. *"I have another clip in my purse. We can kill him with that."*

"Cyra!" the dragon called. *"Finish my trae-*

chea. Damnation! I need the fire. Hurry, I can't keep the bear from Thomas much longer."

The gun, or the dragon?

The dragon spoke again: *"Cyra, Thomas will die if you don't help me. And if I take the power from you myself, you'll die too! Help me."*

"I'll die no matter what if you take any more."

She looked over, and through the dark tunnel of her failing vision she could see that the bear had Thomas trapped against the rock face, pushed flat against another set of old bones. The crowbar in his hands looked small and useless. She glanced back toward her purse, uncertain of where she had dropped the gun.

There was no time to search for it.

A claw ripped through Thomas's shoulder, flaying Cyra's nerves as it tore his flesh. She could feel him going into shock, losing blood.

"Thomas!" she gasped. And then she decided. *So be it.* If she had to die to save Thomas, then she would die. Finding a last vestige of strength, she reached into her soul and sent what was left of her energy, her life, her breath, into the dragon. And at the very end, she felt a tiny spark of life—of *other* life—give itself too.

Cyra collapsed completely on the ground, trying to understand. She pulled her cloak about her. Other life? *A baby,* she thought. And then the dragon pushed that spark back.

"Thank you, Cyra. But not this."

And suddenly there was fire. Everywhere. It bathed the walls of the canyon. It filled the sky. If Cyra had been breathing, the heat would have seared her lungs as it passed over her. Her flesh should have burned, but her cloak somehow protected her.

Twin roars, one from the bear and one from the dragon filled the red air, and Cyra could feel the moment when the two titans met in battle in the heart of the flames.

She wanted to cry out when the bear's claws ripped into the dragon's flesh—she could feel it like she felt Thomas's wound—but she had no breath, no voice to scream with. She began to float.

And then Thomas was beside her, a gory sight of burns and bloody wounds, but a welcome sight nonetheless. In an instant her gun was in his hand and he was slapping in another clip. Without hesitation, he turned and ran toward the battling monsters. He moved around the dragon and fired into the bear's head. The bullet somehow pierced its enormous skull.

The dragon, bleeding from a wound in its side, closed in and finished the job, tearing the bear's head from its long neck. It gave a roar of triumph.

"Cyra—sweetheart, answer me!"

"I'm fine," she answered, wishing it were true but knowing it wasn't. She couldn't breathe and couldn't hear her heart. *I love you, Thomas. I said it before, when you . . . I—*"

"I love you, too."

Cyra had waited for these words, and she closed her eyes in happiness.

From the bear and dragon, the appalling sounds of snapping bones, and pain that welled up like a spring. Cyra's soul began to sail away, a kite whose string had snapped.

But Thomas was instantly there, catching at the string. *No! You aren't leaving. My name is Thomas Marrowbone, the quiet man. Say my name! Cyra, if you truly love me, say my name!*

"Thomas . . . Thomas Marrowbone, the quiet man," she thought—and then felt him catch hold of her spirit in a firm grip. He began ruthlessly reeling it back toward her pain-wracked body.

Reaching out, Cyra grabbed hold of the *other*, the girl, and pulled her back from the void too.

Chapter Twenty-one

"We aren't home free. We still have issues to deal with," Cyra warned, shrugging her cloak off so she could feel what little breeze there was. She was singed and dusty, her face as black as the scorched rocks around them, but her cloak sparkled, undimmed. Her brief nap had not healed all her physical or psychic wounds, but she was able to stand again.

"Doesn't everyone?" Thomas asked.

"Probably, but their *issues* don't breathe fire and have claws."

"I wouldn't count on that," Thomas answered. "If it's an *issue*, it has claws of some form or another."

Cyra shook her head, reluctantly amused. "Okay, but the literal fire thing . . ." They turned to face the dragon, who was washing the wound in his side. The cut had already closed and was healing. *"What are we going to do with him?"*

"Well, for starters, don't piss him off until you blow out his pilot light."

The admonition was purely for form. The dragon was at ease and doing his best to look benign. Thomas tore off a strip of his ruined shirt and set about binding up the tear the coyote had made in his arm. Cyra did her best to ignore the sound of his blood pattering on the rocks. Instead, she offered him some mental anesthetic. She was getting good at it.

"Stop," Thomas said quickly. "I appreciate your concern, but don't. You've come too close to the infinite today. Let's not press our luck. Stop using your magic."

Exhausted, Cyra did as he asked. She dragged a sleeve across her face, wiping up her own trickles of blood. She needed to start thinking about the welfare of the *other*, the life she carried within her.

"I don't suppose we can just leave him here?" Cyra suggested, feeling unequal to the task of conveying a dragon to Cadalach—assuming that they could think of something to do with him once they got him there.

"Yessss, you can," the dragon hissed with his

half-completed vocal cords. He was completing himself rapidly, however.

Frowning at the pained sound, Cyra reached inside for a last bit of energy and helped him. She couldn't do otherwise. She was not going to destroy her first conjuration, even if he was probably a little bit evil. Anyway, killing him might have some horrible effect on Thomas. If she had felt the dragon's wounds, Thomas must also have experienced them.

"Leave a dragon living outside a populated area?" Thomas asked, dubious. He turned back toward the cobbled-together beast. He looked tired, too, with eyes as hollow as a dead man's. Battling the minions of evil could do that to a person, Cyra knew. "What are you going to do with yourself, dragon, if we leave you? What will you eat? How will you live?"

"I'll eat goblins. There will be plenty fleeing Sin City now that their water is gone," the smug serpent rumbled. He puffed experimentally, belching a tiny flame. Apparently satisfied that his "pilot light" hadn't been "blown out," he added: "I shall live in a cave and collect treasure. There's lots of it hereabouts. I can smell it. And I can visit you at Yule and bring presents to your children."

The dragon turned its eyes upon Cyra, and she suddenly recalled that it was aware of her pregnancy, that it had felt the tiny spark of life that had almost been sacrificed to make him whole, and his refusal to take it had been deliberate.

"Oh, goddess!" Cyra closed her eyes and laid a protective hand over her belly. She said distractedly: "It's enough to make me give up Christmas."

"He's kidding," Thomas assured her. Then, with exasperation: "What did you give him vocal cords for?"

"I don't know. Just make him stop talking. I'm tired and sunburned—just plain burned too—and in no mood for jokes or making decisions. He's your dragon, anyway," she snapped back.

"Not anymore. Sorry." Thomas shrugged when she glared at him. "Look, making him obey isn't my job anymore. I can kill him, but I can't control him. He's filled with . . . different magic now—yours and the bear's. I guess the coyote's too."

Cyra said a bad word, then faced the monster she had created. "Okay, here's the deal, dragon. You get to keep your body and your freedom—but no eating Orel! I want your word on this. And no attacking any humans either. Or feys. They're just tourists trying to get out of the city."

330

The dragon glanced at the damp crevice where the burned goblin had returned to hide. The red flames in his pupils danced crazily. His lips weren't designed for it, but he smiled anyway. The sight was unnerving.

"No, ma'am. I'll leave your pet goblin alone since he helped us."

"You better," Cyra warned, forcing strength into her tone and spine. "And humans too. And feys. I'm not kidding. I made you. I can unmake you too. Now give me your word."

"I promised," the dragon answered, managing to sound hurt by her lack of trust. The innocent disclaimer was slightly hampered by the thin line of drool leaking from the corner of his jaws. "Anyway, I have better things to eat just now."

Cyra swallowed, but she didn't turn to look at the smoking remains of the bear. She knew she'd never be able to eat barbecue again.

"I guess that's that, then," she said, slumping. Her head hurt fiendishly and she thought she might be sick to her stomach. Again. "Let's go find the Harley. I think it's okay. I didn't dump it that hard."

She and Thomas turned, but they were interrupted.

"What? No virgin sacrifice to show your gratitude? No kiss goodbye? Not even words of

331

thanks?" the dragon asked. "I'm hurt. Especially when I played matchmaker for the two of you."

"Don't press your luck," Thomas advised. Turning back, he draped his uninjured arm around Cyra and walked her toward the road. He called over his shoulder, "I could tell her your real name. With that, she could turn you into a pink skink."

The dragon snorted once, but held his peace.

Cyra wasn't reassured. The dragon knew she was pregnant, and she sensed that this was somehow significant to him. She wondered why. She also was suddenly certain as sunrise that she and Thomas had not seen or heard the last of this reptilian problem.

But it would all have to wait. She had no more miracles in her.

It took an effort to scramble over the rockslide, now considerably larger than it had been on her arrival, and get back down to the toppled Harley, but at last they were in the kind shade as they labored.

Thomas tightened the arm he had draped around Cyra as they rested near the bottom. They stood quietly for a moment, listening to the slowing drops of his blood spatter on one of the few patches of shady ground.

"You're healing, aren't you?" she asked worriedly.

"Yes. It wasn't that bad." And compared to the last time he had battled goblins, he was telling the truth.

"And you feel okay without *him?*"

"I feel a little strange without the dragon," Thomas admitted. "Lighter. But don't worry, I'm glad he's gone. Frankly, I don't know how I lived so long with someone else inside me."

"Good. I'm glad you're free of him. I was never quite at ease knowing there was a witness to all our . . . *conversations and plans.*"

Thomas nodded. "I'm free. And next we're going to work on finding out how to get you proficient with *your* magic. None of this luck stuff, or borrowing mine. You're a Kloka. You're healing now, but after you're better we can try. You won't be truly whole until you have full use of your power the way it was meant to be. Anything else is slowly killing you. It has to stop. You are doing damage to yourself. And the baby."

Cyra signed. "I know. And I've said it a lot today, but: Never again. I just didn't know what else to do. It was the only way I . . ." Then: "*The baby?* You know?"

"Yes. I've known for a while," he said gently. "Thank the goddess we saved it."

"You've known for a while? Well, I feel a little stupid. I didn't know until just . . . How can I be a mother and not know it? What's wrong with me?"

Thomas stared at her, bruised eyes filled with compassion and something else Cyra wasn't ready to address. They stood there, bleeding in the desert.

Cyra touched a strand of hair that had fallen over her eyes. It was pure white, like her hands. The dragon had really sucked her dry. There wasn't any pigment left. She sighed. "Is all of it . . . ?"

"Yes, I'm afraid so. You look ghostly pale all over."

"But do I look good?" she asked wryly.

Thomas stared at her for a moment and then laughed. His sudden explosion of mirth echoed on the walls of the canyon, and a few more small rocks lost their precarious perches and tumbled to the ground near the overturned Harley.

"Yes, you look good," he assured her at last, kissing her for luck and then once again because he felt suddenly joyous. "We've won, Cyra. I know the price was high—we may pay it forever! But, damn. We did it! We saved California and we stopped Lilith and Fornix."

"Good." Cyra smiled tiredly, not truly elated, but unable to resist responding to Thomas's pleasure. "Now let's get the hell outta Dodge. I've had enough of Sin City and goblins."

Epilogue

Cyra snuggled into her lumpy pillow, feeling sleepy after her steak dinner. Sadly, they hadn't been able to get gorgonzola butter for the T-bone—but on the other hand, they hadn't had to drive all the way to California to eat either.

The bedding on the old mattress, like this motel itself, was clean but shoddy. The mineral rich water had stained the linen a pale rusty shade. The pillows were so flat that they were merely a gesture, worn down by the weight of all the heavy heads that had rested here. Staring at the flattened bolster, Cyra was glad that her newfound talents did not include divination. The memories of all the people who had rested here before her would have kept her awake. As it was, she hoped to leave some of her nightmares of Sin City behind when they left.

Her eyes shifted over to the small window that looked out on the desert. The building that sheltered them was also busy blending into its surroundings, a little more of it eaten away each day, its adobe sills and walls being worn away by airborne particles that assaulted it nightly when the winds picked up. The glass of the windows was nearly opaque, being slowly embedded with the tiny, sharp chips of stone broken off from the petrified dunes around them.

The landscape was wretchedly hostile and hard on the eyes—and suited Cyra fine. If it was nearly too wretched for her and Thomas, it was too hostile for goblins. They'd be able to safely sleep through the rest of the day before going on to Cadalach, and then to California to hunt for her missing selkie skin. It would be the first sound sleep she'd had since finding out that the goblins of Sin City were bankrolling Bracebridge.

Still, the location of the motel had to make a person wonder what strange urge had caused the first humans to build there. It was one of the most geographically and climatically un-suitable places in the world. Maybe the first settler had seen a mirage and imagined that this was paradise. No—no one was that delusional, were they? But then, the motel's current manager had been wearing a polyester suit and bow tie on a day when the temperature had climbed well over 110 degrees, which only proved that there was no end to human inappropriateness in hostile situations—if not out and out stupidity.

Cyra smiled a little to hear herself thinking of *humans* as something separate from herself. Who would have ever thought to see the day?

The smile made her face hurt, and she wished that she hadn't had to leave behind the wonderful and expensive cosmetics she'd bought. This would have been the ultimate test of the hydrating moisturizer she'd gotten in Sin City.

Thomas turned from the phone jack, portable in hand. He was carrying scars from their battle and looked more than a little windblasted. There were worse scars too. The area right below his heart was marked by a ridge of flesh that resembled a lightning bolt. The dragon had needed an exit for its heart, and the wound was slow to heal—probably because there had been no time to just sit still and let the skin knit. His arm would never be a thing a beauty again either.

"What is it?" When Thomas stared at her expressionlessly, Cyra stopped smiling and pushed back her snowy-white hair. It was actually very pretty, ethereal even, but she wasn't sure how she felt about the physical reminder of her battle with the goblins. She probably would have preferred a t-shirt as a memento. She supposed there was always dye if she just couldn't get used to it.

"I've just had an e-mail from Jack. There are two things. First of all, though eyewitnesses place Fornix and Lilith in the Yucca Mountain caves when they flooded, no bodies have been recovered."

"Do you think they could have survived?"

"No. But I would still feel a lot better if we had proof that they were dead."

Cyra nodded. "And the other thing?"

"Chloe gave birth last night." Thomas's tone was grim as he set his portable computer on the end table and sat on the edge of the bed.

"Is she all right?" Cyra asked, rolling toward him as the mattress dipped. She looked at the computer screen but couldn't read the strange glyphs that glowed there.

"Physically, yes. Mentally . . ."

"The baby? Is it . . ."

"Alive. But as we feared, it's half-troll."

Cyra understood the implications immediately. It explained why the girl had seemed so broken in spirit as well as in body. "So, she *was* raped?"

"Apparently. She claims to have no memories of that time, but this is certainly proof enough of what happened while she was captive."

"That poor child," Cyra whispered, speaking not just of the infant but of Chloe. "And Zayn? How is he handling this?"

"Zayn is okay. He's worried about Chloe. He's had a while to think about this and to prepare mentally if the worst happened."

"And this is almost the worst. What *will* happen to the child?" Cyra asked bluntly.

"They'll keep it, of course. It's a risk, raising an enemy among us, but what is the alternative? They can't give a half-human child to trolls—they'd eat it." Cyra flinched, but she knew it was true. Thomas stared into the distance, and she knew he was thinking about what the trolls had done to Annissa. Then, sensing that she could read his thoughts, he pulled his gaze and mind back to the present. "Anyway, it's a girl. Girls are less violent, at least until adolescence. Puberty is not pretty in either gender—"

"Good Goddess! A hormonal teenage troll," Cyra gasped.

"Yes, a time to truly go in fear of PMS." Thomas's words, though not truly intended to make Cyra laugh, still lightened the mood. "And there is some good news, which is that in these cases, trolls almost always take their intelligence from their mothers."

"Well, thank heavens. The thought of a stupid, PMS-ing, teenage troll is terrifying. More than any family should have to face. I wonder how much chocolate they'd eat at that time of the month. Or maybe it'd be live chickens or fish. What do trolls crave when their hormones rage—do you know?"

It was Thomas's turn to smile and shake his head.

"I love you, you know," he told her. "I didn't have the chance to tell you properly before. Or show you. But I do."

Cyra looked into his eyes as if to be sure his words weren't counterfeit, a sop to an injured comrade and the mother of his child. Not that she thought they were, but—

Thomas shook his head. *"They're not. I love you."*

"Good. Because I love you, too."

Thomas reached out a hard hand and cupped her chin. Cyra laid her own hand over the place where his second heart had been and they looked into each other's eyes, letting each other see everything that was inside.

"Thomas, let me heal you. I—"

341

"Cyra," he warned as she leaned in to kiss him.

"I won't do it that way," she promised softly. "But you know that love can be *therapeutic.*"

When she drew back, Thomas was half smiling.

"See?" she said.

Thomas looked down. His wound had lessened a shade or two. He nodded: "Very therapeutic. Okay, then. Heal me any way you will."

Cyra pulled him down beside her, smiling herself. The bed swayed alarmingly beneath them.

"I'm glad you're strong," she told him, pushing his shirt open.

"I may be, but I am less certain about this bed."

"Just so long as I don't break you."

Thomas fisted a hand in her hair. His golden eyes glowed softly. "Don't worry. That'll never happen. We are meant to be together."

Thinking of her dream and the child she carried, Cyra nodded. "Yes, and nothing will ever part us again."